DAMNED

JANA DELEON

For I do not do the good I want to do, but the evil I do not want to do—this I keep on doing. - Romans 7:19

1

SATURDAY, MAY 14, 2016
  St. Mary's Cathedral, New Orleans

FATHER NICOLAS CHATRY pushed himself out of his dressing chair and twisted his entire body when he was upright, then dropped into the wheelchair. It had been two years since the car accident that had left him partially paralyzed. Physical therapy had resulted in a tiny bit of improvement every month, but it was excruciatingly slow as well as painful. With every session he kept reminding himself that now he was able to stand, even if only for ten seconds at a time. And he could manage a few steps with the help of a walker. They were the halting, shaky steps of a drunk, but Nicolas was thrilled to have them.

Standing, even for seconds, and walking like a drunk,

even for a handful of steps, had made a huge difference in his independence. And at only twenty-six years of age, that had been of monumental importance. Those few seconds and steps had allowed him to do everything he needed for basic living without assistance. Things like using the restroom and changing clothes. Things normal people took for granted.

Things he had taken for granted before the accident.

His therapist believed that if he kept up his therapy regimen and did his daily exercises without fail, he would be able to walk without the walker soon. He'd look like a baby taking his first steps without his parents' hands, and a lot of tumbles were probably in his future, but that was all okay. As long as he was making progress, Nicolas wouldn't stop believing that he could live a completely normal life again.

Pull his weight.

The senior priest at St. Mary's, Father Bernard Abshire, had taken Nicolas under his wing out of seminary, despite his limitations, and had assigned him duties that could be conducted while seated in order to allow him recovery time. Nicolas was grateful to the senior priest for creating the position for him and making adjustments to his duties to fit his situation. He suspected it was because Bernard was a biblical and historical scholar, like Nicolas, and appreciated the dedication Nicolas had to knowledge. They had indulged in many a spirited discussion over the nuances of Scripture in regard to historical context, and Bernard appeared pleased that someone could engage anywhere near his level.

Father Malcolm Warner, seven years Nicolas's senior and the other junior priest in residence at St. Mary's, was more progressive than historian, which was common among the younger generation of priests. Bernard called Nicolas an old soul. He called Malcolm "necessary for the future of the church." Nicolas assumed that meant Malcolm was in touch with the younger generation and could prevent the congregation from becoming one that eventually died off.

Nicolas exited his apartment and wheeled himself down the cloister toward the church. Immediately following the accident, he had a motorized wheelchair, but he'd found that using it made him complacent—less inclined to work on his recovery. So he'd given the motorized chair to a senior church member who didn't have the funds to purchase one, and he'd picked up his manual form of transportation. At first, his upper body had protested all the use. Nicolas had always played sports, but he'd never spent this much time utilizing just one area of his body. But after many months of ice packs and heating pads, his arms adjusted, and now he could propel himself around all day without tiring.

But all that exertion was not necessary today, because he was scheduled for one of the duties his body was completely suited for—confession. He was pretty sure the chair in the confessional was as old as the church, which made it slightly less comfortable than the wheelchair, but it was a task he could handle without assistance. Malcolm had been more than happy to turn over his confessional duties and take additional turns at mass in exchange. But then everyone knew Malcolm was hoping to be made senior priest, even though he'd have to leave St. Mary's if he wanted to head his own church. Bernard, at fifty, showed no inclination that his retirement was on the horizon.

The confessional was located in a private section on the side of the cathedral. A stone wall separated the confessional from the main part of the cathedral where mass was conducted. A narrow hallway traversed the length of the wall with the confessional on the back side, allowing those coming to confess—penitents—to enter the hallway from the cathedral and to exit at the other end, either back into the cathedral or through a door opposite that led into the courtyard. Nicolas loved the architecture of the 250-year-old building, despite the challenges it sometimes presented him. The sheer beauty of the structure sometimes held him captive for hours, just studying the artistry that had gone into the construction.

When he reached the confessional, he pushed himself out of the wheelchair and slid it into a tiny alcove next to his booth. He then managed, by clutching a cane and the stone wall, to make the four steps around the corner into the confessional. He turned around and dropped into the chair, winded from even that small bit of walking, but rather than view it as something to be distraught about,

Nicolas chose to view it as one small victory for independence.

He pulled his phone out of his pocket and accessed a book on ancient Egypt that he'd been reading. Ten minutes went by before he heard the shuffle of footsteps pass him and enter the confessional. The familiar sounds of the oak door closing and the chair squeaking let him know it was time for the unburdening of souls. He flipped the switch that triggered a small red light in the cathedral, alerting congregants that the confessional was currently occupied. Then he pulled back the small door that covered the screen between the two booths and saw the silhouette on the other side.

"Bless me, Father, for I have sinned," a voice whispered. "It has been a week since my last confession."

"Welcome," Nicolas said. "What do you have to confess?"

"I killed her."

Maybe it was the simple statement of fact or the whisper, but Nicolas felt the hair on his arms rise. He forced himself to focus. Of course, the penitent did not mean that statement literally. Clearly, they were upset about the death of someone close to them and feelings of self-doubt had manifested.

"Death often brings about guilt in those left behind," Nicolas said, trying to find the correct opening. "We wonder if we could have done something that would have made a difference. But that's rarely the case."

"It's not what I could have done. It's what I did. I

strangled her. Watched the life drain out of her until there was nothing left but her imperfect body in an imperfect world."

Nicolas's pulse shot up and he felt suddenly short of breath. "You're saying you willingly took the life of another person?"

"Yes. Do you think God makes mistakes, Father?"

Nicolas tugged at his collar, feeling as if he were being choked. "No," he finally managed, his mind racing with a million horrible thoughts. "God has a reason for everything He does."

"I agree. You see, God is the reason I killed her."

"I don't understand," Nicolas said as panic began to course through him. As incomprehensible as it sounded, the person on the other side of the wall might be a murderer. And Nicolas was all but defenseless—trapped in a stationary chair. He fumbled with his phone, typing a text to Father Malcolm.

"I didn't want to do it at first," the penitent said. "But he kept calling. Whispering in my ear."

Nicolas finished the text and hit Send, praying that Malcolm was nearby. It was Father Bernard's day off.

Emergency in confessional. Come now!

"You know how in the movies," the penitent continued whispering, "when people die, they look like they're at peace? It's not really like that. When you kill someone, that terror they feel as the life drains out of them is permanently frozen onto their expressions. It's beautiful. Art, really. Only God could create something that perfect. That's how I know for certain it was his will."

Nicolas struggled to take a breath and choked.

"Will you absolve me, Father?"

"I...don't..." Nicolas stuttered. "I can't..."

He heard the chair in the booth squeak and a shadow passed in front of the screen. Nicolas could feel his pulse pounding in his temples and he started to sway, dizziness washing over him. Malcolm wasn't going to make it in time. He was going to die in the confessional at the hands of a murderer asking him for absolution.

Then he heard the quiet echo of footsteps quickly walking away.

Gathering all his strength, he shoved himself up from the chair, not even bothering to grab the cane, and staggered to the door, pushing it open. He clutched the frame, the pain in his legs like daggers stabbing him from every angle. He was moving too fast, too harshly, but he had to know who had confessed. He took one more step to the side and peered around the doorframe, but the hallway was empty. He pushed himself away from the frame and twisted in time to catch the other side. Tears formed unbidden and rolled down his face as he forced himself around the corner and into his chair.

A wave of nausea washed over him as he dropped onto the seat, and he drew in a deep breath, trying to control his ravaged body. The breath barely alleviated the dizziness, but he didn't have time to wait. He grasped the wheels and propelled the chair as fast as he could manage down the hallway, every bump on the uneven stone causing him to flinch.

At the end of the hall, he leaned right and shoved open the door to the courtyard, but he only saw the landscaping crew at work. He turned left and flung open the door to the cathedral, almost catching Father Malcolm in the face.

"Nicolas?" Malcolm took one look at him, heaving for air, and paled. "I'll call an ambulance."

"No," Nicolas said. "I just need a minute."

Malcolm didn't appear remotely convinced. "You've lost all color, you're not breathing properly, and you're clearly in pain. Please let me call."

Nicolas shook his head, taking in another deep breath, trying to force his body into compliance. "I need some air."

Malcolm moved behind him and maneuvered his wheelchair out the courtyard door. "You need more than air," Malcolm said as he scrutinized him. "What happened? Did you fall?"

Nicolas looked up at Malcolm, his concern so clear in his tone and his expression. "Did you see someone enter the cathedral from the hallway?"

Malcolm looked confused. "No. But I was in the electrical room beyond the choir loft. Did someone hurt you?"

Malcolm's voice went up several octaves, and Nicolas could see the panic starting to set in. The text and his behavior had the other priest's imagination working overtime. Nicolas hadn't been physically attacked, but he had been spiritually and emotionally. And both had done a number on his already-weakened body.

"I need to speak to Father Bernard," Nicolas said.

"He said he had an appointment," Malcolm said. "I don't think he's back yet, but I'll call him. Just try to calm down. Keep breathing. Do you need water? Your pain medication?"

Nicolas shook his head. "I need Father Bernard."

Malcolm pulled his cell phone out of his pocket and dialed, his watchful eyes never leaving Nicolas's face. All the while, that horrible whisper echoed through Nicolas's mind.

God is the reason I killed her.

2

FATHER MALCOLM SAT A MUG ON THE TABLE NEXT TO Nicolas. "It's chamomile tea," he said. "I know you think it sounds a bit snooty but it will help calm you."

Nicolas picked up the mug and took a sip, but he doubted the tea would have any effect at all on his racing emotions. Everyone was fond of saying time healed all things, but Nicolas wasn't certain he had enough time on earth to forget the sinister whisper and the words the penitent had said.

Father Bernard sat in the chair next to Nicolas. The three of them were in the senior priest's personal study at the church, where Malcolm had taken Nicolas when Bernard returned. Nicolas was certain Malcolm was hoping Bernard would insist on Nicolas getting medical care, but so far, that hadn't happened. Bernard studied Nicolas as he drank but said nothing. He was a very patient man. He would wait until Nicolas was ready to talk, regardless of how long that might take.

Finally, Nicolas steadied enough to speak. "I'm sorry you had to be called back on your day off," he said to Bernard.

"Don't worry about that," Bernard said gently. "Clearly something is very wrong. Will you tell me what has upset you so?"

Nicolas bit his lower lip. The sanctity of the confessional was indisputable. He couldn't repeat anything he'd heard. That was his vow, and Nicolas took that promise seriously. But surely there were exceptions? Extreme circumstances where he couldn't be expected to keep what he'd heard to himself? And even though he already knew the answer, he didn't like it and hoped Father Bernard knew of a loophole.

Nicolas glanced at Malcolm, then looked back at Bernard. The senior priest clued in on his hesitation and looked up at Malcolm. "Can you please check on the workers in the cathedral? They were due to start cleaning the sculptures this afternoon."

Malcolm glanced back and forth between the two of them. It was clear that he didn't want to be dismissed, but he wasn't going to argue with Bernard, either. "Is there anything I can do for you before I go?" he asked.

Nicolas shook his head. "Thank you for helping me earlier and for the tea."

"Yes," Bernard said. "It's good to know I can depend on you to handle things while I'm away."

Malcolm looked a tiny bit pleased at the senior priest's praise and gave them a nod before heading out of the study. Bernard waited until he heard Malcolm's footsteps in the hallway before he leaned forward and looked Nicolas straight in the eyes.

"What happened?" Bernard asked. "I've never seen you this upset."

"I...the confessional..."

"Ah," Bernard said, and nodded. "You heard something that upset you. It happens to all of us from time to time."

"Yes, but this was more than just upsetting. I know I can't tell you. I know my responsibilities. But the burden on my heart is overwhelming."

"Do you know the person who confessed this thing that has upset you so greatly?"

"No. I didn't see the person or recognize the voice. I couldn't even tell you if it was a man or a woman, as they whispered."

"Then you can't follow up with them. That makes things more difficult."

It did make things more difficult, but not in the way Bernard believed. Nicolas was certain he didn't want to follow up with the penitent. The potential of a follow-up to the confession was what had sent him straight into a panic attack.

"I know my duties," Nicolas said, "but I have to ask if there exists a situation where my moral obligation to all of society outweighs my vows."

Bernard frowned. "You graduated at the top of your seminary class. You already know the answer. I think, perhaps, it's simply not the answer you wish it to be at this moment."

"So even if a person confesses to a crime, I am bound to my silence?" Nicolas asked, even though he already knew the answer. "An awful, horrific event that might happen again?"

Bernard's eyes widened and he drew in a deep breath. "And you think this person was truthful?"

"How am I to know? I felt no deception. Only my own overwhelming fear and panic. If my instincts are to be trusted, then I would say that the person was truthful."

"I can see why you were upset," Bernard said. "Especially as you felt the confession was sincere."

"It wasn't just being upset at what I heard." Nicolas looked down at the floor for a couple seconds, then back at Bernard. "I'm ashamed to admit it, but I was afraid for myself. If they had decided to...with my condition..."

Bernard's eyes widened. "Yes. Yes, of course. I apologize that I hadn't even thought about it in those terms, but I can see why it would be particularly distressing in your case. And with the confessional being so isolated, it made your fear more acute."

Nicolas felt a bit of relief pass over him. He was afraid the senior priest would find fault with his fear. Would tell him that he should have faith that all things happened for a reason and not to question the way God worked. Both of which would have been a normal response, and neither of which would have done a thing to help Nicolas with his current mental state.

"I sent a text to Father Malcolm telling him I had an emergency so that he would come straightaway," Nicolas said. "The penitent asked for absolution. I didn't—couldn't—do it. And before I could find my voice they were gone."

"And you didn't see this person when they exited?" Bernard asked.

"I tried. But by the time I got to the doorway, the hallway was empty. It took me time to get to my chair and then to the exit. I saw only the landscapers outside and when I opened the door to the cathedral, Father Malcolm was just on the other side, responding to my text."

"And you didn't see anyone other than Father Malcolm and the landscapers?"

"I didn't see anyone else in the courtyard, but someone could have slipped behind the hedges. For that matter, they could have been behind a statue in the cathedral or simply sat down and pretended to be praying with the others. There were several people inside."

Bernard nodded. "I suppose one of those is the likely answer."

"What do I do, Father?"

"You take the rest of the afternoon off to collect yourself, devoting a significant amount of time to prayer. Next week, I will split your confessional duties between myself and Father Malcolm. After that, we'll talk about whether or not you're ready to resume."

Nicolas drew in a breath and slowly let it out. "I meant what do I do about the confession. This person did something horrible. I'm as certain of that as I am my own name. I can't tell you why, but I simply know."

"And your instincts may be right, but you know your duties."

"But if a crime has been committed—"

"Your duties are the same."

Nicolas knew the senior priest was right. He had known about the sanctity of the confessional since he was a child. But during all of his preparation, he'd never once imagined that he'd be in this position. Even when he'd thought about the possibility of hearing more than he ever wanted to know about one of his congregants, he'd always imagined his faith and prayer would allow him to maintain control of his emotions. Would allow him to separate his base human instinct of revulsion from his duty as a priest.

He'd been wrong.

"You understand what I'm telling you?" Bernard said.

Nicolas nodded, unable to speak lest his voice betray his true feelings.

Bernard narrowed his gaze. "Consider this, Father Nicolas. Even if you were willing to break your vows and risk excommunication by telling the police what you heard, what could you offer them? You saw no one. You didn't recognize the voice. You have no information other than someone confessed to a crime they may or may not have performed. If a serious crime has been committed, it is likely the police are already aware. If they are not, then you must have faith that they will become so and investigate."

Bernard was right. Nicolas didn't have anything to offer the police but wild speculation. And without a name for the police to follow up on, they would probably dismiss Nicolas's report as the act of a crazy person or someone simply looking to rile up the young priest. It wouldn't be the first or last time that pranksters had targeted the church with their play. All Nicolas had was his belief that the confession was not a joke. That it was truth.

It wasn't enough.

3

TUESDAY, MAY 17, 2016
French Quarter, New Orleans

SHAYE ARCHER POURED herself another cup of coffee and headed back to her office to tackle invoices once more. She'd spent the past three days catching up on paperwork, and despite the fact that she was an introvert, she was beginning to get a little stir-crazy. At some point today, she had to venture out of her apartment. Unfortunately, the internet, cell phones, Amazon Prime, and food delivery had made it super easy to stay locked inside one's home for long periods of time without the necessity of venturing out. And when she was in between jobs, the reasons to leave her apartment all but disappeared.

Except, apparently, for her sanity.

But then, the overwhelming need to escape was probably due to the stack of paperwork on her desk and not the burning desire to interact with the public at large. Of course, she could avoid the public entirely by visiting her mother, and if she didn't show up soon, Corrine would take it as a sign that she needed to drop by Shaye's apartment and drag her out to a new trendy restaurant, or even worse, a boutique. Despite Shaye's overwhelming lack of interest in all things fashionable, Corrine still wasn't ready to entirely give up hope. That tenacity made her who she was, so a couple times a year, Shaye indulged her and actually purchased a dress that would languish in the back of her closet until she was obligated to attend a charity event.

She picked up the next file in the stack and accessed her accounting software, ready to break out the hours she'd spent on an insurance case into the billable bits that the company wanted to see. It had been almost three months since she'd had a case that wasn't insurance-based. She had known when she started her agency that it would be a slow build, especially as she had no interest in getting in the middle of divorce proceedings, which is where many private investigators made their living. So she worked for the insurance companies and took the occasional oddball case that fell into her lap, hoping that her reputation would build to the point that the more interesting cases would increase and the insurance work would be shoved completely out.

She just had to be patient. Which wasn't really in her wheelhouse.

As she began to type in a description of the surveillance hours, her cell phone rang. She didn't recognize the number.

"Archer Investigations," she said when she answered.

"Is this Shaye Archer?" a man asked.

"Yes. How can I help you?"

"I need your services. I think I do, anyway. I'm not sure. Can we talk?"

The level of anxiety in the man's voice was palpable.

"I'd be happy to talk," she said. "Would you like to schedule a time to meet at my office?"

"I was...I hoped that we could meet now. I know it's sudden, but I can't get away easily."

Shaye's interest was piqued. Whatever had caused the man's stress was apparently something he needed immediate attention for.

"Now is fine," she said. "Let me give you my address."

"I was hoping you could meet me at a café. It's more accessible for me. I'm in a wheelchair, you see."

"Yes, of course. Just tell me where."

The man named a café in the French Quarter that Shaye was familiar with and said he'd be there within twenty minutes. Shaye changed from her wrinkled yoga pants and tee into jeans and a non-wrinkled tee, grabbed her laptop, and headed out. The café was only five blocks away, but Shaye didn't feel like jogging in jeans, so she hopped in her SUV and headed that direction. Given that it was lunchtime, she had to circle the block twice, playing the parking game, but finally managed to nab a spot right across the street from the café.

She headed inside, figuring her client should be easy enough to spot, but gave a slight pause when she spotted the man in the wheelchair at a table in the back of the café. He hadn't mentioned he was a priest.

Her curiosity spiked into overdrive.

He'd spotted her as soon as she entered and lifted a hand to wave. She made her way through the mostly empty tables and took a seat next to him, then extended her hand. He was young and had a pleasant face, but the dark circles under his eyes and pinched, weary expression let her know that whatever was worrying him had been present for a while.

"Shaye Archer," she said.

"Nicolas Chatry," he said. "Thank you for meeting me on such short notice."

"No problem. Should I call you Father Nicolas?"

He gave her a small smile and shook his head. "Nicolas is fine. Truthfully, the Father thing still throws me off a bit."

"How long ago did you take your vows?"

"Twelve months."

She nodded. He looked awfully young to be wearing a collar. "How can I help you?"

Before he could answer, an older woman stepped up to the table with a pad. "What can I get you, Father?" she asked.

"Coffee, please," he said.

Shaye ordered the same and the server headed into the kitchen. Nicolas waited until the swinging door had closed behind her before turning his attention back to Shaye.

"I have a problem, but it's an extremely delicate matter," he said. "The truth is, if anyone finds out I talked to you, I could be excommunicated from the church. I need your word that you won't repeat what I tell you. Ever."

Shaye hesitated a couple seconds before answering. On the one hand, if Nicolas wanted to hire her, an investigation would be tough without divulging what she was seeking answers to. On the other hand, she was fairly certain Nicolas would thank her politely and leave if she didn't agree to keep his secret. Finally, she nodded. If maintaining secrecy would prevent her from doing the job, then she'd simply tell him that. Then the ball would be in his court.

"My clients have full confidentiality," she said. "I will never share information that I've been asked to withhold. But you need to be aware that not being able to broach certain subjects could make an investigation difficult."

"I understand. To be honest, I don't even know why I'm doing this. I doubt you'll be able to help me, but I can't ignore the burden of this knowledge any longer. I haven't slept more than twenty minutes in one stretch for the past three days. I can't eat properly. The tension in my back and neck has me reaching for pain medication that I haven't used in well over a year. In short, I didn't know what else to do."

He was so clearly distraught that Shaye immediately felt sorry for him. Whatever was bothering the young priest was clearly a huge burden on his conscience, especially if he was taking action that could force him out of the life he had chosen.

"I will do whatever I can," she said. "And if I don't think I can help you, I'll let you know that as well."

The server returned with the coffee, then hurried off to attend to a table of four up front. Nicolas picked up a packet of sugar and added it to his coffee, his hand shaking as he completed the task. He lifted the cup with one hand, then grasped it on the side with his other hand to steady it before he sloshed the coffee outside the mug.

He took a sip, then sat the mug back down. "Three days ago, I was assigned to confession."

Shaye stiffened a little. She'd thought this might be where the problem stemmed and was anxious to hear what had made him willing to break his vows.

Nicolas stared at her for several seconds, then told her what had happened, including explaining the extent of his injuries and the limitations they placed on him. Shaye listened intently, horrified at what the priest had endured. The amount of fear he'd experienced was enough to have produced his haggard appearance, but the content of the confession was what had burdened his conscience.

When he was done, he took a deep breath and slowly

blew it out. He reached for the coffee, which was cool by now, and took another drink. When he sat the mug back down, Shaye placed her hand on his.

"First," she said, "I want to say that I'm sorry that happened to you. It was both frightening and horrifying, I'm sure."

Nicolas nodded. "Is there anything you can do?"

"I honestly don't know. You feel certain that the penitent was truthful, but we can't be 100 percent sure of that. It's possible that no crime was committed. If we assume that a crime *was* committed, we have no idea of the identity of the perpetrator, not even the most basic of information to go on, like sex. Therefore, there's no way to narrow down the suspect list from that angle."

She stared across the café for a bit, then continued. "The other side of things, of course, is the victim. If we knew who the victim was, it might be possible to track her killer that way. But I haven't seen anything on the news about a recent strangulation death. At least, not in the city."

"I know," Nicolas said. "I've been haunting the news. Every station. It's been like an addiction, but there's nothing. I even tried searching the internet in case the crime wasn't committed in this area."

"It's possible there is a victim but it hasn't made the news yet. Or won't. Not all do. It's also possible it happened some time ago, which makes things even more difficult."

Nicolas stared at Shaye, his expression bleak. "Yes, it

does. Do you have any idea how many women are strangled every week in this country? The statistics were overwhelming. I know more than most that evil exists in the hearts of men, but I never thought..."

He blushed. "I'm so sorry. You know all too well, and I didn't think—"

"Don't worry about it. And yes, I do know all too well, but I've had a lot of help in finding ways to keep it in perspective. I doubt you'll have many instances like this one, and maybe never again one this severe, but you need to find a way to handle exposure to the ugly side of humanity. I'm afraid this isn't the first or last time you'll be upset by something someone has said or done."

"I am not sure what it would take to top this. Is there nothing you can think of to do about it?"

"That depends. You said there were people working in the courtyard when you exited. It's possible they saw this person leaving. Or it's possible the penitent exited through the cathedral and someone praying inside or entering from the sidewalk or parking area saw them. Did you recognize anyone inside the cathedral?"

"No. When I opened the door, Father Malcolm was there. When he saw I couldn't breathe properly, he pushed me outside, so I didn't get a good look inside although I did see several people in the pews."

"What about Father Malcolm? Did he see anything?"

"I didn't ask. I wasn't sure how to without having to explain. But I doubt it would have done any good anyway. The electrical room doesn't have direct access to the cathedral or a view into it, so this person could have already been gone by the time Malcolm got there. And it didn't occur to me at first, but they could have easily entered the cathedral and simply taken a seat before Father Malcolm arrived and left when we exited. It's a horrifying thought. That they could have sat pleasantly in God's house..."

"Evil is often very clever," Shaye said quietly. "But it's also egotistical. That's usually its downfall."

"It's small comfort, but at this point, I'll take any that I can get."

"You said there were workers in the courtyard, right?"

"Yes, but I don't see how you can do anything with that information. You'll need to provide a reason for questioning people in order to gain their cooperation, and you can't give them that." He sighed. "I understand now what you meant about the limitations. Everything circles back to my doing something I am not supposed to do, and in asking you to keep my secret, I've tied your hands as effectively as mine are."

"There is another way. But it requires me to be less than honest."

He frowned. "I don't understand."

"I could present myself as working for a congregant who left her purse in the cathedral but didn't find it when she returned later to retrieve it. If it contained an item of great personal value, then it wouldn't be unheard of to hire a private investigator to see if it could be recovered. Even if it's a long shot."

"So you would lie to the people you interview about why you're asking the questions?"

"It's the only way I know to get the information I need without divulging the truth."

"And you have no problem doing this?"

"No. The greater good is my concern. Not the white lie that might help catch a murderer. Do you think we're judged on action or intent?"

Nicolas smiled. "I think God has a special place reserved for you already. Okay then. Go ahead with your plan. Do I need to sign a contract? I know I need to pay you a retainer."

"No contract. I don't want anything on record between the two of us...for your sake."

"I can pay you cash."

"That's not necessary. I know the church doesn't pay high wages."

"It doesn't," he agreed. "But I was a millionaire before I took my vow of poverty. Successful parents, you see. My father passed when I was in high school of a heart attack. My mother died of cancer when I was in seminary. She knew I would be compelled to give away my inheritance, so she planned ahead. It's all in a trust and I am allocated a monthly allowance and allowed to draw more for certain expenses, like my medical care. I am free to donate my allowance, of course, but she didn't want me to be able to give it all away at one time."

"She thought you would change your mind?"

"Probably. Many do. More importantly, I don't think she felt the church had the means to take care of me in the way I needed after the car accident that caused my injuries. My therapy has been extensive, and I've learned the best of medical care is rarely covered by health insurance. I am thankful that my mother didn't take my lifelong vows as seriously as I do. Without the ability to cover those costs myself, I would not have progressed as far as I have."

"Sounds like she was a wonderful woman and a good mother."

He nodded. "You would know about that, wouldn't you? I've met your mother at fund-raisers. She's a special lady."

"She is."

"Okay, then. So it's settled. Will two thousand get you started?"

"That will be fine, but please don't get your hopes up. This is a huge long shot. From every direction."

"I understand."

"Do you have private email?"

"Yes."

"Good. Email me a list of everyone you think was present around the church that day. You don't have to know the names of the people. The company will do. I'll start running down employees and see if they can tell me anything."

"I...I only know the landscaping company." He gave her the name.

"That's okay," she reassured him. "It's a starting place."

A tiny flicker of relief passed over Nicolas's face. Shaye immediately understood its origin. The chances of her finding anything was slim, but at least he was doing something about it. It was only a tiny burden lifted off his conscience, but even that little bit helped. Shaye, on the other hand, was troubled.

No matter how things eventually turned out, the answer wasn't going to be a pleasant one. If a victim surfaced whose cause of death matched Nicolas's description, then hopefully the police would have enough evidence to find her killer. If a victim never surfaced, then he had to allow that the whole thing might have been a horrific prank. Unfortunately, Shaye didn't think that would happen. If she found nothing, Nicolas would go on believing that a murderer was walking free in New Orleans, probably looking for the next victim God had instructed him to kill.

She was an excellent judge of character. Nicolas was clearly distraught and the stress he was under was visible. But she didn't think he was untruthful, fanciful, or dramatic. Whatever reality might be, she knew for certain that Nicolas believed the penitent was telling the truth. And unless he got answers, that confession would haunt him the rest of his life.

4

JACKSON LAMOTTE SAT ON THE FLORAL-COVERED chair, looking at the two distraught parents sitting on the couch across from him. Their sixteen-year-old daughter, Hailey, had been missing since the day before. Normally, when a teen disappeared, it was usually because they were mad at their parents and had left on their own accord. They were usually collected at a friend's house, but the officer who'd responded to the call had already paid a visit to the known friends and had come up empty.

In the less common case where the teen had taken off and not informed any of her friends of her plans, she could often be tracked by her cell phone, which was usually always on and mostly slotted into her hand like it had grown there along with her fingers. But a trace on Hailey's phone had yielded nothing. Either it was out of charge or turned off. It was currently being monitored so that if it came back online, Jackson and his partner Grayson would be alerted.

And forensics was working on getting the records from the phone company, but that always took a bit of time.

Time Jackson wasn't sure they had.

Sharon Pitre clutched her husband's arm as if squeezing it would produce their daughter. Michael Pitre's expression flickered between worried and agitated, but then, circulation in his arm had probably been cut off a minute or two before.

"I know this is very stressful," Detective Grayson said. "But Detective Lamotte and I are going to do everything possible to find your daughter. The picture will help but we also need information."

"What kind of information?" Michael asked.

"Friends, for starters," Grayson said.

"We gave that information to the other officer," Michael said.

"I understand," Grayson said, using his most patient voice. "But the officer who took your report is not a detective. We need to cover everything again in case anything was missed."

Sharon Pitre shot a frustrated look at her husband and gave them two names and addresses, her voice breaking as she talked.

"That's it?" Jackson asked. "Just these two?"

"She was a shy girl," Sharon said. "She had trouble making friends."

"She was too smart for girls her age," Michael said. "If I had the money, Hailey would be in a private school with other gifted children. She doesn't belong in public schools, but business has slowed the last couple years and commissions aren't what they used to be."

Jackson nodded. He had done some checking before they'd left the police station for the interview. He knew Michael was an outside sales rep for an office supply company. Jackson imagined that with more office work conducted online and digitally, it had seriously cut into the sales of office supplies, particularly paper products. Pitre had gotten behind on his mortgage on their previous home and had sold it to avoid a foreclosure. They were renting this house, which was a step down from where they lived before, and the school district wasn't quite as good, but it was still a decent neighborhood.

"What about a boyfriend?" Jackson asked.

"Hailey is not allowed to date," Michael said. "She is to concentrate on her studies. In order to get a scholarship, her grades have to stay up. I don't want her saddled with student loans for the first half of her adult life, and tuition at a suitable school is out of my reach."

"Does Hailey participate in any sports or clubs?" Grayson asked. "Things that would keep her after school?"

Sharon shook her head. "Hailey isn't fond of group things. School let out at three and she came straight home. She sent her father and me a text as soon as she locked the door."

"And you both work outside the home, correct?" Grayson asked.

"I went back to work when we moved here," Sharon said. "Hailey was older and Michael said she could get her own snack and do her homework until I got home. I'm usually here by six."

Michael's expression flashed with a flicker of irritation. "It was only a couple of hours. Hailey isn't a baby. She's a responsible girl. There should have been no problems."

"Did you receive a text from her yesterday?" Grayson asked.

"Yes," Michael said. "At the usual time. It said she was home and was starting her studies. Her mother asked her to set chicken out to thaw as she'd forgotten to that morning."

"And was the chicken thawing?" Jackson asked.

Sharon nodded.

"You told the officer who filed your report that Hailey's purse and cell phone were also missing," Grayson said. "Have you discovered anything else that's missing since you called the police? Clothes, backpack?"

Michael straightened and flashed an angry look at Grayson. "My daughter is not one of those emotionally unstable children who run away when they have a dispute with their parents. Hailey knew that all the decisions we made were in her best interest."

"Okay then," Grayson said. "I'd like to have a forensics team go over the windows and doors of your home.

We didn't spot any sign of forced entry in our review, but I would prefer specialists go over everything as well."

"Is there anywhere else you can think of that Hailey might have gone?" Jackson asked.

"No," Michael said firmly. "Hailey obeyed our instructions. She would not have left this house unless someone forced her to do so."

Jackson looked at Sharon. "If Hailey decided to disobey, is there someplace she would have gone—a store, café, library?"

Sharon glanced at her husband before shaking her head. "Hailey went to school during the week and to church with us on Sundays. Sometimes, on Saturdays, she went to Gina's house to help her with schoolwork. But usually, Gina came here after school if she had an exam to prepare for. Hailey always helped her with her science tests."

"What church?" Jackson asked.

"Merciful Trinity," Sharon said. "Just a couple blocks over."

Grayson rose from his chair and Jackson followed suit. "If you hear from Hailey, call me immediately."

"Yes," Michael said.

"And if you think of anything else that might help, please call," Grayson said.

"Of course we'll call," Michael said, his frustration evident in his voice "We want our daughter back. If there was something we knew that could make that happen, we'd tell you."

"I don't mean to upset you, sir," Grayson said. "Detective Lamotte and I will be working full time to find your daughter, but we don't know her like you do. Even things you think are insignificant might help us locate her."

Michael barely nodded.

They exited the house and headed for the car.

"Whew!" Jackson said as he climbed inside. "I feel for the guy with his daughter missing, but I don't like him."

"His obvious superiority and condescension make it difficult to," Grayson agreed.

"Why are you bothering with a forensics team? No one broke into that house and you know it. That girl lived under a microscope every day. It's far more likely that she'd simply had enough and walked."

"I agree, and that's what worries me. This isn't a safe place for an inexperienced teen to wander around, and it doesn't sound like Hailey had much of an opportunity to develop street smarts."

"Probably not. Hopefully, she'll be hiding in one of these friends' closets. I know they've already denied any knowledge, but teens don't always tell the truth."

Grayson nodded. "I've seen it before. A teenager hid his friend for over a week in his bedroom. His parents had no idea and only figured it out because food kept disappearing from the pantry when none of them were home."

Jackson looked at his notes. "Then I guess we better go see if Marcy's or Gina's pantry has some gaps."

"Not in only one day. Not most girls, anyway. A teen boy can put gaps in a pantry in thirty minutes."

"Well, she left that house to go somewhere, and I don't think she was forced. There's no sign of struggle. Besides, what kind of abductor waits for his victim to get her purse and cell phone? And we know she made it inside the house because the chicken was thawing."

"I'll be interested to see the trace on her phone. In the meantime, we'll run down the obvious places. She probably chose to leave the house and I seriously doubt it was the first time, but something could have happened to her afterward."

Jackson nodded. No city was safe for a young girl to wander about, and the fact that Hailey had been missing overnight bothered him. He hoped she was hiding at a friend's house. Because a lot of things could go wrong on the streets of New Orleans, especially for a young, naive girl.

NICOLAS WHEELED himself out of the cathedral and into the courtyard. He'd passed his absence off to Father Malcolm and Father Bernard as needing to get out for some air and to calm himself down. It wasn't a lie but it wasn't the whole truth, either. And he hated lying to the priests, even by omission. Despite the fact that he was certain he was doing the right thing, he still felt guilty.

So he'd spent a good bit of time in prayer when he'd

returned to the church, then an hour poring over his favorite historical texts in their private library after he'd finished his administrative duties in the business office. But he felt only marginally better as he wheeled himself down the walkway to the building that housed the priests' living quarters. He was still convinced he'd done the right thing, and he was fairly certain that was the crux of his despair. How could doing the right thing be in such huge conflict with his vows? In seminary, they'd been required to ponder such things so many times, but nothing of this magnitude. But then, how could the church have prepared him for the uncertainty he now had about every choice he'd made, when before, he was just as certain they'd all been absolutely correct.

Time, he kept telling himself. Time and prayer would restore things back to normal. And the likelihood of anything like this happening again had to be small. He'd just been unlucky. In the wrong place at the wrong time. It sounded good, anyway, but he was certain that if Father Malcolm or Father Bernard had been taking confession that day, they wouldn't have heard the confession Nicolas had. Someone had taken advantage of the fact that his lack of mobility would prevent him from identifying them.

And that bothered him the most. Because it was insidious.

He opened the front door and rolled into the common living room that they shared. Each of their apartments had a small living space, but this one was larger and allowed for them to sit and visit with one another and visitors. It was open to a kitchen with a small dining area, something they did not have in their apartments.

Fortunately for Nicolas and Bernard, Malcolm was an excellent cook and actually enjoyed the process. Nicolas was handy enough to help prep for Malcolm as he'd always done for his mother but couldn't be depended on to cook much beyond grilled cheese sandwiches, which he'd lived on most of his time in seminary. Bernard's great-grandmother had been full-blooded Italian and he could make a mean pasta, but the food was so heavy, they reserved it for special occasions. Nicolas had been watching his diet ever since the wreck. It was too easy to gain weight when your movement was so restricted.

Country music was blaring on the radio and Malcolm stood at the kitchen island, chopping onions. He looked up when Nicolas entered and turned down the volume on the music before he called out an enthusiastic hello. Malcolm smiled as he issued the greeting, but his eyes also searched Nicolas's face for the strain he'd clearly been under the past couple days.

"Are you feeling better after this morning's walk? So to speak, I mean," Malcolm said.

Nicolas nodded. "That and a good bit of prayer have improved my outlook."

"Excellent. Dinner should help as well. I know we're supposed to watch our calories most of the time, but I thought your favorite would cheer you up."

"You're making enchiladas?"

Malcolm smiled. "I thought you might be willing to make a dietary exception."

"Okay. But just this once."

Malcolm laughed. "You'd eat enchiladas every day if I'd make them."

"Probably, but then you'd need a trailer to get me around. Do you need any help?"

"No. I finished up early so the prep is already done. Your mail is on the table. This will be ready in about an hour."

"That gives me time for a shower. Thanks, Malcolm... for everything."

Nicolas gathered the mail from the table and continued down the hallway to his quarters. There were four apartments on the first floor and another four on the second floor. At one time, attendance had been so great that six apartments had been occupied. Now St. Mary's could get by with only two priests, but Bernard had argued that three were necessary to give the appropriate amount of focus to the congregation as well as the business end of things, which seemed to increase in time consumption every year.

The apartments on the second floor were all furnished but remained closed unless a visiting priest was in residence. The unoccupied apartment on the first floor had been repurposed as a small gym, complete with a treadmill, stationary bike, and weight machine. Nicolas had paid for the extravagance himself, with some argument at first from Bernard. When Nicolas insisted that it was his circumstances that made the equipment necessary, Bernard had acquiesced. Malcolm and Bernard had both dropped their gym memberships and enjoyed the option of a workout right in their own home and more often than before, as it was now possible to sneak in some exercise in between their duties. Bernard had thanked Nicolas so many times for insisting on the room that it had become a joke between Nicolas and Malcolm.

He entered his apartment and decided to check the mail before showering. It was just after 4:00 p.m. and that way, if anything needed addressing during regular business hours, he still had time to make a phone call. The first couple of envelopes were junk mail—offers for things that were completely unsuited, like women's shoes and lingerie. He wondered briefly if businesses bothered to screen addresses before they did mail-outs, but he doubted it. The next letter was an account statement from his attorney that he received monthly. A quick check of the bottom of the paper let him know he still had plenty of money, and he tucked the paper back into the envelope for filing.

When he saw the handwriting on the next envelope, he sighed.

He was deliberating whether he wanted to open the letter at all when there was a knock on his door. He called out for the person to enter and Father Malcolm stepped inside.

"I apologize for the interruption," Malcolm said, then

noticed Nicolas's expression. "Is everything all right? Did you receive bad news?"

"I'm sure it's not good news, but I haven't actually opened it yet."

"I don't understand."

"This is from my third cousin. He and his parents are the only living relatives I have, although my parents never spoke to them and I've never met them."

"Then what do they want from you?"

"Money."

Malcolm frowned. "It seems forward to ask a stranger for money, even if you're related."

"It *is* forward, and I know we're not supposed to judge, but the reason my parents had nothing to do with them is because of the way they chose to live. They're all addicted to drugs. And despite many offers of help in the form of rehab and counseling, they have refused. They only want cash, and I know it will go straight up their arms. I'm sure they're suffering in their own way, but I cannot be party to their deaths."

"Of course not. I'm sorry you are in that position. Would you like for me to address the letter for you?"

Nicolas hesitated for a moment. He'd had his attorney handle these for the past year, thinking that if his family understood that they would receive no access to Nicolas, they would find someone else to beg money from. And the letters had lessened, but he still received one every couple months.

"You know what," Nicolas said, mind made up as to

how to proceed from now on. "I'd love for you to address it for me. Please put it into the kitchen garbage."

"You're sure?"

"Positive." He handed Malcolm the letter. "Now it's my turn to apologize. You came here clearly seeking something and the conversation has become about me once again."

"Oh, yes! I completely forgot to tell you that the florist for the Donahue wedding called earlier in a snit. He wants to know what time he can deliver the flowers and to make sure the temperature will be correct, so they won't wilt before the ceremony."

Nicolas sighed. "The panic surrounding a wedding that doesn't take place for three weeks is somewhat overwhelming. I dread the last few days leading up to the actual ceremony."

Malcolm grinned. "People lose their minds over weddings. This is your first one officiating, but you'll get used to it."

"That's a frightening thought."

Malcolm laughed. "Yes, well, I have to call him about the Miller christening, so I figured I'd answer his question about the wedding as well and save you one tiny hassle."

"Then tell him I will adjust the temperature that morning. The guests will be freezing, but you can assure the florist that the flowers will be beautiful. He can deliver them any time after noon."

"Very well," Malcolm said and ducked out, closing the door behind him.

Nicolas looked down at the last envelope and frowned. It hadn't gone through the regular postal system. There was no address or return address. Not even a stamp. Only his name written on the front in a handwriting he didn't recognize. He opened the envelope and pulled out the paper.

When he saw the words, he gasped. Then he grasped the arms of his wheelchair and stifled a cry. When he was certain he had control, he looked down at the paper in his lap, the horrible words staring up at him. Shaming him. Mocking him.

She can't help you.

5

It took Shaye several hours and trips to four different locations before she found the landscaping crew who'd been working at St. Mary's. Some of the wasted time appeared to be because of a completely horrible administrative system, but the rest appeared to be employees closing ranks. Despite her protesting, they sensed trouble and didn't want to put others in the line of fire. Finally, she'd convinced one young man that she was not looking to make trouble for anyone, and he'd told her where to find the men who'd been working at the church that Saturday.

It was late afternoon when she located them in the courtyard at the university. It seemed a lot of work for five people, but they moved quickly and transformed the shrubbery from scraggly into compliant. She saw an older man with black-and-silver hair giving instructions to the rest and assumed he might be the foreman, so she made her way over.

When she introduced herself, the man gave her a wary look and glanced at the other employees.

"You the cops?" he asked.

"No. I'm a private detective. And no one is in trouble. I'm simply looking for information."

"What kind of information?"

"My client was at St. Mary's on Saturday when your crew was working there."

"Did someone make a complaint? Because we don't speak to people when we're on the job except the clients. It's company policy."

"No one has made a complaint," she assured the man. "My client was in the cathedral praying and when she left, she forgot her purse. When she went back to get it, it was gone. I wondered if you saw anyone leaving the cathedral through the courtyard around 2:00 p.m.?"

"We don't go in the cathedral." The man looked slightly panicked.

"I don't believe you did." Shaye's frustration began to grow. The man was so worried about being accused of something that he was no help whatsoever. "My client doesn't want to press charges anyway. But there's a string bracelet her niece made her in that purse. Her niece passed away a month ago. She just wants the bracelet back. There are two exits from the cathedral, and one leads into the courtyard. Since that's where you were working, I hoped you could tell me if you saw anyone leave that way."

"There was several people," a young black man said. "An older black lady with silver hair, blue dress, and a hat with flowers on it. A white dude, maybe late 50s. He was tall and had on black slacks. Got into a Mercedes S-Class. There was a younger Asian guy with hair in a pony-tail and a little girl with him. The girl was maybe five or six. Two average white dudes were there—one came out the courtyard door and one came down the sidewalk from the front of the cathedral. Probably in their twen-ties. They got into a van for an electric company. After that, the younger priest pushed the one in the wheelchair out. He looked like he was sick. The one in the wheel-chair, I mean."

"And all of these people exited into the courtyard around two o'clock?"

"Sometime around then," he said. "I wasn't looking at my watch really. Some might have been before and some after, but they was all around that time."

"You have a really good memory," Shaye said.

"Thanks. My moms says so too. That's why I'm taking night classes. She don't want me working lawns forever."

"Your mom is a smart lady," Shaye said. "I'm sure you'll do fine. What's your name?"

"Jamal Thibodeaux."

She pulled out a card and handed it to Jamal. "If you think of anyone else, please give me a call. Do you think

above committing murder, but it took strength to strangle someone. So unless the victim was very young and weak, it was unlikely the older lady was the perp. She'd focus on the four men instead, although the man with the child wasn't exactly a good fit, either. People *had* inserted children in the middle of their crimes before, but it was risky. Still, she'd move him just in front of the older lady.

It wasn't a lot to go on, and it only covered one exit, but it was a start.

6

As Grayson pulled away from the curb of the café where they'd just had a late lunch, Jackson's cell phone rang. It was the forensics unit, so he answered right away and put him on speaker.

"Please tell me you got something on the phone," he said to Matt, the tech.

"Not much," Matt said. "This girl was not a normal teen. Hardly any texts and it looks like she deleted most everything as soon as she read it. We retrieved the texts, but I don't see anything of interest. They're all to her parents or a girl named Gina."

"No talk of being mad at the parents, or a secret boyfriend, running away, nothing?" Jackson asked.

"Not even a peep," Matt said. "There was plenty of complaining about a calculus teacher, and the other girl is afraid her grades are going to drop below an A in science, but mostly it's school stuff or about shows they're watching on television. It's weird."

"What do you mean?" Jackson asked.

"What sixteen-year-old girl isn't talking about boys?" Matt asked. "Or bitching about her parents?"

"Probably the kind whose parents read all her texts," Jackson said. "The father seems determined to ensure that his daughter is not corrupted by outside influences."

"One of those," Matt said. "Then I'd bet on another phone. She's talking regular talk somehow, and I doubt it's all in person."

"If she has another phone, then it's gone along with her because forensics didn't turn up anything," Jackson said.

"Well, if you get something, let me know and I'll do another trace."

"Thanks." Jackson hung up and looked over at Grayson.

"You think he's right?" Jackson asked. "You think there's another phone?"

"Maybe. Given the situation, I'm sure she'd want one, but she'd need the funds to pay for it."

"Most kids figure out a way to get a hold of some cash. Babysitting, dog walking, tutoring, whatever. If she was helping Gina with school then she might have been helping others."

Grayson nodded. "We'll be sure and ask the friends. One of them should know."

Jackson checked his phone—4:30 p.m. School was

out for the day, but that didn't mean either girl was at home. If they weren't, then Jackson and Grayson would spend whatever amount of time it took to track them down. The first forty-eight hours were critical in a missing persons case. And despite the fact that both girls claimed no knowledge of Hailey's plans, teens usually covered for each other until they realized things had crossed the line from a bit of fun away from the watchful eye of parents to a dangerous position for a young woman to be in.

Hailey's parents had stressed the fact that she didn't have a boyfriend, but if she was hiding someone from her parents—someone they would deem inappropriate— there was a 99 percent chance one or both of her closest friends knew about it. Then it was just a matter of convincing them to talk and hoping that the inappropriate boyfriend wasn't the stuff nightmares were made of.

Grayson parked in front of a Spanish-style home and they climbed out. The area was mostly middle-class families, often with both parents working. If they could catch either of the girls at home and question them without their parents present, they were far more likely to get the answers they were looking for.

They rang the doorbell, and a tall, thin girl with brown hair pulled back in a ponytail opened it. Grayson explained who they were and her eyes widened. She responded in the negative when Grayson asked if her parents were home, and Jackson thought she was going to refuse to speak to them, but then she gave them a long-suffering sigh and waved them inside. She flopped on the couch and started picking the polish on her thumbnail.

Grayson indicated for Jackson to sit and they sat across from the girl in two chairs. Towering above her was only likely to make her nervous and that often equaled silence, especially with teens. However, Jackson was fairly certain that Marcy wasn't nervous at all. She looked more bored than anything.

"Have you found Hailey?" Marcy asked.

"No," Grayson said.

She shrugged. "I guess it was stupid of me to think you had. I mean, if she'd come home, she would have called, right? Unless something bad happened. Did something bad happen?"

"I don't know," Grayson said. "We don't know where Hailey is or what happened to her. We were hoping you could help us with that."

Marcy shook her head. "I don't see how. Gina's sent a million texts but they don't go through. She even tried calling and it goes straight to voice mail. It's like her phone isn't even turned on."

"Would it be out of character for Hailey to turn her phone off?" Grayson asked.

Marcy gave him a look of slight disdain. "We don't turn off our phones. How can people live without a phone? Our whole lives run by these things. Appointments, reminders, friends, social media—and parents calling all the time. 'Where are you?' 'Did you remember to lock the door?' 'Don't eat the cookies before dinner.' And how would we take selfies?"

Properly chastised, Grayson tried a different line of questioning. "And you have no idea where Hailey might have gone?"

"She wouldn't have *gone* anywhere," Marcy said. "Hailey was so boring even her dog ran away. She never did anything that mattered. She never said anything that mattered."

Grayson glanced at Jackson. For someone who was supposed to be friends with the missing girl, Marcy's attitude was strange.

She noticed the glance and rolled her eyes. "You think I'm being mean, right? Just like Gina. 'Be nice to Hailey. She doesn't have many friends.'" She threw her arms in the air. "Well, that's a big lie and I assume you want the truth. The truth is Hailey doesn't have *any* friends except Gina."

"So you're not her friend?" Jackson asked.

"I'm *Gina's* friend. Have been since we were five years old. Hailey came along a year ago when her family moved to the neighborhood. Gina was nice to her one day and Hailey's been clinging to her like a parasite ever since. I never get to do anything with just Gina anymore." She perked up a bit. "Until now. I guess I can now."

"Okay," Jackson said, slightly uncomfortable with the teen's complete lack of concern about a missing girl. "So we can rule out other friends. Is there any place in particular that Hailey liked to spend time—a library, store, coffee shop? Somewhere she might have gone? If we can narrow down where she was right before she disappeared, it might help find her."

"She did like to read," Marcy said. "But why would she go to a library when you can read on your phone?"

"Of course," Jackson said. "I suppose it's safe to assume Hailey doesn't have a boyfriend?"

Marcy snorted. "Are you kidding? She was afraid to talk to boys. She blushed seventy shades of red and purple if one accidentally spoke to her."

"So there was no one she was interested in?" Grayson asked.

"I didn't say she wasn't interested," Marcy said. "Everyone notices a cute guy. Even geeks. But no cute guy was going to notice Hailey. Not with her staring at her feet all the time."

Grayson rose and pulled a card from his pocket. He handed it to Marcy. "Please give me a call if you think of anything that might help. Her parents are really worried, and New Orleans is no place for a young girl to be alone."

Marcy looked a tiny bit contrite. "Okay. I hope you find her. I mean, I don't really want to hang out with her, but I don't want anything bad to happen to her, either."

Grayson nodded and they headed out of the house. When they climbed in the car, Jackson looked over at his partner and shook his head.

"Remind me to never, ever have a teenage girl," Jackson said.

Grayson snorted. "They're not all as bad as that, but yeah. She definitely makes one rethink being a parent."

"You didn't ask about a second cell phone."

"That girl doesn't know anything about Hailey, except that she wanted her to disappear, which is exactly what happened."

Jackson shook his head. "If she wasn't so forward and was a bit more clever, I might consider that she'd killed Hailey just to get Gina back to herself."

"It wouldn't be the first time a teen committed a murder over something that silly, but I agree. Marcy appears to be all talk. I'm sure her mouth does plenty of damage but I'm not ready to peg her as a killer."

"I'm not ready to strike her off the list, either."

"No. It's too early for that."

"Let's hope Gina doesn't feel the same way Marcy does. We don't know anything more about Hailey now than before we went in that house."

"We know Hailey's dog found her uninteresting."

"Fine. We don't know anything relevant."

Grayson pulled away from the curb. "Let's go see if we can get something, then."

Jackson found himself scanning the neighborhood as Grayson drove. It was an average middle-class sort of place. Modest homes with modest cars in the drive. Some with nice landscaping and well maintained. Some with beds that had been taken over by weeds and a lawn that needed a good round of fertilizer. It was so typical that it could have been any neighborhood in any city anywhere.

Except a girl had gone missing from this one.

Maybe.

The reality was, they needed to narrow down exactly where Hailey was when she dropped off the radar. Her phone last pinged in her house, but with no sign of forced entry and her cell phone and purse missing, everything pointed to her leaving voluntarily. Where she'd gone was the question.

Gina's house was a classic, boring red brick with white shutters and decent hedges. There were no cars in the drive, so unless one was stored in the single-car garage, they might have lucked out again and would catch Gina at home alone. Grayson knocked on the door and they waited a bit, but there was no answer. He knocked again and Jackson saw a blind slat lift a bit. He took his badge out and put it in front of the window. A couple seconds later, the door opened and a young girl peered out.

While Marcy had looked somewhat athletic and had a bit of a tan, Gina was thin and had no color to her skin. Her lips were a natural bright pink and her hair a mousy limp blond, making her look somewhat fragile.

"May we come in and speak to you?" Grayson asked.

She nodded and stepped back to let them in, then immediately closed the door, locked it, and drew the dead bolt. As she walked into the living room and sat on the fireplace hearth, the contrast between her and Marcy was all the more defined.

Gina was scared.

Grayson and Jackson took seats on opposite ends of a sofa facing the fireplace. Gina stared at the ground and chewed on her fingernails.

"Detective Lamotte and I are trying to find Hailey," Grayson said. "We'd like your help."

She looked up at him and nodded.

"We just talked to Marcy," Grayson said. "She said you were Hailey's only friend."

She nodded again. "People didn't get her. She was smart...too smart to be cool, you know?"

Grayson nodded as if all this teen angst made sense. "There's no indication that Hailey was taken from her home, so we're assuming she left on her own accord. Do you have any idea where she was going?"

"No. I didn't know she'd gone anywhere until her mother called me panicked because she wasn't at home. I thought maybe she went for a run or something, but then it got late and she never came back."

"Did she go for a run after school often?" Jackson asked.

"Yeah. She wasn't supposed to, but she said she couldn't stand sitting in that house staring at the walls all the time. She liked to run and she was good at it. She would have done track if her dad would have let her, but he didn't like anything that wasn't academic."

"Did she take a particular route when she ran?"

"I don't know. She never said and I never asked. I wish I would have now."

"Is there anywhere else you can think of that she would go besides running?" Grayson asked. "A favorite hangout spot? Or somewhere she went to be alone?"

"Sometimes we'd sit on the bench under the big oak tree in the park when we were done studying," Gina said. "But never after dark. We're not allowed out after dark."

"The park a couple blocks from here?" Jackson asked.

She nodded.

Jackson had been through the park on a missing persons hunt for a toddler. Fortunately, the child had simply wandered off and had been located asleep under a hedge at a house across the street. It was an open area, about a block in size, and while it had some large trees and some shrubs, there were no heavily wooded sections and it was surrounded by houses. Not typically the kind of park setting that kids disappeared from. But still, it wouldn't hurt to knock on doors and see if any of the people who lived in the homes that surrounded the park had seen Hailey.

"What about a boyfriend?" Jackson asked.

Gina shrugged. "Hailey wasn't allowed to have a boyfriend. Her parents said she was too young."

Jackson glanced at Grayson, who frowned. Her answer was total deflection, which meant she was hiding something that might be important for them to know. Especially if it involved a boy that Hailey had a romantic interest in.

"Young girls don't always do what their parents tell them," Jackson said. "Especially when they think their parents are wrong. Like the running."

Gina looked at him and bit her lip, then looked back down at the floor.

"Gina," Grayson said gently. "I think there's something you're not telling us. And I understand covering for your friend, but she's missing and might be in danger. She's not going to get mad at you for trying to help us find her."

Gina looked at Jackson, then Grayson, and finally blurted out, "She was seeing a guy."

"You're sure?" Grayson asked. "Because Marcy said Hailey didn't have a boyfriend."

Gina blew out a breath. "That's because Marcy doesn't like Hailey and mostly ignores her. If Hailey sprouted wings and flew around the block, Marcy wouldn't notice."

"Do you know who the boy is?" Grayson asked.

"Sorta. I mean, he's not a boy really. He's not in school anymore."

Jackson tensed a bit. An adult male and an underage, inexperienced girl was never a good combination. "Can you give us his name?"

Gina shook her head. "Hailey never said. I...I wasn't supposed to know. But last week she was being weird after school. We had a chemistry test on Thursday and she always helped me study, but she said she had to go to the doctor. It didn't sound right."

"So you followed her?" Jackson asked.

Gina looked down at the ground, clearly embarrassed. "Yeah. I hid in the bushes across from her house and followed her to the convenience store two blocks over. I thought maybe she was just mad at me for some reason and was going for a soda or something."

"But she met a guy?" Jackson asked.

She nodded. "He came out of the service station next to the store. He had one of the shirts on like the other guys that work there. They went around the corner between the two buildings and I saw him kiss her. Like, a real kiss, you know?"

Grayson nodded. "What else did you see?"

Gina blushed. "Nothing. I turned around and ran home. I was mad. I couldn't believe she'd kept a secret like that from me. And I couldn't believe she was kissing some guy that old."

"How old do you think he is?" Jackson asked.

"I don't know," she said. "Old. At least twenty."

"Can you describe him?" Jackson asked.

"Taller than Hailey by a good bit," Gina said. "The top of her head came to his nose. He was thin but had muscles. Longish brown hair in a ponytail, and a tattoo on his arm."

"Could you tell what the tattoo was?" Grayson asked.

She shook her head. "I could just see the ink from where I was, but it was a band that went all the way around."

"That's a big help," Grayson said. "Thank you. Is there anything else you can think of that might help us?"

"No," she said. "Do you think she's going to be all right? I mean, that guy looked strong. Do you think he hurt her?"

"We don't know what happened," Grayson said. "But we're going to find out. Does Hailey have a second cell phone—one she keeps secret from her parents?"

Gina slowly shook her head. "I've never seen one, but I guess she might." Gina sighed. "I'm beginning to think I don't know Hailey as well as I thought I did."

"That's usually the case." Grayson handed her his card as they rose. "If you hear from Hailey or think of anything else that can help us, please give me a call."

As Grayson pulled away from the curb, Jackson accessed a picture of Hailey on his phone. "She's a pretty girl," Jackson said. "But she has only one friend and a secret boyfriend who is likely an unsuitable age."

"You mean old?" Grayson grinned.

Jackson laughed. "I guess if twenty is old that makes you and me ancient."

"I might be prehistoric."

Jackson smiled, then sobered. "A pretty girl but fairly new to the school, brainy and probably an introvert. So she meets Gina, who is nice to her and is safe, but she comes with Marcy, who probably spent most of her time poking at Hailey."

Grayson nodded. "Because Hailey is as pretty as Marcy. She didn't like sharing the spotlight."

"So Hailey meets this mechanic at some point, and he gives her attention and says the right things, and she's taken with him."

"Don't forget the bad-boy thing. Her parents wouldn't approve of the relationship. That makes it all the more exciting."

Jackson blew out a breath. "I hope to God that guy has just been foolish enough to let her stay at his place. Otherwise..."

Jackson didn't finish his statement. He didn't have to.

7

"Well, let's go find out just how smart this mechanic is," Grayson said and pulled into the parking lot for the auto shop. "Be on the lookout for the tattoo. If this guy likes to play with fire, he'll probably be able to spot cops a mile away."

"I hope he doesn't run," Jackson said as he exited the car. "These are new shoes. They're not broken in."

"They might be by the end of shift."

As they approached the shop, an older man stepped out of one of the bays and greeted them.

"Afternoon," he said. "Name's Silas. Can I help you with something?"

"You have an employee," Grayson said. "Young guy, around twenty, brown hair, tall, a band tattoo on one arm?"

Silas nodded. "That would be my sister's boy, Hudson. What's he done now?"

"What makes you think he's done something?" Grayson asked.

"You're cops, right?" Silas asked. "Boy has been a bit of trouble since his father died. Not serious trouble, but the general sort. He needs to grow up. I'm trying to help that process along. So what did he do?"

"We're not sure he did anything," Grayson said. "But we think he was involved with a young woman who is missing. She's sixteen, so there's some urgency in finding her. We're hoping she's having a young adult moment and is hiding out with your nephew."

Silas frowned. "Don't see as how that's possible since the boy's been living with me for the last two years. You said this girl is sixteen?"

Grayson nodded.

Silas sighed. "Damn it to hell. He's back here doing an oil change. We best figure this out."

Silas headed into the shop for the back corner, where the guy Gina had described was checking the oil in a sedan. He looked up as Silas approached and his eyes widened when he spotted Grayson and Jackson behind his uncle.

Yep, Jackson thought. *He knows cops.*

"Hudson," Silas said as they stepped up. "These men are police and they want to ask you some questions about that young girl you've been messing around with. The operative word being 'young.'"

Silas's frustration was so evident in his voice that

Hudson looked a bit ashamed. That was a good sign. Defiant was a much harder nut to crack.

"You've been seeing a young woman named Hailey Pitre," Grayson said.

Hudson glanced at his uncle, and it was clear that he wanted to lie but was trying to gauge if he could get away with it. Given how horrible he was at hiding what he was thinking, Jackson was going with no, he couldn't get away with it.

"Don't even think about lying," Silas said. "This is serious business."

Hudson shuffled his feet and stared down at the ground. "Yeah. I see her sometimes. What of it?"

"Do you know where she is now?" Grayson asked.

Hudson looked up at him, his expression uneasy. "No. I haven't talked to her since yesterday morning."

"You're sure about that?" Grayson asked.

"Yeah," Hudson said. "Usually she sends me a text or calls after school, but I haven't heard anything."

"Have you tried calling her?" Grayson asked.

He nodded, looking guilty. "I'm not supposed to. You know, in case her parents are around, but when I didn't hear from her yesterday afternoon, I called then and today when she would have been at school. It went straight to voice mail."

"You didn't go to her house?" Grayson asked.

"No!" Hudson said. "She'd be in serious trouble with her parents if they found out about us."

"And rightfully so," Silas interrupted. "She's a girl.

You're a man. If I caught you seeing my sixteen-year-old daughter, I'd be loading my shotgun."

"It's not like that," Hudson said. "Hailey is different. Grown-up. She doesn't act like a kid, and she's really smart."

"Ha," Silas said. "If she was smart, she wouldn't be wasting time with you."

"Hailey is missing," Grayson said before things could get off on too much of a tangent.

Hudson's eyes widened. "Missing? You mean like disappeared?"

"Yes," Grayson said. "Since yesterday afternoon. That's why we're here."

Hudson ran a hand through his hair. "I didn't know. I thought maybe her parents found out and took her phone. Or maybe she'd ditched me. But I never thought..."

"Do you have any idea where Hailey might be?" Grayson asked.

"She has some friends," Hudson said.

"We've already spoken to them," Grayson said. "One of them gave us you."

Hudson scowled. "Marcy, right?"

Jackson glanced at Grayson. "You know Marcy?" he asked.

"I know her all right," Hudson said. "She's been coming by here for months, trying to get my attention. I told her I ain't interested."

"Why not?" Jackson asked. "She's a pretty girl."

"She's a bitch," Hudson said.

Silas popped his nephew on the back of the head.

"Well, she is," Hudson said. "And I ain't apologizing for saying so. She was always nasty to Hailey."

"How long have you been seeing Hailey?" Jackson asked.

"Two months," Hudson replied.

"And how long has Marcy been coming around?" Jackson asked.

Hudson shrugged. "I don't know. Since January, maybe. I did the oil change on her mom's car and she was with her for the pickup. She's been hanging around ever since."

"So Marcy knew you were seeing Hailey?" Jackson said.

Hudson frowned. "I don't know. I didn't think so, but who else would have told you about me? I figure she must have seen something."

"And you have no idea where Hailey might be?" Grayson said. "No other friends that you are aware of? Anyone who might let her crash for a few days?"

"She didn't have nobody else," Hudson said. "Her parents were crazy strict, and Hailey said Gina was nice, but she wouldn't tell her about us because she didn't think Gina would keep it secret. Hailey said Gina's sorta afraid of everything, especially getting into trouble."

"Did Hailey have any money?" Grayson asked.

"Yeah, a little probably," Hudson said. "She would babysit sometimes and her aunt in Seattle sent her money for her birthday. I know she helped kids study some. But I doubt she had a lot. Her parents didn't give her any."

"What phone number did Hailey call you from?" Grayson asked.

Hudson recited the number and Jackson took it down. It wasn't the same as the cell phone her parents provided her with.

"What's your last name?" Grayson asked.

"Landry," Hudson said.

"You have any trouble with the law?" Grayson asked.

Hudson shuffled his feet. "A little. Just stupid kid stuff —joyriding, stealing some beer."

"Okay," Grayson said and handed Hudson and Silas each a card. "If you hear from Hailey, call me. Don't even think about keeping it a secret. Not even if she asks. This is a police matter now and she's a minor. You could be in all sorts of trouble if her parents find out about your relationship. Don't give them even more reason to make it an issue."

"He won't," Silas said. "I'll make sure of it."

Hudson nodded and went back to the car engine, but Jackson could tell he was nervous and worried. The question was, about what? Did he know something about Hailey that he wasn't telling? Was he involved in her disappearance somehow? Or was he simply worried that the girl he was dating with was missing?

Jackson dialed the second cell phone as soon as they got into the car, but like the other phone, it went straight to voice mail. He called Matt and gave him the new number.

"The ole secret cell phone wins again," Matt said. "Give me a few minutes for a trace. I'll get the warrant for the records moving as well."

"Thanks," Jackson said. "And I need a background check on Hudson Landry and his uncle who owns the repair shop." Jackson gave him the name of the shop.

"I'm on it," Matt said.

Jackson disconnected. He looked over at Grayson. "So? What do you think of 'old man' Hudson?"

Grayson shook his head. "I'm not sure. He was nervous and worried, but that could swing a lot of different ways."

"Yeah. What do you think about the uncle?"

"Seems like a straight shooter and frustrated with Hudson. But there's clearly a lot he doesn't know about his nephew, especially since Hudson's managed to keep a two-month relationship hidden from him."

"He's not going to make much of an alibi, either," Jackson said. "We have no idea when Hailey dropped off the map or where, and even if Silas said Hudson was at home all night, I don't think we can buy it. I'm not saying Silas would lie for him. I just think a lot of people have no idea what goes on after they're asleep."

"That's true enough. Besides, Hudson could have met Hailey after work and either stashed her somewhere or worse and still been home for dinner."

"It's interesting," Jackson said. "Hudson thinks Marcy

is the one who tipped us off but Marcy was adamant that Hailey didn't have a boyfriend. You think she was lying?"

"It didn't seem like it, but now I'm not sure of anything."

"If Marcy saw Hailey and Hudson together, and she's been pursuing Hudson for a while now, that's a really bad combination."

"I know. Shit. If this is another case of one teen killing another over a boy, I'm taking all of my vacation when this is over."

Jackson nodded. "Where are you going? I might go with you."

SHAYE CLIMBED into her SUV and sent a text to Nicolas.

Please call me tomorrow when you can. Need more information. Nothing urgent.

She added the last bit so Nicolas wouldn't panic thinking she'd discovered something when that was not the case at all. Well, that wasn't exactly true. She'd gotten a list of potential suspects, such as it was. But in order for it to matter, she needed to figure out the names that went with the descriptions. The electric company would probably be the easiest to identify.

She checked the time on her dash and frowned. Late for dinner with her mother again. It was becoming a habit, as Corrine had pointed out the last time she showed up twenty minutes late. Corrine wasn't necessarily upset at her tardiness but more that her carefully prepared dinner had gotten cold. She'd decided that from then on, she'd wait for Shaye to arrive before she started cooking, but Eleonore, Corrine's best friend and Shaye's therapist, had argued that she was old and had a bedtime. Corrine had finally relented and agreed that she and Eleonore would eat on time and if Shaye was late, she'd have to eat reheated food.

Given that the majority of Shaye's personally prepared meals were things she popped in the microwave, it wasn't exactly a scary proposition. Corrine's cooking was exceptional, even reheated. But still, Shaye regretted that she'd lost track of time again and was behind schedule. She enjoyed her dinners with Corrine and Eleonore and hated missing part of them.

She let herself in and made her way to the back of the house, where she found Eleonore sitting at the kitchen island eating chips and salsa and Corrine checking the oven. Eleonore looked over as she walked in and shook her head.

"Your late habits are rubbing off on your mother," Eleonore said. "She was just starting dinner when I got here."

"I got held up in a meeting at the center," Corrine said. "The tamales just need another ten minutes."

"Mexican night?" Shaye asked. "Yum!"

Eleonore sighed. "If there were predinner cocktails, like the old days, all this waiting would be a lot more pleasant."

"Not for you it wouldn't," Corrine said.

Eleonore was an alcoholic. She'd gotten sober decades ago when she finally admitted her problem, but she'd fallen off the wagon last year when Shaye's past had returned full force. She was sober again, but it was a tenuous thing and the struggle would always be there.

"I can make virgin margaritas," Shaye offered.

Eleonore shook her head. "Best to avoid it altogether. It brings back too many memories—good ones at the bar and not so good ones afterward. So what's your excuse for tardiness?"

"A new case," Shaye said.

"More insurance work?" Corrine asked, her voice clearly hopeful. Her mother would prefer Shaye do only boring insurance work.

"No. It's a private client," Shaye said.

"What kind of case?" Corrine asked.

"I can't say," Shaye said.

Corrine sighed.

"I mean it," Shaye said. "Clients have confidentiality. But don't start your worrying. This case is likely to go absolutely nowhere."

"Why is that?" Corrine asked.

"Let's just say the whole thing might have been a prank," Shaye said. "And that's all I'm saying. Next subject."

Corrine frowned. She wasn't satisfied with the answer but she knew when she'd reached Shaye's information limit.

"What's new with the center?" Eleonore asked, changing the subject. "Do you have an opening date yet?"

"Sort of," Corrine said. "The counselors will be able to move out of their temporary offices and into the building in a couple weeks. The dorms are still not complete and I'm ready to strangle someone if I could just latch onto the responsible party. But since they all keep pointing the finger at one another, it would have to be a mass murder for me to ensure I got the culprit."

Shaye looked over at Eleonore, who raised her eyebrows. Given the things that Corrine had seen on a daily basis during her time as a social worker, it was difficult to ruffle her feathers. The building contractors must have really mucked things up for her to be this angry.

"You know how it is," Eleonore said. "You've done enough improvements to this house to know you take a contractor's estimate and add 30 percent more money and 50 percent more time."

Corrine sighed. "I know, but this is not a bathroom remodel in a house that has five others to use. These kids are living on the streets. I want them inside and safe. And I want more time spent on approving foster homes before we toss kids into them. There's been too many issues with foster parents the last several years. We're missing things and the kids are paying the price."

"You know a lot of the street kids will never stay there," Shaye said. "They're too worried about being found. And as much as I support what you're doing, staying there would allow abusive parents to easily find them. I imagine everyone actively seeking a runaway will haunt the doors to see if their kid is there."

"I'll have security," Corrine said. "No one will be able to hang around without being noticed. I'll follow all the laws concerning these kids, but I know their rights and I intend to exercise every one of them. Trust me, I have the best attorneys on staff and they are eager to get started."

Shaye smiled. "I'm sure they are. I think it will work out fine. I'm just warning you that getting started might be a little slow. You have to build up a reputation for trust on the street. Then the kids who really want help will ask for it."

"And you have to remember that they're not all like Hustle," Eleonore said, referring to a street kid that Shaye had met during one of her investigations. Shaye and Corrine had been instrumental in getting him off the street and with a good foster parent, and Shaye and Hustle remained close.

"I know they're not all like Hustle," Corrine said. "But I still believe most of them can be helped. You just have to guide me in screening out the bad apples."

Eleonore was heading up the psychiatric division of the center and had handpicked the counselors and worked with them on the more difficult cases. "My people know what they're looking for. If they spot someone questionable, they'll inform me."

During one of Shaye's investigations of missing street

kids, one of the perpetrators had turned out to be a kid himself. Sociopathy and plain old evil didn't discriminate when it came to age. All three of them were aware of the horrible things that kids could do. Fortunately, those cases were the minority. Still, emotional or mental issues were common in street kids, usually because of the things they'd endured before they'd chosen to live on the streets.

Eleonore's staff would try to ensure that any horror they'd experienced didn't affect the rest of their lives and more importantly, the other kids staying at the facility. Shaye was a living testament to Eleonore's ability. Corrine had saved Shaye's life, but Eleonore had given it back to her.

"So what's the hunky Detective Lamotte up to these days?" Eleonore asked.

Shaye grimaced. "Hunky?"

Eleonore waved a hand at her. "Whatever you call good-looking men these days."

"Hot," Corrine said. "One of the teens in the group counseling session last week said I was hot enough to be a cougar. I almost died right there. The counselor explained why it was inappropriate, but I don't think he cared. Or any of the rest of them standing there. They thought it was hilarious."

"You are pretty hot for an older woman," Shaye said.

"I'm not that much older," Corrine said. "But I'm far too old for teens to be gawking at. Where do they come up with these things?"

"Movies, the internet, other teens," Eleonore said. "I wish someone would call me hot enough to be a cougar."

"If you'd let me take you for one of those makeovers I keep suggesting..." Corrine said.

Eleonore cringed. "I'll just stick with old lady looks."

Shaye laughed. "I tell her the same thing all the time."

"That you'll stick with old lady looks?" Eleonore asked.

Finally, Corrine couldn't hold it in any longer and started to laugh along with them. "I know it sounds funny now, but I swear when it happened I was mortified."

"You need to get out more," Eleonore said. "With a man. And I'm not referring to a contractor. I mean a man with the potential for romance."

Corrine shook her head. "You know my stance on that one."

Shaye felt her heart tug. "It *is* possible to find a man who's not only there for the money. I found Jackson. Or he found me. Whatever."

"Jackson is one of the last good ones," Corrine said. "Don't you worry about me. I'm not lonely. I have a beautiful daughter that I force to eat with me once a week and a best friend who hates dealing with dirty dishes and wouldn't miss a meal she didn't have to prepare. I've got all the companionship I need."

"All you're missing is a dozen cats and a closet full of bathrobes," Eleonore said.

Corrine looked slightly horrified. "I wouldn't even go

onto the patio in a bathrobe, much less out of the house."

"You wouldn't go onto the patio without full make-up," Eleonore said.

"I'd go out there with a cat," Corrine said. "Maybe I'll consider one. *Just* one."

Eleonore smiled. "Every collection starts with the first."

8

HAILEY PITRE WOKE IN A PANIC. HER HEAD THROBBED and her body ached like she'd been in the same position for far too long. She pushed herself up and as her hands struck the cool stone, her fuzzy mind cleared enough for her to realize she wasn't in her bedroom. She put her arms in front of her and moved them around, trying to connect with something, but all she found was open air. It was pitch-black in the room so she couldn't see anything.

Her heart began to race as she forced herself onto her knees and started crawling, her bare feet feeling every bump and crevice in the floor. She hadn't gone far when her head connected with a stone wall, and she yelled out as the throbbing launched into full-blown migraine. A wave of nausea passed over her and she struggled to maintain control of her stomach. She turned into a sitting position and clutched her head as the room started to spin.

What was wrong with her? The hit hadn't been that hard, but her head hurt so bad. Even worse than that one time she'd drunk whiskey with Marcy and Gina. Marcy had stolen it from her father's liquor cabinet and insisted that they all do shots. Hailey and Gina hadn't been as excited about the prospect as Marcy, but neither had wanted to tell her no. Hailey's room had whirled all night and she'd been so sick her mother had kept her home from school for two days. With the help of a heating pad, she'd managed to fake a fever and convince her mother she had the flu, but Hailey had promised herself right then that she'd never drink alcohol again.

And she hadn't.

But something was seriously wrong. She didn't know where she was or how she'd gotten there. The last thing she could remember was putting the chicken in the sink to thaw. Then something...a phone call?

Her phone!

She felt her pockets for her cell phones but neither was there. Had her parents discovered her secret cell phone? Had they seen the texts between her and Hudson? She always deleted everything but she knew there were ways to retrieve them. But even if her parents had found out about Hudson, that didn't explain where she was. Their house didn't have a space with stone floor, and this one had no light coming in at all. Like a basement. And besides, her father was strict, but he wasn't crazy. He wouldn't lock her in a cold, dark room.

She turned around to face the wall and balanced herself against it to pull herself up. Rubbing her hands across the stone surface, she inched down the wall, looking for a light switch. She found the first corner and turned. Then the second. Then the third.

That's where she found the door.

It was made of a thick, heavy wood. As she passed her hands over it, feeling for the doorknob, a splinter jammed into one of her fingers, and she cried out. She yanked her hand back and stuck the finger in her mouth, trying to suck the splinter out. She managed to get the tiny shred between her teeth and pulled, wincing as it tore her skin. Then she patted the door rather than rubbing her hands on it until she located a knob. She twisted it and it turned easily in her hand, but the door wouldn't budge. She couldn't find a dead bolt anywhere along the edge, so it must be on the other side.

She was trapped.

She'd been panicked before but now she was on the verge of a breakdown. There was absolutely no explanation for the situation she was in, except that someone had put her here and intended for her to stay. She'd been kidnapped. She was a hostage.

All the things that happened to young girls raced through her mind. Her parents made her watch the evening news with them. Her father thought it was important that she understand the things happening in society, but so many times, the things she'd seen had given her nightmares. Now she was living one of those nightmares. She was going to be one of those horrific, sad stories that everyone watched on television and shook their heads about before going on with the rest of their evening.

Because it wasn't happening to them. Because it wasn't really real.

But this was real. And she wasn't prepared to deal with it. She started to sob, her entire body shaking with the effort, and slid down the door back onto the ground. She drew her knees up to her chest and circled her arms around them.

What had she done to deserve this? Where had she gone wrong?

If only she could remember.

9

SHAYE PULLED INTO JACKSON'S APARTMENT COMPLEX AT 11:00 p.m. It would have been late for most people, but Jackson had texted Shaye when he was on his way home from work thirty minutes before. Shaye knew that meant he'd caught a bad case and figured he had been working nonstop all day. She was loaded with leftovers from Corrine and wanted to drop them off so at the very least, he could have a decent meal before getting some sleep.

He smiled when he opened the door but she could tell he was exhausted and worried. She gave him a quick kiss and headed to the kitchen to unpack the food. He lifted the lid on a container of tamales and gave a sigh of pleasure.

"I owe Corrine big-time," he said as he grabbed a fork and started eating right from the container. "I think I remember lunch, but I'm not certain."

"Let me heat that up," Shaye said.

"It's good like this," he said as he grabbed a beer and a diet soda from the refrigerator. "Hell, it's great like this. What else is in there?"

"Chips, queso, tortillas, black beans, and pineapple cake."

"Okay, maybe heat the queso while I polish these off." He handed Shaye the soda and sat at the kitchen table with the container of food.

Shaye popped the bowl of queso in the microwave and set the timer, then placed the rest of the food on the kitchen table and pulled out the cake. "How big a slice do you want?"

Jackson glanced at the container that held a quarter of the cake that Corrine had baked and frowned. "Just bring the whole thing over. I'll know more once I start eating."

Shaye shook her head and slid the container on the table, then grabbed the steaming queso before taking a seat across from Jackson.

"I take it you caught a bad one?" she asked.

He nodded. "Missing girl. Sixteen. It will be on the news tomorrow. I hate it when it's kids. Especially girls."

Shaye's stomach clenched. "Me too. You have any leads?"

"Not really. We're at that point where everyone looks suspicious and no one looks more suspicious than someone else."

Shaye frowned. "When did she go missing?"

"Yesterday afternoon. Sometime after school. We

you'd recognize any of the people if I showed you pictures?"

"Yeah, I'm pretty sure," Jamal said. "I'm good with faces."

She looked around at the other workers. "Did anyone else see someone exit into the courtyard besides the ones Jamal mentioned?"

The other workers and the foreman shook their heads.

Even if they had noticed someone, Shaye doubted they'd say so. They all had that look she ran into often that said they weren't sticking their necks out.

"Well, it was nice meeting you, Jamal," she said. "Good luck with your studies."

He nodded. "It was nice meeting you too. I know who you are. My moms is going to be excited when I tell her. You help people. There's not enough in this city that do."

"There's a lot more than you know. They just don't make the evening news. But you're right. We could always use more."

"You have a nice day, Ms. Archer," Jamal said. "And I hope you find your client's purse."

Shaye headed back to her SUV and immediately made notes based on Jamal's descriptions. The young man had noticed a lot, but none of it was enough to send her to someone's doorstep. She hoped Nicolas could help her narrow things down. The senior lady could go last on the list. Shaye didn't think for a minute that women were know she made it home because she put chicken out to thaw per her mother's instructions, but after that, nothing. Her purse and phone are gone. No sign of forced entry. No indication that she's a runaway."

Shaye nodded, feeling a tiny bit relieved. At least the missing girl wasn't the one Nicolas was concerned for. The confession had been before this girl disappeared.

"You have that look," Jackson said.

"What look?"

He studied her a couple seconds more, then nodded. "You got a case."

"Sort of. Do you know if there have been any female victims found recently that were strangled?"

"Not offhand, but with an average of ten murders a month, I don't hear about them all. Is that what your case is about?"

"I think so."

Jackson frowned. "Strangulation is a fairly specific form of death to not be certain about it."

"Yeah. It's sort of a weird situation. My client is afraid a crime was committed but he only knows the how, not the when or the who."

"Did he report it to the police?"

"No. He can't. He shouldn't have reported it to me, either."

Jackson stared at her for several seconds, then groaned. "Damn it to hell."

"A fairly accurate sentiment given the circumstances."

"Those vows are a thorn in the side of law enforcement. Do you think there's anything to your client's story?"

"I don't know. He feels the person was telling the truth but he has no means to identify them, so I'm starting in a big hole. At this point, I figured finding the victim would probably be easier. And at that point, the police would be handling it, so my work would be done and his conscience would be clear."

Jackson nodded. "I guess it's something that he hired you, at least. Most stick to their vows like glue. I can't wrap my mind around it myself, but whatever. I'll check tomorrow and see if anything matches. Unless it's a state secret, I should be able to give you basics."

"Thanks."

"You know, it could have been someone just messing around. That would be optimum. Not that messing with a priest that way is cool by any means, but you know..."

"The alternative is a murder. I'd be happy with uncool prankster myself."

"But the priest doesn't think that's it?"

She shook her head. "It's just a gut feeling, of course. But he thinks it's real."

"I'm hoping his gut is off."

"Me too."

10

Because Father Bernard had excused Nicolas from confessional duties for the rest of the week, he had the opportunity the next morning to call Shaye and see if she could meet with him. It would be far easier in person to have a conversation about what she'd discovered and what had transpired with him the evening before. He struggled a bit to move from the bench at the foot of his bed and into the wheelchair. He had no issues falling asleep, but the sleep was often restless and filled with confusing dreams. It was draining him, making him weaker. Something had to give or he would fall behind on his physical progress.

As he wheeled himself out of the church and toward

the street, he glanced around, looking to see if someone was watching. Clearly, the penitent had seen Nicolas meet with Shaye in the café because they'd sent the note. Had they been watching the church, waiting for him to exit? Were they watching now?

For this reason, Nicolas had derived a plan for this meeting. His attorney had a conference room that he was happy to lend to Nicolas. He was certain the staff might have some questions when they caught sight of Shaye, but he didn't worry about them asking. Nicolas's estate was a big account for the firm. They wouldn't do anything to jeopardize their stewardship.

Despite the fact that he'd offered her no detailed explanation, Shaye was more than happy to arrive at the law firm before Nicolas did and enter the building from the rear. If someone was watching today, it would appear that Nicolas had visited his attorney. Since he did so on a fairly regular basis, nothing would appear untoward. Assuming the penitent had been watching him prior to now. And for some reason, Nicolas felt that was the case. He just couldn't offer up any evidence to support the feeling. It was simply there.

He located his taxi service at the curb and the driver assisted him with the lift. It was a short drive to the law firm and Nicolas checked his watch when they arrived. If Shaye was on time, she would have arrived fifteen minutes before and would be waiting for him now. He made his way into the building and to the fifth floor where his attorney's offices were located. The receptionist gave him a big smile as he entered.

"Good morning, Father Nicolas," the young woman said. "Ms. Archer is in the second meeting room. I just took in coffee and bottled water. Please let me know if you need anything else."

"Thank you," Nicolas said and continued past reception and down the hall.

Shaye was sitting at the table, facing the door, so she could see him when he came in. A space at the table was already cleared for his chair. He greeted her as he closed the door behind him and pushed himself up to the table.

"How are you feeling?" she asked, giving him a critical eye.

"I wish I could say I was feeling better, but I can't lie. I was feeling better after our talk, but then something happened to make it all worse."

"Tell me."

Nicolas told her about the letter, then pulled it from the portfolio he was carrying and passed it over to her.

"You put it in a plastic bag," she said. "That's smart. Most people don't think about it."

"I don't know how much good it will do. So far, my penitent appears to be steps ahead of me, so I doubt there are fingerprints on it. And the envelope has been handled by myself and Father Malcolm and who knows how many others."

"True, but it was still smart thinking. You never know what might provide the break you need. Even clever criminals don't get everything right. Those slipups are how they get caught."

"He's watching me, isn't he?" Hating that he had to ask. Hating that he already knew the answer.

"I don't see any other explanation."

"Maybe he could have hacked your computer and read the notes?" The slightly desperate tone in his voice annoyed him, but he was also beyond frustrated with the fact that someone had been watching him and he'd never noticed.

"Because of the special circumstances," Shaye said, "I haven't made notes in my computer. And even when I do, the clients are listed by a number, not a name. In this case, the notes that I've made are on my phone and they all reference my client with the missing purse."

She accessed her phone and showed him the notes. "Look. I even put a picture of the missing string bracelet from the deceased niece that I'm touting as the mitigating reason for hiring me to look into this."

He looked at the image of the twisted strings, then at Shaye. "You really put a lot of thought into this."

"That's my job." She smiled. "I know you consider it lying but in my line of work, playing a role is often necessary."

"You mean undercover stuff. Like cops."

She nodded. "It's an untruth that hurts no one and helps you. At least, that's my hope."

"Mine too."

"So first things first. Who could have slipped the letter in with the mail?"

"Anyone. It's one of those boxes with a slot and we have to open it from the back. But it's out next to the sidewalk. Anyone walking by could have shoved a letter in there and not been noticed."

His frustration and disappointment must have shown on his face, or maybe she could hear it in his voice, because she leaned forward and stared him straight in the eye.

"You're going to get through this," she said. "Even if we never find out who the penitent is."

He shook his head. It seemed completely insurmountable. "I don't think I know how. We're told that prayer will heal anything over time, but I've prayed myself hoarse and I don't feel any relief. My stomach is still in knots and every time I close my eyes, I see this faceless woman..."

She nodded. "I spent a lot of years waking up screaming. I still leave lights on in every room at night. The security at Corrine's house and at my apartment is better than Fort Knox, but I had to leave those walls. And every time I stepped among people, I wondered, 'Is that him? Is that the man who held me captive?'"

She took a deep breath and slowly blew it out, and he could see that her mind was revisiting some of those dark places. "But even not knowing," she continued, "even though the fear sometimes took my breath away, I kept moving forward. Refusing to give up on the future I knew I could have. I'm an excellent judge of character. You have the strength to get past this, with or without an answer."

He felt tears well up. The woman across from him had lived a nightmare that was beyond comprehension, yet not only was she a functioning member of society, she was making a huge difference in the lives of the people around her. If he could manage one-tenth of her fortitude, he'd be perfectly satisfied.

"Thank you," he said. "Your belief in me makes me stronger. Now, what can I offer you?"

Shaye relayed her conversation with the landscaper. "I need to know the name of the electric company that the church uses. Can you get that?"

"It's Freeman Electrical. I coordinated the additional outlets needed for the Easter display and spoke to the owner many times. A very nice older gentleman. I don't know the employees, though. Father Malcolm was overseeing the recent work due to placement of the wiring and my limited mobility."

"The company name is good enough. I'll just head to their office and have a conversation with the owner. If he's as nice as you say, he won't have a problem telling me who was working at the church that day. What about the others?"

"The man in the Mercedes might have been Robert Croft. He's a big donor and is involved in most of our fund-raisers. He usually meets with Father Bernard, but that couldn't have been the case that day as Father

Bernard was out. So I might be entirely wrong in my assessment, but he's the only person who comes to mind that I'm certain owns a vehicle like the one described."

Shaye frowned. She knew Robert Croft. He'd been a business associate of her grandfather's. She'd met him a couple times and always thought him arrogant.

"Is something wrong?" Nicolas asked.

"No. I, uh, know Robert Croft. He did business with my grandfather."

"It doesn't sound like you are a fan."

"I wasn't. I haven't seen him in years. I suppose anyone could change..."

"But you doubt it in this case. And you're probably right. I never bought Mr. Croft's sincerity and I'm not certain Father Bernard does either, but his money makes a difference."

"So don't delve too deeply?"

"It sounds cowardly, I know, but unless he's committed a sin larger than his ego, it's sometimes easier to allow them their feelings of helping the huddled masses. It's hard to get people involved these days."

"That's true. Anyway, he'll probably see me," Shaye said. "So there's that. If he wasn't at the church that day, then I'll figure out another tactic to try to track down the Mercedes owner. What about the guy with the ponytail?"

Nicolas gave her a small smile. "These days? You just described half the young men in our congregation."

"Yeah, I guess I did."

"But Asian narrows it down a bit. I can think of three that match that description, but I don't know all the names. I can try to get them."

"You know what? Don't worry about it just yet. I don't think he's our guy. What the penitent did was dangerous to attempt with a child tagging along."

Nicolas nodded. "So that leaves you three people to check up on. It's not a lot, is it?"

"No. But that's how investigations go. You pick at the tiny threads until you find the one that unravels everything."

"That sounds tedious and frustrating."

"It can be, but it's also rewarding. I would guess the same could be said about your chosen profession."

"I suppose it could." He glanced behind him, making sure the door was still closed tight. "What do I do about being followed? I can't exactly add a security system to our living quarters without Malcolm and Bernard wanting to know why. Even if I covered the cost, they'd think it unnecessary and would insist on an explanation."

"Can you make sure you're only there when one of the other priests is as well?"

"Probably so."

"Then do that. I think it's important that you're in the company of other people as much as possible."

Nicolas felt a bead of sweat form on his brow and he wiped it with his hand. "So you think he's going to come after me?"

"I don't know what he's going to do, and that's why I

want you to be very careful and very aware. God telling someone to kill is not exactly revolutionary. It's been documented in some cases of schizophrenia. But someone with that type of illness is not predictable because they're not following a logical process like we do."

He nodded. "It makes it difficult to determine what he'll do because his motivations don't follow those of a sane person. But that begs the question of whether or not any murderer is sane."

"Plenty of them are. Some people are simply evil. Surely you believe that."

"I do, although I wish I didn't have to."

"So do I."

A thought flashed through Nicolas's mind and his stomach rolled. "If the penitent knows about you, then that means you could be in danger as well. He could see you as someone attempting to stop the work God called him to do."

"That's true and it's something I've already considered. The confession might have been his way of furthering his connection with God—letting you know that he was a warrior who had been called. Or it could have simply been him wanting to brag. Since your vows prohibit you from repeating what you hear, he probably considered it a safe option. The truth is, there are a lot of potential reasons for his choice. Some assuming he's sane and some assuming he's not. But I don't think you'll know why until he's caught."

"I'm so sorry," Nicolas said, his stress level rising. "I didn't even consider that in breaking my vows, I would be putting you at risk. I never thought he'd be watching."

"You couldn't have known, and I don't need you worrying about me. You have enough on your mind. Trust me when I say I can take care of myself. I have the best security money can buy. I am an expert at martial arts and an excellent marksman. Plus, I date a cop who is very protective. If anything seems even remotely off or too dangerous for me to approach alone, I'll get backup."

Nicolas nodded, feeling a bit more relieved. The fact that Shaye had chosen this line of work, despite everything she'd been through, told him she was confident and capable. But it wasn't going to stop him from worrying about her safety. Or for praying for her several times a day.

"Is there anything else I can do?" he asked. "I feel like I should be doing more, but I have no idea what more might be."

"Like I said, be aware. I'm convinced the penitent either did his research on you beforehand or knew about your condition and your limitations before he entered that confessional. It's possible he's someone you know."

It was a thought Nicolas had already processed a time or two before but one he'd tried not to dwell on. It made him overly anxious and then his thinking got foggy.

"We both keep saying 'he,'" Nicolas said. "Do you think the penitent is a man?"

"Killing women is usually a male crime, but given that

you couldn't peg the voice as male or female, it's possible it was a woman. I only have a description of people leaving the church through the courtyard door. Unless I find a witness who can describe those leaving through the front door, there's an entire pool of suspects that we have no description for."

Nicolas felt despair start to creep in again. This was an impossible situation with too many variables. It was unfair of him to even hope Shaye could find answers. It probably hadn't been fair of him to ask her to try in the first place. But he hadn't been able to come up with another solution.

"I know it seems an impossible task," Shaye said, clearly clueing into his thoughts. "But I've been asked to do the impossible before and I've found solutions. Don't give up just yet."

He nodded but he couldn't help but fear that the next turn of events would be the police finding the young woman's body. Or even worse, never finding anything at all.

The swamp didn't always give up its secrets.

11

MARCY CHECKED THEIR USUAL SPOT IN THE SCHOOL cafeteria, but Gina was nowhere in sight. Marcy knew that when Gina wasn't feeling social, she hid in the library, so she headed for what she considered the most boring place on the face of the earth besides church and school and walked the rows until she spotted Gina huddled on the floor behind a statue at the very back of the building.

"What are you doing hiding back here?" Marcy asked, as if she didn't already know.

"I don't feel like talking to people," Gina said. "Everyone's heard about Hailey. They keep asking questions."

"Oh, I'm well aware," Marcy said as she sat in a nearby chair. She'd been fending off questions and faking outrage all morning long, and she was just about done with it all. But the last thing she needed was this bunch of losers to think she was a bitch. Cheerleader tryouts for next year were coming up and the students still picked. Marcy had every intention of wearing that short skirt straight to the popularity train.

"What if something happened to her?" Gina asked.

"Like what?"

"Something bad. What if someone hurt her?"

"Did you ever think she might have gotten what she deserved for being stupid? You don't just run off from your home with your cell phone dead. Who does that?"

"Maybe someone kidnapped her. Maybe it wasn't her choice."

"Like who? Who would want to kidnap Hailey? Someone who needed a math tutor and couldn't pay?"

Gina shrugged and looked down at the carpet.

Marcy narrowed her eyes. She'd known Gina for a long time and she knew when something was up. Gina wasn't asking the questions at random. She suspected something and she wasn't telling.

"What do you know?" Marcy asked.

Gina looked up at her and widened her eyes. "Me? I don't know anything."

"You're lying. I know that look. Tell me."

Gina stared at Marcy for a while, biting her lower lip, then sighed. "I saw Hailey with that tattooed guy with the ponytail. The one who works at the mechanic shop next to the convenience store."

Marcy blinked. Of all the things she'd thought Gina

might say, that was not anywhere on the list. Surely Gina was mistaken. "Saw her doing what?"

"Kissing him."

Marcy shook her head. No way did that happen. Gina was wrong. Or crazy. "You're telling me Miss Goody Two-Shoes was kissing a guy? That guy?"

Gina nodded and Marcy felt her stomach flop. Gina was shy and often a doormat but she wasn't a liar.

"I don't believe it," Marcy said. "You must have been mistaken. Maybe she'd fallen and he was helping her up. Maybe he needed both arms to lift her."

Gina gave her a defiant look. "Unless he needed to lift her with his lips, I know exactly what I saw. They were kissing and it was not a friends sort of thing. They were seriously locked."

Marcy's head spun. This couldn't be. Hudson and Hailey? She couldn't make the picture form in her mind.

"That guy is a lot older, right?" Marcy asked. "Hailey barely speaks to guys in school. How did she even hook up with him?"

"I don't know. I don't know anything except what I saw that day. And I never asked. I can't believe Hailey was keeping that from us."

"You mean from you."

Gina shrugged. "Fine. I can't believe she was keeping it from me."

"She was probably afraid you'd tell her parents."

"I wouldn't do that."

"Sometimes you get spooked and do things you

shouldn't. Are you sure you wouldn't have told? Hailey's dad would flip his shit if he knew. He'd probably ship her off to a convent on an island of only women."

"Which is exactly why I would never tell her parents."

Maybe she wouldn't have, Marcy thought. But Gina had never been the sort of person you trusted with big secrets. The little things she could handle fine, but the big things tended to send her into full-blown anxiety until she ended up blurting everything out. She'd been that way since kindergarten.

"But you told the police?" Marcy asked.

"Of course! Hailey's missing. That guy could have kidnapped her or killed her or worse."

"I don't think there's anything worse than death."

Gina's face flashed with rare anger. "You know what I mean. I know you never liked Hailey, but you could at least try being a human being and caring about something besides yourself for once in your life."

Gina jumped up from the floor and practically ran down the aisle. Marcy didn't bother to follow. She'd gotten everything she could from Gina. And as she had no intention of caring about Hailey, she saw no reason to stick around school any longer, being forced to pretend. Her next conversation would go right to the source.

She headed out of the library and around the side of the building, where she eased behind the row of hedges and followed them to the spot with the break in the fence. She pulled the chain link aside and slipped through, then took off across the street, already fuming.

Hudson Landry had been ignoring her for months. He wasn't going to ignore her again.

IT DIDN'T TAKE Shaye long to track down the electricians who'd been working at the church that day. A single call to the company and a quick explanation to the owner about what she was trying to accomplish for her fake client yielded the two men's names and their job location that day. She'd made the drive across town to an old warehouse in the Upper Ninth Ward that an investor had purchased and was redoing as public housing.

Shaye's investigations had taken her to the area before so she was somewhat familiar with it, but she still made sure her nine-millimeter was ready to go before she got out of her SUV and headed into the building. A handful of contractor trucks were out front, so several repair items were being addressed at one time. That was a good thing for her because it meant more people.

In the entry, she found a man with a sledgehammer knocking out a wall. He stopped when he caught sight of her and pulled off his goggles. "Can I help you?"

"I'm looking for two guys with Freeman Electrical," she said.

He nodded. "They're upstairs checking the wiring in

the attic. Take the staircase up, and the attic access is in the hallway."

"Thanks," she said, and headed up the stairs. The sound of the sledgehammer on the wall started up again. At the top of the stairs, she saw pull-down steps for the attic. Two men's voices carried out of the opening. She had no way of knowing how long they'd be up there so she climbed up the steps and scanned the attic.

She spotted the two men about twenty feet to her right, inspecting a set of wiring.

"This shit is toast," the one with sandy-blond hair said.

The other one, a man with dark hair and features, nodded. "It all has to be replaced. He ain't saving no money on wiring. Not if he wants to pass inspection."

"You know he's going to bitch," the blond said.

"So let him," the one with dark hair said. "I ain't losing my license to make some rich dude richer. He has to follow the rules like everyone else or he can find someone else to break them for him."

"Fine by me," the blond said, then looked over and caught sight of Shaye. "Can we help you?"

"I hope so," she said. "My name is Shaye Archer. I'm a private investigator and wondered if I could have a couple minutes of your time."

"Just mine?" the blond asked.

"Both of you, actually," she said. "I promise it won't take long."

The blond looked over at the dark-haired man, who

shrugged. "Might as well break now anyway and call Pops about this. He's gonna have to order in a bunch of stuff before we can start rewiring."

Shaye backed down the steps and a couple seconds later, the two men descended and stood in the hallway looking at her. They both appeared curious but not remotely nervous.

"Private investigator, huh?" the blond said. "You spying on a cheating husband or something?"

"Nothing like that," she said, and extended her hand.

The blond shook her hand and nodded. "Mark Phelps."

"Jeff Breaux," the dark-haired man said as he took her hand. "I seen you on TV. You caught that guy selling people."

"I helped the police catch him," Shaye said.

"They need all the help they can get in this city," Jeff said. "Place is bad."

"So what are you investigating?" Mark asked.

"Nothing nefarious this time," she said and smiled, hoping to keep them at ease. She told them the story about her fake client's missing purse and the bracelet with sentimental value. "Since you guys were working there that day, I thought maybe you saw someone in the cathedral or someone who left there around two that afternoon."

"We was chasing a short through the church," Jeff said. "Finally found it in the choir loft. Didn't see no woman there, though, so your lady must have already gone. That was probably a bit before two, though."

Shaye nodded. "Was anyone else in the cathedral?"

Jeff frowned and looked over at Mark. "There was a couple guys, maybe one with a kid, but I don't remember what they looked like or anything. Do you?"

Mark shook his head. "When I was carrying in wire, I saw that priest in the wheelchair go through, but he went in the door at the back of the church. I talked to Father Malcolm sometime after that in the electrical room. Sorry, but I didn't pay no attention to the people praying when I walked through, so I can't help you there."

"Did you see which way Father Malcolm came from?" Shaye asked.

"I think he came down the hallway from the cathedral," Mark said. "He might have seen someone. Have you talked to him yet?"

"I haven't caught him yet but hope to this afternoon. Is there anyone else you can think of? Maybe someone who went down the hall to the confessional? Or to the courtyard exit?"

They both shook their heads.

"I guess we're not much help," Jeff said.

"That's okay," Shaye said. "My client knew it was a long shot when she hired me but she has to feel like she's doing something. I appreciate your time."

"Good luck," Mark said, and they headed back up the ladder.

Shaye went back downstairs and exited the building.

She made a note of the men's names on her phone and figured she'd do a background check on them later. Neither had given her any indication that they were involved in anything but the job they'd been hired to do, but she'd dealt with those skilled in psychological control before. It was frightening how normal they could appear.

Next up, a visit to Robert Croft.

She wasn't looking forward to it.

12

A CLANG ON THE ENGINE OF THE CAR HE WAS WORKING on startled Hudson, but he decided to ignore it. If his uncle was looking for another round of telling Hudson how much he'd fucked up, he wasn't in the mood to hear it. The conversation with the police hadn't exactly gone well yesterday, and the conversation with his uncle at home afterward had been even worse. Then his uncle had called his mother and they'd both spent until almost midnight chastising him for what they considered idiotic choices.

He'd told them that he and Hailey were serious. That she wasn't like other girls. That she was mature and knew what she wanted. That he wasn't "leading her astray" as his mother accused him. But neither would hear it. They continued to drone on about his irresponsibility and how he better pray every day that Hailey was found safely, and that when she was, he was never to speak to her again. He wasn't even to look in her direction.

Maybe. *Maybe* when she turned eighteen, he could revisit things.

They said it like Hailey was going to pop into the garage one day as if she'd been on vacation and everything was all right. But Hudson knew things weren't right. He figured the police thought she'd run away, and they'd assumed it had been with him. Good thing he lived with his uncle and didn't leave the house much. He didn't figure his uncle was a great alibi as far as the police were concerned, but he was pretty sure they didn't think his uncle would allow him to hide the girl out in his house, especially a minor. No way would someone offer up themselves for that sort of trouble. At least no one in their right mind. And his uncle was a pretty straight shooter.

The loud clang came again, but still, no one spoke. Now annoyed, Hudson shoved himself out from under the car and looked up at the fuming face of Marcy Long. Jesus H. Christ. Could his life get any worse?

"What do you want?" he asked, not even bothering to sit up.

"Is that any way to greet a lady?" Marcy gave him a flirty smile.

"When I see one, I'll greet her differently."

The smile disappeared and Hudson got a full view of the nasty side of Marcy that Hailey had always talked about.

"Don't pretend to be all innocent with me," she said. "I know you were messing around with Hailey, and I'm sure her parents didn't know. But I guess they know now."

Hudson clenched his jaw. He didn't need Marcy the Bitch reminding him of other things he didn't want to deal with. He'd already spent most of the night worried that something bad had happened to Hailey and trying to think of something, anything, that could help find her. Then he'd worked on convincing himself that she was all right and going to be found safe and sound, so he thought about ways to convince his uncle, his mother, and Hailey's parents that they were serious and he wasn't taking advantage of her. So far, he'd come up with absolutely nothing.

Based on what Hailey had told him about her father, Hudson might be better off just leaving the state and taking on another identity. He wouldn't put it past the man to press charges, especially if he believed Hudson had anything to do with Hailey's disappearance. And Hudson would bet money that once her father heard about their relationship, that's exactly what he would think.

"I don't remember inviting you into my business," he said. "I need to get back to work. Customers aren't supposed to be in the garage."

Marcy gave him an evil smile. "You think you can get rid of me like that? Like I don't matter? Well, you're wrong. You're going to talk to me now and any other time I want you to."

"I don't think so."

"You don't have a choice."

Hudson frowned. Where was Marcy going with this? She didn't have anything on him because there wasn't anything to have. Well, except his relationship with Hailey, but the police already knew about it and he figured they'd inform her parents.

"I'm pretty sure I can decide who I'll speak to," he said.

She shrugged. "If you don't want to speak to me that's fine. Of course, I'm sure the police would be interested to hear about how you keep asking me to have sex with you. And how you pulled me into the back seat of a car one day after the shop was closed and touched me all over before I could get away."

Hudson popped upright. "I didn't do any of that."

"Who do you think they will believe? The sweet, innocent minor or the adult with a sketchy past whose girlfriend is missing? I own you. You're mine until I'm bored. Pick me up tomorrow night at seven at LeBlanc Dress Shop. My parents have a charity thing and there's a movie I want to see."

Hudson felt the sweat form on his forehead and he started to panic. The last thing he needed was to be alone with another teen, especially one of Hailey's friends. If the police found out, it would look bad. Really, really bad. But if Marcy went to them with her lies, it would look worse.

Marcy stared down at him, clearly pleased with his discomfort. "I'll see you tomorrow. Make sure you shower before you pick me up. I hate the smell of grease."

She turned around and strolled out of the garage. Hudson took a deep breath and blew it out. What the hell was he going to do now? He couldn't take Marcy out but he couldn't afford not to, either. Maybe he should tell his uncle what happened.

He shook his head. His uncle would never believe him. Who would?

I swear, she blackmailed me into taking her to the movies because she's jealous of her missing friend who I really care about.

Yeah, that sounded convincing.

He threw the rag he was holding across the shop and cursed. One of the other mechanics glanced over at him, but these weren't the sort of men who asked questions. What the hell kind of game was Marcy playing? What good did it do to force him to go out with her? He didn't like her and had made that clear months ago.

His head started to ache and he rubbed his temples. He was already worried sick about Hailey and now he had this crap to deal with. His mind was already a mess and this situation looked like trouble from every angle with no way out. Silently, he let another string of curse words fly, damning the day he'd laid eyes on Marcy Long and her mother. Then fear gave way to anger and his jaw clenched so hard it hurt. No way was that little bitch getting away with blackmailing him. She thought she had him trapped but she was wrong.

He was going to do the one thing no one would ever expect him to do.

FATHER NICOLAS GUIDED his wheelchair into the cathedral. Father Malcolm and Father Bernard were both busy with their church duties as well as some of Nicolas's, so the apartments were empty. Normally, when he didn't have duties, Nicolas read in the common living area of the priests' quarters. The lighting was good and he had purchased a recliner—a luxury—that was particularly easy on his back and hips.

But since Shaye had admonished him to remain in the company of others as much as possible, he was doing his studying in the cathedral. Even if he'd wanted to, Nicolas doubted he could have sat alone in the living quarters and maintained his sanity. The fear was too great. His vulnerability had always been there but now he'd been made fully aware of the extent. He'd thought he had protection —being a priest, living in the church—but he'd learned the hard way that anyone was a potential target.

In the middle of the cathedral at the end of a pew, he pushed himself out of the wheelchair and slung his backpack over his shoulder. Using his cane and the back of the pew in front of him, he made his way ten feet or so down, then turned around and dropped onto the seat.

The little bit of walking and the stress of the situation had exhausted him more than it should have, but he knew that the lack of decent sleep was starting to affect him.

And his appetite hadn't been on point either, something Malcolm had commented on the night before. Normally, he had to carefully watch his portions when Malcolm made enchiladas, but he'd only managed half of his usual consumption. Attempting sleep was even worse. His bedroom, with the one exterior window and no lock on the door, had felt unsafe. Penetrable. He'd fallen asleep easily but had been tormented by his dreams. He couldn't remember them at all when he awakened but he was covered with sweat, and his mind was so anxious that he knew he'd been restless most of the night.

Even in the cathedral, every little noise had him flinching and looking around to locate the source. His senses had always been excellent but now they were heightened even more. Every step was the bang of a drum. Every cough was a clap of thunder. It made it almost impossible to concentrate but at least he didn't have to worry that someone would sneak up on him.

He glanced around to make sure no one was looking, then removed the text from his backpack that he'd gotten from the library after his conversation with Shaye. It was a book on sociopathy and had a chapter on those who thought God was speaking to them. He opened to the first chapter and started to read. He was well into chapter two when he heard the door to the confessional hallway open and close. He glanced back and saw Father Bernard emerge.

The senior priest spotted him and paused for a second, frowning, then headed his direction.

Crap.

He closed the sociopathy book, then picked up the text on ancient Roman history off the pew next to him and opened it on top of the other text. Father Bernard stopped at the end of the pew where he was sitting, and Nicolas saw him wince when he turned. His limp was slightly more pronounced, and Nicolas wondered if taking on Nicolas's work as well as his own had taxed the older man. He hoped not. He already had enough to feel guilty about.

"May I sit for a minute?" Father Bernard asked.

"Of course. I see you're favoring your knee a bit more."

Bernard entered the pew and sat beside Nicolas. "Yes. I'm afraid I might have twisted it a bit this morning moving some office supplies."

"You need to be careful of twisting with that kind of injury. Have you had it checked lately?" Two months prior, Bernard had fallen prey to the many street problems in New Orleans and had stepped on a curb that gave way. He'd taken a tumble into the street but luckily no cars had been passing. His knee had caught the worst of it as it had broken his fall. But a bump on the head, a gimpy knee, and a pair of torn slacks were better than the alternative.

The senior priest gave him a fatherly smile. "As a matter of fact, I had a checkup this week. My doctor happens to be of the same opinion you are about twisting. I promise I've been careful, but I lost my balance and overcompensated. These things happen when you age and refuse to admit you can't lift a box of copy paper like you could when you were younger."

Nicolas nodded. He understood. He wasn't dealing with aging issues yet, but he often pushed too hard with his therapy and paid for it later.

Bernard looked him over. "How are you feeling today?"

"Fine, I suppose."

He raised one eyebrow. "This isn't a casual conversation among strangers. The polite response is not the one I'm looking for. It doesn't appear as if you're sleeping well and you're not eating well, either."

Nicolas sighed. "I suppose I meant I'm as fine as I can be given the situation."

"But are you?"

"I'm doing everything I can. I'm praying for hours extra every day. I want this burden lifted, but I can't seem to get it out of my mind. When I close my eyes, I can picture everything the penitent said. I manage to sleep, but it's restless and I awaken even more tired than before. During the day, I can focus on my work and my studies, but I can't force my mind to cooperate when I'm asleep."

Bernard gave him a sympathetic look. "I'm not a big

fan of medication, but perhaps it's time to try something along those lines. Or maybe more of Father Malcolm's tea."

Nicolas nodded but he had no intention of taking anything for sleep. The last thing he needed was for something to happen while he was looped out. He was already at a huge physical disadvantage. No way was he adding to it.

"It worries me," Bernard continued, "to see you so troubled."

"I'm working through it," Nicolas said. "I think it was the shock, really. I suppose there's no way to prepare for everything one might encounter."

"That's true enough, but the only real preparation we need for all that we face is our faith. You've got the tools to get you through this, Father Nicolas. It's up to you to rely on and trust in them."

Bernard reached over and lifted the Roman history text from Nicolas's lap and leaned over to see the title of the book beneath. He frowned.

"You won't find the answers you seek here," Bernard said.

"Why not? Do you not believe in the study of the mind?"

"Of course. But that is not our field. It is not our calling. We don't heal minds. We heal hearts and protect souls."

"But surely understanding how people are motivated allows us to do a better job."

"Undoubtedly. But in this particular case, I fear that this book will not give you the relief you seek but will instead only cause you to be more troubled."

"I seek understanding. Not relief."

"There are a lot of things about the mind that doctors and scientists can't explain, though they have often worked a subject for years. Even the best in their field couldn't diagnose someone they had never met based on a whispered confession that they can't even be sure is true. So if the experts in their field often can't give you answers about the people they use for case studies, why do you think you can find those answers yourself?"

Nicolas sighed. "I guess I was hoping. I've always found comfort in knowledge, and perhaps I was seeking to find it there again. I figured it couldn't hurt and at least I'd feel that I was doing something."

"I felt the same way. With my brother's addiction, I thought if I knew what made him the way he was, I could fix it. I thought I could somehow overcome all the hurt he'd built up inside that he drowned out with drugs. Our father's death while we were young. All the struggles my mother had keeping food on the table. After all, I had overcome all of them. Why couldn't he?"

Bernard shook his head. "I was guilty of pride," he said. "Of thinking I knew more than all those who'd spent decades studying the behavior. But nothing I did made a difference and eventually, I stopped trying. My conscience was clear when he died."

Nicolas felt his heart clench. Bernard's brother had

died of an overdose just a couple months before. The senior priest hadn't seemed in the least bit surprised, but he'd been sad. Nicolas figured the sadness was mostly for their mother, whom his brother had lived with.

"I suppose I could pray all day long," Nicolas said, "but I'm not inclined to think it will make a difference."

"No. I'm not either. What we need to do is get your mind occupied with other things. I know I released you from most of your work duties, but perhaps that was a mistake."

Nicolas sucked in a breath.

Bernard placed his hand on Nicolas's arm. "I'm not asking you to return to the confessional. But the summer festival is coming up and I need someone to oversee the committees and make sure everything is organized. I think you should be that person. The festival is one of our major fund-raisers, so I'm entrusting you with one of the most important tasks we have set before us."

Nicolas was momentarily taken aback. Father Bernard wasn't overstating the importance of the festival. A large percentage of the church's operating and fixed improvement costs were derived from that one event. In the past, Bernard had always been in charge of the organizing. For him to pass that responsibility on to Nicolas was huge.

"I'm honored that you think I'm capable," Nicolas said. "Especially to follow in your footsteps. You've set a high bar."

Bernard nodded. "I'm sure you can scale it. I have

faith in you, Father Nicolas, even when you're not entirely sure of yourself. The first meeting is tonight at 8:00 p.m. It will be you and the five committee chairpersons."

"Will you also attend?"

"Only to make an introduction and announce your position as lead. You will take over from there. I have a notebook with all the information I intended to cover tonight. Are you planning on sitting here for a while longer?"

"I think so. I find the company of others comforting, even if they are going about their own business."

Bernard nodded. "Then I'll retrieve the notebook and bring it to you here before I resume confessions. That way you have time to review my notes and cover any questions you might have with me." He rose from the pew. "Take heart, Father Nicolas. This is merely a test. I have every confidence that you will pass it."

Nicolas watched as Bernard exited the cathedral, thinking about the senior priest's words. Was this a test? Would God really send a murderer to his doorstep just to test his faith? He didn't think so. The truth was, Nicolas didn't believe God controlled any of man's actions. He believed in free will. God was there if you sought him out, but he wouldn't stop someone from committing a sin.

Even murder.

But Nicolas didn't believe he sanctioned it, either. At least, not in recent times.

He opened the book on sociopathy again and picked up reading where he'd left off. Father Bernard might be right in saying the book couldn't help him, but he doubted that at this point it could hurt him, either. He'd covered two more chapters when he heard footsteps in the aisle.

"Father?" A child's voice sounded to his right and he turned to see a young boy, maybe twelve or thirteen, standing at the end of the pew. He was dirty and his clothes too small and threadbare. His hair needed a cut months ago, but so many were choosing to look that way these days that the clothes and general cleanliness were often the only way Nicolas could differentiate the street kids from those with homes. That and the fact that the street kids usually avoided adults.

"Can I help you?" Nicolas asked.

"A man said to give you this."

The boy extended his hand. Nicolas took one look at the envelope he held and his stomach rolled. It was from the penitent. He knew it.

"What did the man look like?" Nicolas asked.

The boy appeared taken aback that Nicolas hadn't simply taken the envelope. It was clear that he was uncomfortable being there and just wanted to leave. Nicolas expected him to drop the envelope on the pew and run but instead he studied Nicolas for several seconds, then frowned.

"He was creepy," the boy said quietly.

"Can you describe him?"

The boy shook his head. "That's why he was creepy. He wore black pants and a black hoodie that was pulled over his head. It was pulled so far over his face, and he was looking down, so I couldn't really see him. Not until he got close enough to give me the envelope."

Nicolas's pulse shot into the stratosphere. "What did you see?"

"He had no face."

"What do you mean? Everyone has a face."

"He was wearing this mask thing, except it didn't look like nobody. It was just solid black. Like I said, creepy. I grabbed the envelope and the money and ran."

"What about his hands? Was he wearing a watch or a ring? Did his hands look like an old man or a young one?"

"He was wearing gloves. Even though it's hot outside." The boy glanced back at the exit door. "I gotta go."

The boy dropped the envelope on the pew, spun around, and took off.

"Wait!" Nicolas cried. He tried to rise, but even if he could have gotten out of the pew, there was no way he could have caught up with the boy.

Frustrated, he forced his legs down the pew until he reached the end. He sat again and looked at the envelope lying on the shiny wood. It was wrinkled and had small dirty fingerprints on it. It didn't look like something that should cause fear, but Nicolas could feel his heart pounding in his temples.

He drew in a breath and slowly blew it out, closing

his eyes and saying a prayer for strength. When he opened his eyes, he grabbed the envelope and tore it open. He unfolded the piece of paper inside and choked back a cry at the single world it contained.

Sinner.

13

GRAYSON HUNG UP THE PHONE AND LOOKED OVER AT Jackson as he started the car. "That was Hudson Landry. He wants to talk to us in private. Now."

"Interesting. You think he's 'remembered' something he didn't bring up in front of his uncle?"

"Maybe. Probably. You saw the kid. He definitely didn't want to get on his uncle's bad side. I know he's legally an adult, but he didn't seem all that mature."

"I don't think he is, which is probably part of the reason he thinks Hailey is so grown-up. I'm kinda surprised he called, though. I didn't think he was smart enough to hold anything back."

Grayson nodded. "He definitely isn't the sharpest tool in the garage. Maybe it wasn't anything he held back. Maybe he remembered something that Hailey said and thinks it could be important."

"You don't think he's heard from Hailey, do you?"

"I doubt it. If he had, that would have been the first thing he blurted out, or he wouldn't have called at all, assuming she wanted to stay hidden."

"Well, then it's a mystery. Where are we meeting?"

"A bar two blocks from the shop. Shouldn't be busy this early."

Grayson was right. The bar held exactly one bartender and two patrons, one of them Hudson, who sat in the back corner of the room as far away from the bar as he could get. He had a glass of whiskey in front of him and Jackson noticed that his hand wasn't steady when he lifted the glass. He caught sight of them as they made their way across the room and Jackson could see the nervousness and a slight bit of panic in his expression.

Jackson's senses went on high alert. Maybe this was going to be something important.

They took seats at the table across from Hudson and the bartender popped over. He gave them a once-over and Jackson was certain he knew they were cops. They both ordered a soda and he glanced at Hudson before heading off to grab the drinks.

"You said you had something to tell us?" Grayson asked.

Hudson nodded and looked over his shoulder. A couple seconds later, the bartender sat the sodas on the table, then left. Hudson looked at them, indecision written all over his expression. Finally, he took a drink of his whiskey and slowly blew out a breath.

"This is going to sound crazy and maybe you won't

believe me," Hudson said. "But I don't know how else to handle it. And I don't want any more trouble."

"Why don't you tell us what's wrong and we'll figure out what to do about it," Grayson said.

Hudson stared down at the table and nodded. He was silent for so long that Jackson wondered if he was rethinking the entire meeting. Finally he looked back up and blurted out the entire exchange that had happened between him and Marcy Long.

"She's been coming around for months," Hudson said. "But I swear I never gave her any reason to think I was interested. Just the opposite. Toward the end, I was rude. Really rude. But it only seemed to amuse her. I know this all sounds bad coming from me, but I swear it's true."

Grayson looked over at Jackson, who gave him a slight nod. Jackson believed every word of Hudson's story. Marcy Long had struck him as exactly the type of person who would do whatever it took to get what she wanted. And she wanted Hudson. Even worse, Hailey had attained what Marcy hadn't managed, and that had probably pissed her all the way off.

"You were smart to contact us," Grayson said. "Going along with Marcy's plans would have only led you to more trouble."

Hudson looked back and forth between them. "So you believe me?"

"We do," Grayson said.

Hudson let out a huge rush of breath. "Oh my God.

You have no idea. I couldn't think…didn't know what to do. That girl…"

"Do you know why some policemen become detectives?" Grayson asked.

Hudson shook his head.

"Because we have a knack for understanding human motivation and for reading people. Some of us are better at it than others. Jackson is better than me, which is why I like partnering with him. He might pick up on something that I miss. But rest assured, both of us clued in on Marcy Long's personality. Your story doesn't surprise me in the least. But it disturbs me."

Hudson frowned. "Disturbs you? Why?"

"Because I wonder just how far Marcy will go to get what she wants," Grayson said.

Hudson stared for a moment, then his eyes widened. "You think Marcy did something to Hailey?"

"It's possible," Jackson said. "There's just one thing that doesn't align."

"What's that?" Hudson asked.

"You thought Marcy tipped us off about your and Hailey's relationship," Jackson said. "But it was actually Gina who saw you. Do you think Marcy knew?"

Hudson shrugged. "I don't know. When you showed up asking questions, I just assumed it was Marcy that knew because she was bugging me."

"There's our dilemma," Jackson said. "Either Marcy knew and said nothing to us because she was waiting to use that information to her advantage, or she didn't know and found out, probably from Gina. Then she confronted you and decided to take advantage of the situation."

Grayson nodded. "We really need to know which one is the case."

Hudson ran his hand through his hair. "Because one means she's an opportunist and the other means she might have done something to Hailey. Damn. I didn't even think about all that. How do you figure out which one it is?"

Jackson glanced at Grayson, who nodded. "You take Marcy to the movies," Jackson said.

Hudson's eyes widened. "No way! I don't want trouble, and that girl is nothing but trouble."

"She can't make trouble for you if you're working with us," Grayson said.

"Working with you?" Hudson asked.

"You'll wear a wire," Jackson said. "We'll be nearby. It's a movie so there won't be much talking during, but on the drive over and before it starts, you might be able to get something out of her."

"How?" Hudson asked. "I'm no detective. I don't know how to make people confess to shit."

"My guess is if you bring up Hailey, it will make Marcy mad," Jackson said. "When people get really angry, they sometimes blurt out things they never meant to say."

"Okay." Hudson nodded. "So I just say stuff like how I'm worried about Hailey and miss her...stuff like that?"

"Exactly like that," Jackson said. "Make sure Marcy

knows that you're only there because she blackmailed you, but all of your thoughts are about Hailey."

Hudson stared down at the table and shook his head. Then he looked back up at them. "Do you really think Marcy could have done something to Hailey? Over me? Because I don't know if I could live with that."

"We'll cross that bridge if it comes to that," Jackson said. "The only thing you need to know is that you've done nothing wrong. And you did the right thing by calling us. It helps your credibility."

"Yeah, I guess," Hudson said. "I just want Hailey back. Even if I can't see her anymore. I want her safe, you know?"

Jackson's heart went out to the young man. He clearly had feelings for Hailey and was struggling with how to deal with everything. Jackson understood more than most how it felt to worry about a woman you cared about who had run up against evil. It was a difficult thing for anyone to deal with, but for a man used to protecting people for a living, it was even harder.

"We all want her back safe," Grayson said. "Hailey's case is our full-time job. We're doing everything we can to locate her."

"I hope it's enough," Hudson said.

Jackson nodded. He hoped so too.

SHAYE MADE her way into the building that contained

Robert Croft's corporate offices. She hadn't called ahead, hoping to get lucky and catch him by surprise. When certain types of people had time to prepare, they could convince almost anyone of their lies. And Robert Croft hadn't made his many millions by telling the truth. His reputation was well known by the whispering at parties and charity events, but as was typical of society people, no one dared say anything to his face.

The receptionist's eyes widened as Shaye walked inside the office and she knew the young woman was well aware of who she was. "Can I help you?" the receptionist asked.

"I'd like to see Mr. Croft for a couple minutes. If he's available."

"Do you have an appointment?"

It was a useless question. The receptionist was already aware that she didn't, but it was the sort of thing that managed to get rid of most people who thought they could drop by and interrupt people at their place of business. It wasn't going to work on Shaye. Interruption was how she got some of her best information.

"I'm sorry, but I don't," Shaye said. "I was just in the area and thought I'd give it a try. I promise it won't take long."

"Let me see if he's available." The receptionist lifted the phone and dialed. "Mr. Croft, Shaye Archer is here and would like to speak to you. She said it wouldn't take — Oh, okay."

The receptionist hung up the phone. "He can see you now. Down the hall, all the way at the end."

"Thank you." Shaye set out down the hall, noting the expensive paintings lining the hallway. If Croft purchased collectible art to hang in his hallways, the business of lying must be doing very well indeed.

She knocked on his office door and he called out for her to enter. As she stepped inside, he rose from his desk and moved forward with a big smile. He kissed her cheek and motioned for her to sit in one of the two overstuffed leather chairs in front of a beautiful antique desk.

"It's good to see you," Croft said. "It's been a long time. I'm so sorry about...things. I'm not sure how to phrase it. I apologize. You'd think someone with a law degree could come up with words."

"It's okay," Shaye said. "I know exactly what you mean. And thank you. It's been difficult, but my mom and I are moving forward."

"That's all you can do, right?"

Shaye nodded, even though his statement wasn't true at all. Plenty of people, when faced with horrible circumstances, never moved forward again. Some sank into a depression that lasted a lifetime. Some decided that the role of perpetual victim was to their liking and remained cemented within it. But she didn't see any reason to point that out to Croft, who'd probably never considered himself wrong.

He studied her intensely and Shaye knew he was trying to figure out why she was there and what she could possibly want from him. Hoping to set him off-kilter just a bit, she remained silent during his scrutiny.

"How can I help you?" he asked, curiosity finally getting the better of him.

"It's a case I'm working. It's rather a long shot and I feel bad asking for your time on it when I know how busy you are, but if it turns out you could have helped and I didn't ask..."

A flash of uncertainty passed over his expression but he recovered quickly. "Of course. Whatever I can do."

Shaye launched into the tale of her client and the missing handbag. She could see Croft visibly relax as she talked. He'd probably been afraid her investigation was along the cheating husband lines—she'd heard those rumors forever along with the shady business practice ones. But a stranger forgetting her handbag was completely innocuous.

"One of the church workers said they were pretty sure you came out of the cathedral that afternoon shortly after my client left, so I just wanted to know if you saw anyone."

He nodded, now completely relaxed. "I'm sorry for your client. The handbag can be replaced but the bracelet, while of no marketable value, was significant to her. It's a tragedy that it's lost."

Shaye frowned. The sincerity and empathy in his voice was so convincing it gave her pause. If she didn't know this man, she would swear it was genuine.

He caught her expression and gave her a small smile.

"I know what you're thinking—the barracuda of business has a heart. I know what my reputation is and I'm sure you've heard plenty, as I ran in the same circles as your grandfather. But sometimes something happens that changes your perspective."

"That's true. May I ask what changed yours?"

"I found out I had a daughter. Six years old. My wife, of course, was far less than pleased. We're currently separated. Working on things, but I'm afraid I have a lot of sins to overcome."

"You weren't aware of the child before now?"

He shook his head. "The woman was married—here in town on business for the weekend. I never heard from her again. Until two months ago." He stared out the window, his expression becoming sad.

"She contacted me because the girl was ill. She needed a kidney transplant and none of her family was a match. It was during the testing that the woman realized the child wasn't her husband's. Unfortunately, her husband realized it as well."

"That must have been hard on her."

"I'm sure it was but when she contacted me, her sole focus was ensuring our daughter lived. She wanted me to get tested...to see if I could be a donor. At first, I was so shocked, I couldn't even answer."

Shaye nodded. "That was a lot to process in one conversation."

"It was, and at first, I was hesitant. I know it sounds awful, but I knew there was no way to keep this hidden.

All of my sordid behavior had just walked up and slapped me in the face, and I'm ashamed to admit that I considered ignoring her altogether. Then I saw the picture. It was me. The features were feminine but the eyes, the smile... I couldn't deny that she was my child. I knew if there was anything I could do to save her, I had to do it."

"Were you a match?"

"Yes. I had the test done before telling my wife, but when I came back as a match, I knew it was time to lay it all out. She took it badly but she didn't disagree with my decision. We'd never wanted children, you see. But when I looked at my daughter, I wondered if we'd made a mistake."

"And did the transplant work?"

He shook his head and Shaye could see tears forming in his eyes. "Her body didn't accept my kidney. She had the best doctors—I made sure of that—but in the end, there was nothing they could do. I was at her side when she drifted away."

Shaye's chest tightened. How heartbreaking it must have been. First, to find out you had a child you never thought you wanted, then to find out she was horribly ill. Then to risk your marriage, go through the surgery, and lose her anyway. That was a lot for one person to deal with in a short amount of time. Croft's personality switch now made sense.

"I'm so sorry," Shaye said. There were really no other words to say.

"Thank you. I hear it a lot, but you know more than

most about personal tragedy and loss. People's sympathy shouldn't have rank, but I'd be lying if I said it didn't."

Shaye nodded. She understood exactly what he meant. Sympathy over loss was the norm but when you knew someone had suffered something similarly tragic, it somehow hit you harder.

"Anyway," he said, straightening in his chair as part of an attempt to pull himself back together. "You didn't ask to see me to hear about all my failings and sorrow. I don't recall seeing a woman in the cathedral when I was there, but I was up front to light a candle and I close my eyes during prayer. It's possible she could have come and gone during that time."

"And afterward, did you see anyone else that you could identify well enough for me to question?"

He shook his head. "I'm afraid I was in my own head. I know there were lawn people in the courtyard. I remember hearing the equipment, but I couldn't tell you what any of them looked like."

He studied Shaye for a moment and suddenly, everything felt slightly off. "Are you a religious person, Ms. Archer?"

Shaye didn't share her personal beliefs on anything unless she knew someone intimately. But the question was odd, and the look on Croft's face was a little too intense. Too focused.

"I don't practice any religion," she said, avoiding a direct answer.

"You should. We all have sins to atone for. We do

things every day thinking 'it doesn't really matter' or 'no one will get hurt' but that's not the truth. The truth is that every sin takes away a little more of our humanity. It drives a larger wedge between us and our relationship with God. The sinful are ruining our society."

"I thought everyone sinned."

"Of course. But surely you agree that some sin is worse than others. Like sin that puts children at risk. We can agree on that, can't we?"

Shaye chose her words very carefully. "I think it is particularly evil for someone to prey on those who are weaker. Children certainly fall into that realm."

"So many women have children and fail to protect them. Worse, they invite evil in with their choices of drugs and prostitution and the random men they allow access. Those women are not mothers. They're conduits of abuse and neglect. They're Satan's vessels."

As he spoke, his expression grew more intense, more manic, and Shaye felt her discomfort grow as he talked.

"It sounds like you've found your passion," Shaye said. "Perhaps you would be interested in donating to my mother's organization. She's going to be doing some great things for the very children you're talking about."

"Absolutely! I've been following Corrine's organization work on her website. I'm prepared to make a rather substantial commitment each year toward continued operation." He leaned forward and locked eyes with Shaye. "But sometimes, we're called to do more than just write a check, don't you think?"

"We do what we can with what we have."

He nodded. "Exactly. And that's what I'm doing. Everything I can with what I have. I knew you'd understand. Your work is a calling, is it not?"

"Some would see it that way."

"How do you see it?"

"For me, it's like breathing. It's simply part of who I am."

The buzz of the phone startled her a bit and Croft looked at it and frowned.

"Mr. Croft," the receptionist's voice sounded over the speaker. "The clients are waiting on you for the meeting. Conference room 1."

"I'll be there in a minute. Please make sure my jet is ready to leave in two hours," he said as he rose. "I'm sorry to end our conversation. I feel like you would have a lot to say about the power of evil in today's society. I'm leaving this evening for New York, but perhaps we can schedule a lunch next week when I return. I'd love to talk longer."

"Sure," Shaye said, and handed him her card. "If you think of anything else that might help my client, please give me a call."

He clasped her hand in both of his and looked her directly in the eye. "God will protect you as long as you keep doing his work."

She nodded and made her way out of his office. On a bookshelf next to the door, she noticed that amid the law books was a stack of Bibles and other religious texts. A crucifix lay on top of one of the Bibles. She hurried out of the office, forcing a smile and a wave at the receptionist as she traversed the lobby. Even when she was inside her SUV, the overwhelming urge to flee was still present.

She put the vehicle in drive and pulled out of the parking lot, headed for her favorite outdoor café. She needed sunlight and to be surrounded by normal people doing normal things. Right now, she was too jittery to think. Too unnerved to focus.

Croft could be the penitent.

He clicked on his mouse to close the article he'd been reading. The mighty Shaye Archer. Savior of the regular people. In her own category of calling, he had to admit that she was excellent at what she did. She identified evil and brought it to light, and that was something he immensely appreciated. It was a skill set that was needed, and the world could use more of Shaye Archer in that regard.

But she didn't save souls.

He could offer sinners eternal salvation. God had told him how. He'd guided him through the process of choosing the sinner. Then he coaxed the sinner into confession and repentance. And that was when he saved them. Because he knew that given an opportunity, sinners went right back to their old ways. But he offered them eternal life.

Death immediately after repenting was the only way.

Saving lives was an honorable profession, but saving souls was God's work. And God had called him personally. He wouldn't let anyone get in the way of that.

Not even Shaye Archer.

14

JACKSON LOOKED UP FROM HIS COMPUTER AND motioned to Grayson. "Come look at this."

Grayson pushed his chair across the walkway to Jackson's desk and looked at the monitor. "Michael Pitre," he said when he saw the background check. "You got a feeling about the father?"

"I don't know. When we talked to the parents, something felt off to me, but I couldn't put my finger on it."

"Looks like an assault arrest for attacking a man at his place of employment," Grayson said.

"Yeah. This Nathan Greer didn't want to press charges as he wasn't injured. Apparently Pitre can't fight. Based on the police report of injuries to Pitre, he caught the worst of it, but three witnesses said Pitre clearly threw the first punch."

"Any note on what the fight was about?"

"No. And I couldn't find a correlation between their

places of business, but when I checked the home address for the Greer, I found something interesting...it was the same neighborhood where Pitre used to live."

"Okay. So some fight over barking dogs or parking on the street?"

Jackson clicked over to another report and pointed. "Greer had a fifteen-year-old daughter. She disappeared a year ago. The fight happened two months before. And look at this."

He clicked onto the internet and pointed to the Instagram account he'd found for Hailey Pitre. "That is Melissa Greer with Hailey Pitre. See the caption?"

"'Besties.'" Grayson blew out a breath. "What the hell is going on here?"

"I don't know, but I don't like any of it. Pitre didn't think the fact that his daughter's best friend went missing just a year ago was something he should mention? That stinks so bad I could smell it in Utah."

"No doubt. Did you pull the file on the missing girl?"

"Got it printed out."

"Good. You can read it while we go to chat with Mr. Greer."

Jackson nodded. "Maybe get some dirt on Pitre that we can use to break him."

"That's the idea." Grayson rose from his chair and grabbed his keys from his desk. "Did you make a note of the employer? He'll probably be at work."

Jackson took a picture of his screen with his phone. "Got it and the home address, too."

Traffic was light and it was a quick drive to the manufacturing plant in the Seventh Ward where Greer worked. They headed inside, showed the receptionist their ID and asked to speak to a manager. The fact that the badge didn't even elicit so much as a raised eyebrow made Jackson wonder if she was used to cops visiting her place of employment or if her comfort level was on a personal basis.

She made a call and a couple minutes later, a harried-looking middle-aged man with a spare tire around the middle and a balding spot on the back of his head hurried into the lobby. He introduced himself and shuffled nervously. "Is there a problem?" he asked.

"Not with the business," Grayson said. "We'd like to speak to an employee of yours and wanted to keep it quiet, which is why we didn't announce it at reception."

"Which employee?" the manager asked.

"Nathan Greer," Grayson said. "He's not in any trouble. We are hoping he can help us with some information about a person who lived near him a year ago."

The manager visibly relaxed. "Of course. He's on the line. I'll go get him. There's an empty room just down the hall on the right that we use for interviews. You can speak with him in there."

He hurried off and Jackson and Grayson headed down the hall and located the room. About five minutes later, Nathan Greer entered, clearly uncomfortable. Grayson introduced them and asked him to take a seat at the table. Jackson and Grayson sat across from him.

"We're hoping you can provide us with some information," Grayson said.

"About what?" Greer asked.

"Who," Grayson said. "Michael Pitre."

Greer sneered. "What's that asshole done now? Hit somebody else he didn't agree with?"

"Is that what your fight was about?" Grayson asked.

"Not exactly," Greer said. "Before the day he showed up here and started a fight, I'd never met the guy. His problem was with my daughter. He said she was leading Hailey down a path of unrighteousness."

"That's interesting phraseology," Jackson said.

"His words, not mine," Greer said. "The guy was a nut. My Melissa was a good girl...is..." His voice broke, and Jackson's heart went out to the man. His daughter had never been found.

"I'm really sorry about Melissa," Jackson said. "The case is still open and I know the detectives assigned to it. They're doing everything they can."

Greer nodded. "Yeah, that's what they say, but I know the score. After all this time, Melissa's dead and if she's not, then even worse things have happened to her."

"Did Pitre mention anything specific when he complained about Melissa?" Grayson asked.

"He was ranting about them talking to boys," Greer said. "What fifteen-year-old girl doesn't talk to boys? We all had crushes at that age. It's normal."

"It is," Jackson agreed. "But we've gotten the impression that Mr. Pitre's expectations for his daughter are somewhat outside of the norm."

Greer nodded. "Like I said. He's a nut."

"Did you talk to Melissa about what happened?" Grayson asked.

"Bet your ass I did," Greer said. "She said Pitre had come to school to speak to a teacher the day before. Hailey didn't know he was going to be there. He saw the two of them talking to some boys in the hall and made a real scene. Dragged Hailey out of the school and took her home. Called my daughter and the boys some pretty nasty things. One of the teachers was going to call the cops, but Pitre left."

"That's a frightening overreaction," Grayson said.

"Yeah," Greer agreed. "I told Melissa that she needed to steer clear of Hailey. I hated to punish the girls for something Pitre did, but I didn't want any more trouble."

Jackson leaned in a bit. "When your daughter disappeared, did you wonder if Pitre was involved?"

"Of course," Greer said. "Wouldn't you? But the cops said he had a solid alibi. He was home with his wife and kid all night. Two neighbors saw him mowing his lawn late that evening." He scowled. "I still think he could have done something. I mean, Melissa said she was going to one of her other girlfriends' houses after school. They were supposed to be watching movies with some other friends and Melissa was spending the night."

"She never arrived at any of her friends' homes?" Jackson asked.

Greer shook his head. "She could have been taken before dark. Pitre's a salesman. He roams around the city all day."

Jackson nodded. Pitre's job gave him opportunity but not necessarily a great one. He would have had appointments he had to make, and the detectives investigating would have ensured that he'd done so. And there was a lot of difficulty in snatching a teen off the street in broad daylight. Still, it wasn't completely impossible. Pitre could have been clever about it or simply gotten lucky.

Greer cocked his head to the side and looked from Grayson to Jackson. "Why are you asking me all this stuff now? Those other detectives are still assigned to the case. You said so yourself."

"Hailey Pitre has disappeared," Grayson said.

Greer's eyes widened. "I didn't have nothing to do with it. I swear! She was a nice girl and not at all responsible for what her father did."

"You're not a suspect," Jackson said. "We simply wanted to get more information from you. The kind of stuff that doesn't necessarily make it into police reports."

Greer didn't look completely convinced but he nodded. Then he stiffened and gave Grayson a hard stare. "You think Pitre did this? To his own daughter? If that's the case, then he's the one that did it to my Melissa. He's always been the one."

His voice increased in speed and volume as he spoke, and Jackson could see he was getting worked up. Not that Jackson blamed him. Everything about Pitre looked sketchy.

"We don't know what happened," Grayson said. "This is just one avenue we're investigating, but rest assured that we will be pursuing every angle of it. Including revisiting your daughter's case. But it could be someone fixated on them back when they were friends—saw them together around the neighborhood and at local stores. Or even at school."

Greer looked pained. "Someone wanted both of them?"

"It's possible," Grayson said. "Pitre moving his family away might have been what delayed Hailey's disappearance. It might have taken the perpetrator time to find her again."

Greer nodded, the realization of what Grayson said sinking in. "This probably wasn't random. You think they were targeted."

"I think given the circumstances surrounding their disappearances and the lack of evidence in either case, a crime of opportunity in both would be a huge coincidence," Grayson said. "Is there anything else you can tell us about Pitre?"

Greer shook his head. "I wish I could. But I've only seen him the once and he wasn't exactly looking to have a civil conversation. All I know is what Melissa told me, which wasn't much. She didn't like him so she made sure she only visited Hailey when he wasn't going to be there.

And she said Hailey didn't talk about him much. I can't say as I blame her."

"Okay," Grayson said. "Thanks for your time. We might need to talk to you again."

"Anything," Greer said immediately. "Anytime. If you can find out what happened to Melissa...her mother..." He sighed. "I'd like to give her a body to bury at least. But this limbo we're in...it's killing both of us."

Grayson nodded and handed Greer a card. "I understand. Here's my card. If you think of anything else, please give me a call."

Greer took the card and put it in his shirt pocket. "Will you let me know if you find Hailey? I hope she's okay."

"Me too," Grayson said. "But for the time being, I think it's best if you keep the content of our conversation to yourself. Perhaps you tell your coworkers it was a follow-up on an item in your daughter's case. I just don't want things filtering back to Pitre before we're ready to confront him."

"Yeah," Greer said. "All right. Just promise me you'll nail this guy, whoever he is. You'll nail the bastard that hurt Hailey and Melissa."

Grayson nodded.

As they climbed into the car, Grayson looked over at Jackson. "So what do you think?"

"I think Nathan Greer has a lot of reason to hate Michael Pitre."

"And to suspect him."

Jackson nodded. "Pitre hasn't helped his case all that well. And not telling us about this highly relevant situation doesn't make me feel favorable toward him. If he had nothing to do with Melissa Greer's disappearance, then why wouldn't he be shouting from the rooftops that Hailey's friend had disappeared just the year before? If I were a parent, I would have gone straight there."

"Unless I'd done it. Then I wouldn't want anyone to make that connection, especially the police."

"He had to know it would happen, right? And even if Pitre is some kind of religious, controlling psycho, would he really risk the same crime twice? And with his own daughter?"

Grayson shook his head. "I just don't know.

"Me either. But as far as I'm concerned, Pitre just became suspect number one."

"And Greer?"

"I'm not striking him off the list, either."

Grayson started the car. "Amazing. Usually we're scratching to come up with one suspect. This case has given us three already."

"An abundance of leads. That's definitely a new one. And one we're going to need some help on. The clock is ticking. On the chance that Hailey's still alive, we need to narrow things down quickly."

"I'll ask for some help tomorrow. The detectives are all stretched thin, but we can probably get a couple of patrol assigned to doing the background work. That leaves us on the streets."

"Good," Jackson said. Because he knew they weren't going to rescue Hailey sitting behind a desk.

SHAYE SAT at a table in the courtyard of the café, watching two birds bathe in the fountain. A café au lait sat in front of her along with a small plate of beignets. She'd placed her usual order attempting to regain a feeling of normalcy. To quickly rid herself of the icky feeling that she'd had when she left Croft's office. She'd briefly considered showering, but forced herself to stay out in the open, rather than closing herself up behind the safety of her door locks and security system.

She wanted to stay present more and retreat less. Not that retreating was necessarily a bad thing. Sometimes it was the best option, but when she had other choices, she was opting for the harder way out. Pop psychology gurus would say it built character. Eleonore would simply say it was her way of continuing to push herself to become an even bigger badass. Shaye wasn't certain she agreed with Eleonore's sentiment, but she liked the sound of it. There were far worse things than being a badass.

Like being a victim.

And that was a role she never intended to fill again.

Her cell phone rang and she was a bit surprised to see Nicolas's number come up.

"Nicolas?" she answered. "Is everything all right?"

"No. Something happened that I need to tell you about but I can't get away right now."

His voice was shaky and slightly panicked. "Are you someplace you can speak?" she asked. "Can you tell me over the phone?"

"If you're available to listen."

"Yes, please go ahead."

Nicolas told her about the street kid who'd brought him the envelope. His voice hitched several times as he relayed the story, and Shaye knew he was worried about the close watch the penitent appeared to be keeping on him. To be honest, Shaye was worried about it too.

"You did very well," she said, trying to offer him even a tiny bit of relief. "You asked very good questions."

"That offered nothing."

"That's not true. We know for certain that it's a man, right? We didn't know that before."

"His face was covered. It still could have been a woman with a deep voice or disguising her voice."

"That's true, but that's not the impression the child got, and I'm inclined to go with what his instincts told him."

"Great. Then we've narrowed our suspect list down to about two hundred thousand, assuming we're considering New Orleans alone."

Shaye understood his frustration. She'd felt it many times before when she thought she'd run into nothing but dead ends, and she felt it now. "I know how hard it is to remain hopeful. And I'm certain contact from the penitent is the last thing you want, but it gives us an advantage."

"How?"

"More opportunity to get to know him. To pin down a motive. To catch him in the act. If he keeps playing this game with you, he'll slip up."

"What if it's not a game? What if he intends to kill me like the woman?"

Shaye felt her back tighten. It was a possibility that was the penitent's endgame. It was also possible that he was seeking praise from someone he considered a representative for God. It was equally possible that he was showing the priest how powerful he was compared to Nicolas. How his actions produced immediate results.

But the most interesting thing about Nicolas's story was that he hadn't told Shaye what the envelope contained. She didn't think that was by accident.

"You never told me what was inside the envelope," she said. "Was it another message?"

There was several seconds of silence and for a moment, Shaye thought they'd been disconnected. Then she heard a sharp intake of breath.

"Sinner," he said, his voice breaking. "It said 'sinner.'"

All the effort she had put into calming herself went straight out the window. The endgame question had been answered with one simple word.

"Do you have any idea what he's fixated on?" she asked. If they could determine the reason for the penitent's accusation, it might lead them to who he was.

"No. I've done nothing but think about it ever since. Of course, I'm not without sin. No one is, but I can't think of anything that I've done that would have been so egregious it caught the attention of someone else."

Shaye took in a breath and slowly blew it out, trying to control her disappointment. They weren't dealing with a sound mind, she reminded herself. It was perfectly plausible that Nicolas hadn't done anything to merit the attention. The penitent could have imagined the issue or blown something simple out of proportion. Or he could have a problem with priests or the Catholic Church in general. It was impossible for sane people to make the leaps and connections that a damaged mind made.

"Okay," she said. "I don't want you worrying about this. He's probably created some scenario in his mind that labels you that way, and it's unlikely that we're going to figure out what. Are you staying visible?"

"Yes. I've been in the cathedral all afternoon. I'm heading up a fund-raising committee tonight and I'll be in our living quarters afterward. Father Bernard and Father Malcolm should both be there."

"Good." She gazed at the fountain, unsure of her next question, but finally she just blurted it out. "Do you have a weapon?"

"I...uh, no."

Probably because he'd never figured he'd need one.

"I think it might be a good idea if you had some way to defend yourself against an attack," she said. "I'm not suggesting that you arm yourself like Rambo. It doesn't have to be a gun, but even a can of Mace could give you an unexpected advantage."

"I hate this. Physical weaponry is not the sort of thing priests are supposed to have to consider."

"I know. But prayer is not going to protect your very human body."

He sighed. "You're right. As it turns out, you and my mother were of the same mind on things. I just remembered that she gave me Mace after my accident. I thought she was overreacting, of course, but then I decided I was being unfair. Women always have to consider these things, don't they? Things men often don't."

"That's true enough."

"My injury puts me in the same category—an easier target than a healthy male. I don't like it, but I accept the reality of my situation."

"Do you know how to use the Mace?"

"I've read the instructions."

"Good. Then take it out of the back drawer or wherever you tucked it away and keep it on you. And I mean within reach. It doesn't do any good buried in your backpack. You need to be able to reach it within seconds. That's often all the time you'll get."

"What about the child? Should I take a lap around the block and try to locate him?"

"No. Except height, I don't think he knows more than what he already told you. If there were anything else out of the ordinary, he would have said so. Besides, I'd prefer you stick close within the church walls unless you've got a specific appointment somewhere else."

"What about shopping?"

"If you need things from the store, have them delivered when possible. Delay purchase if it's not absolutely necessary and can't be delivered. If it's something you have to have and can't find a courier, then call me. I'll take care of it."

"You really think I'm in danger on the streets, among all those people?"

"I think a crowded street makes it really easy to shove a wheelchair into oncoming traffic."

He was silent for several seconds.

"I understand," he said, and she could hear the defeat in his voice.

"Hang in there," Shaye said. "I'm working full time to figure this out. I won't stop until you are safe."

He thanked her before disconnecting, but she could tell he was overwhelmed. She couldn't blame him. This situation had been far from normal to begin with and it had just launched into the stratosphere. It certainly wasn't the kind of thing his education had prepared him for. She lifted her now-cold coffee to her lips and took a sip.

Sinner.

What did it mean? Something important to the penitent, that was certain. But was it real or imagined? Could Nicolas be hiding something from her? Something he didn't want to admit? She wished they could have had the conversation in person. When someone wasn't a skilled liar, their body language usually gave them away. She put down her coffee and sighed. Now she was going to have to do a background check on her client.

For his own good.

15

Jackson parked in front of Shaye's apartment and trudged to the front door. She must have been in her office and seen him pull up because she had the door opened before he could even knock. She took one look at him and wrapped her arms around him, kissing him soundly. It gave him the same thrill it always did. To know that a woman of the highest quality—this woman in particular—had chosen him.

When they broke off from the kiss, Jackson smiled. "That was the highlight of my day."

"Sounds like your day went as well as mine. I was just about to open a bottle of wine. You interested?"

"Yes. But I'm afraid if I have a glass, I'll end up snoring on your couch, unwashed and unkempt."

"I like you unkempt. It makes me feel less self-conscious about my own lack of desire for girlie grooming. The unwashed part, however, I can help with. I just folded clean towels."

"You don't mind?" Jackson wanted to sit and enjoy a glass of wine with Shaye, but the thought of a hot shower had eclipsed all other pleasures.

Shaye smiled. "The wine and I will still be here when you get out. And as I took my shower earlier, you are free to use every last drop of hot water I have."

"You are the best girlfriend ever."

"If all it takes is the offer of shower to get that title, you really need to raise the bar."

He pulled her into his arms and kissed her soundly. "The bar is all the way to the ceiling and you're sitting on top of it."

She turned around and headed for the refrigerator as soon as he released her, but not before he saw the blush creeping up her neck. Jackson made his way to the guest bedroom and grabbed shorts and a T-shirt he had tucked in the dresser. It had been a casual suggestion of Shaye's that he keep a spare change of clothes at her apartment —both business and casual. Her apartment was closer to the police department and since he usually got off later than her, it was more convenient for him to drop by her place rather than have her drive across town to his.

Plus, the location of her apartment made it far easier to acquire any manner of tasty food in a matter of minutes, and you didn't even have to leave the apartment to do it. Delivery services abounded, so all one needed was a menu and a cell phone and most of the incredible food that New Orleans offered was only a few minutes away.

"I ordered Chinese when you called," Shaye yelled from the kitchen.

Jackson's mouth began to water, his roast beef sandwich from lunch long spent. "Did you get crab Rangoon?" he asked.

"A double order."

He let out a sigh of contentment and headed into the shower. If anyone had told him a year ago that this would be his life today, he would have called him crazy. Back then, he'd been the most junior detective in the department, working with a man who'd gone out of his way to make Jackson miserable. But then, if it weren't for that man's prejudice and stubbornness, Jackson might never have met Shaye.

And meeting Shaye had changed his entire life.

Despite Shaye's declaration that all the hot water was his to utilize, Jackson didn't linger in the steaming bath. The call of good food and wine and an even better woman was too strong to ignore. He dressed and was towel-drying his hair as he walked back into the kitchen. He tossed the towel into the laundry room and looked over at Shaye.

"Is this unkempt enough for you?" he asked, pointing at his hair, which was likely sticking up in all directions.

"Perfect," she said as she unpacked the Chinese food from a brown paper bag. "Do you want to eat at the bar or the couch?"

"The bar makes it easier to share."

"Who says I'm sharing?"

"You got the chicken fried rice, didn't you? Cruel."

She laughed and set plastic forks on the bar next to the boxes. "Fine, but I get my go at the fried rice first. Then you can have a taste. In the meantime, you'll have to suffer with pepper steak."

He slid onto a stool and opened the bottle of wine. "Let the suffering commence."

Shaye took a seat next to him and snagged a crab Rangoon from the box in front of her. She poured soy sauce on a small plate, dipped the crab pastry, then bit off half of it. "These are so good. I keep saying I'm going to make a meal just out of these alone."

"It's definitely possible," he said as he poured the wine. "So your day was as stellar as mine, huh? Any break on your case?"

"I'm afraid it's worse than no break. It appears that my client might be the next target."

Jackson muttered a curse. The last thing he wanted was for Shaye to be in danger, but no way was he asking her to back off, either. He knew how important Shaye's work was to her. He had no right to ask her to change careers so that his worry would lessen, especially when he had no intention of reciprocating.

"That's bad," he said. "Really bad. How serious do you think the threat is?"

She shook her head. "It's impossible to say without

knowing for certain that a crime was really committed to begin with."

"I suppose it could be someone messing with him," he said, silently hoping that was the case. "But who would have that kind of grudge against the guy? Did he strike you as someone who makes that kind of enemies?"

"Exactly the opposite, actually. He's one of those people that even the surliest among us couldn't help but like."

Jackson shook his head. "And yet..."

"I know. Assuming we're not dealing with a sound mind, the offense could also be imagined."

"Or blown out of proportion. Or it could really exist. Have you poked into your client's background any yet?"

"Not yet. That was on the agenda for tomorrow morning. But if he's done something big enough to attract a killer, then I don't know why the Church would have hired him. Given their past issues, you'd think they'd want to avoid potential reputation problems."

"It's probably not going to be all over the internet, that's for sure. But you might find a thread to start unraveling."

She nodded. "Everything starts with that thread. What about victims? Did you get a chance to see if anyone fit the bill for my case?"

"I did a couple searches. One strangulation homicide, but it was two older men over an issue with a cheating wife."

"Dare I ask which one lost?"

"One could argue that they had both already lost long before the strangulation occurred, but the boyfriend has been relieved of his duties."

"No one can be that good in bed."

He laughed. "Yeah. I thought the same, but this sort of thing happens a lot. It usually doesn't end in death, but I can't tell you how many assaults I booked before I made detective. And all over a woman who wasn't worth the cost of a bandage, much less a trip to jail."

"What about missing women?"

"Two. Detectives suspect the first one finally left her abusive husband. Her sister was cagey when questioned. They're pretty sure she knows but isn't talking. The second is a working girl. Roommate reported her missing."

"That's not the norm."

"No. It's not. But she's young. Really young. The one reporting claims she's eighteen, but I don't think the officer who took the statement was convinced. Still, she wasn't the one on the hot seat, so what can you do? The last thing we want is to dissuade women from contacting the police. Poking holes in their own background would do just that and wouldn't help the missing girl at all."

"What about the pimp?"

"They don't have one. She claims they came here from the Midwest somewhere to be artists but they have to make rent...you know the story. Probably runaways."

Shaye sighed. "She sounds like a good candidate for my situation."

"I was afraid that might be the case. I made a note of the info you would need on my phone."

"Thanks. I'll make sure to keep a low profile, but I'd like to talk to the roommate. If this guy is for real, I think it will be easier to figure out who he is once I know who the first victim is."

"Maybe. Maybe not. He might not have a connection to her, and working the streets isn't exactly introverted sort of activity. There's no telling how many people she was exposed to. Your guy could have been watching her from another corner and decided she was the one."

"Stop raining on my potential success parade. This whole thing is like pulling teeth. And it's so much harder because I can't be truthful to anyone I question about why I'm questioning them. Added to that, my client is not openly available for contact. I don't even have his name listed anywhere in my records. All this secrecy is exhausting."

"The deck is definitely stacked against you."

"What about your case?"

He shook his head. "It's a real mess. We have three suspects and they're all good for it. We can't cover that many, so Grayson is asking for some help tomorrow."

"Wow. Three is a lot for this kind of thing. Especially if they're solid."

"They are. And unfortunately, one is a teen girl. Have I told you lately how I sometimes hate my job?"

"That's awful. Any leads on tracking down the missing girl?"

Jackson shook his head. "Except for interviews, Grayson and I spent the entire day checking out every person and every place where the girl might have gone or been seen. We've come up with nothing. It's as if she walked out of her house, locked the door behind her, and simply vanished into thin air."

"Nothing on security cameras?"

"Not so far. We have a couple of injureds on desk duty reviewing everything they can from the businesses surrounding the neighborhood, but a lot of people don't have any cameras at all, and those who do usually have them inside only. They're working to get the footage from a couple of banks in the area. If we can see her somewhere on a street, it might give us a direction to start. Or even better, narrow down which person to lean on if she's not alone."

"That sucks."

"Yeah." There wasn't much else he could say. Shaye knew better than anyone what could happen to a young girl who went missing. She'd lived a horror that most people couldn't even imagine. And every year, more people disappeared from the New Orleans streets, and he couldn't help but wonder how many who were never found were still alive out there somewhere. It was a thought that often kept him from sleeping. And it was a problem with no solution. All he could do was tackle one at a time and hope for the best.

He and Grayson were doing everything they could. But it was of little comfort.

Nicolas shook hands with the last of the committee members as they exited the business office. He'd figured the meeting would run long but when the clock passed 9:00 p.m., he finally suggested they make a list and address the remaining items at the next meeting. Many of the committee members had already put in a full workday and gave him a grateful look. They'd spent another ten minutes putting together that list and finally, everyone was on their way home. He pushed himself outside onto the walkway and locked the office door.

The walkway was well lit and in good condition, but it was some distance from the office to the living quarters. He pushed himself along at a good clip, noticing for the first time exactly how dark the rest of the church grounds were. There were outside lights, of course, but they were sparsely located, leaving large sections of the grounds cast in complete darkness.

He could have called for Father Malcolm to come meet him, claiming he needed a bit of assistance getting back. It wouldn't be the first time he'd worn himself out to the point that he couldn't push himself home, but it had been months since that had been the case. When everything had run so late, he hadn't wanted to bother Malcolm, even though he knew the other priest wouldn't mind.

Still, it was long past time for Malcolm to have finished dinner and showered. Now he would be sitting in the living area watching television or reading and listening to the country music he seemed to enjoy so much. There was no point in rousting him from his rest time. It wasn't that far. Only a couple minutes, really. Well, maybe five. Then he started to wonder if he was right about the timing or simply trying to convince himself that there was no risk.

Calm down. You are freaking yourself out.

But the admonition, although accurate, didn't do much to ease his tension. He turned the corner at the end of the building and continued across the stretch of walkway that traversed the center courtyard. The place where he'd exited the confessional *that* day. In the darkness and without the activity of the landscapers and the hustle of the parishioners and church staff, it was almost bleak, the air stale.

He pushed harder, propelling himself faster along the sidewalk, and then he heard it—a branch cracking under the weight of a footstep. He stopped and whipped his head around, scanning the courtyard. He saw nothing.

But he could feel him.

Watching. Waiting.

The cloak of darkness was his cover and with all the many hedges, he could cross the courtyard unseen and accost Nicolas at any place along the walkway. Fighting the urge to panic, he pushed even harder, but his fear made his exertion unequal. The wheelchair wobbled, then took a hard jerk to the right. He clutched the wheels, trying to steady the rocking chair, but he was too weak. The chair pitched off the sidewalk and he flew out, then slammed onto the ground.

He let out a yell as his shoulder crunched into the hard turf, followed by his head. Pain exploded behind his eyes and he involuntarily clutched his forehead. He'd knocked his breath out when he hit the lawn and now he gasped, trying to drag in air. Finally, his body relented and he managed a huge gulp. He squeezed his eyes shut as his chest contracted, feeling like he'd been put into a vise. As it released, he started to relax.

That's when he heard the footsteps.

They were faint, barely a shuffle on the grass, but they were close. He peered into the darkness, trying to spot his pursuer. Was that movement behind the hedges to his right? With the wind blowing, he couldn't be sure. His hands flew to his pockets. Which one had he put the Mace in? He couldn't remember. And his cell phone. Had he put it in his backpack? And where was his backpack?

"Sinner."

The whisper echoed across the courtyard.

16

RAW FEAR SENT A WAVE OF ADRENALINE THROUGH Nicolas and he shoved himself off the ground, crying out as stabbing pain shot through his shoulder and up his neck. His vision blurred and he forced himself to keep pushing until he was in an upright position. If he could just drag himself close to the walkway, he might be able to use it to stand.

Then what?

He heard rustling behind him and twisted around. And that's when he saw him, standing at the edge of a hedge about fifteen feet away. His silhouette was barely visible in the dim light, but it was enough to send his heart rate into the stratosphere. This was it. It all ended here. The storm clouds above began to move away from the moon and a dim glow was cast over the courtyard. He stared at the man, unblinking as the moonlight uncovered him, and gasped when he got a better view.

It was just like the street kid had said.

He wore a black hoodie pulled over his head, but there was enough illumination for Nicolas to see that he had no face. And even though he knew it was a mask, he couldn't help being terrified. The man took a step toward him, then another, and he scrambled for the walkway, his damaged arms dragging his torso and useless legs across the ground. He clutched the cement and pulled himself up, choking back tears as the pain in his shoulder intensified.

Nicolas might not be able to run from his stalker or even defend himself properly, but he was going to face him standing and showing his true self. This was likely the way it all ended, but at least he wouldn't be a coward, hiding behind a mask and using God as an excuse for evil. He turned around, ready to face the penitent.

But the courtyard was empty.

Every muscle in Nicolas's body began to collapse and he started to sink. A couple seconds later, Malcolm's frantic voice rang out.

"Nicolas!" Malcolm jumped into the courtyard and put his arms around Nicolas, helping his weakened body into a sitting position on the walkway. "I heard a scream and came out to see what was wrong. What happened?"

"I fell."

Malcolm pulled out his cell phone. "I'll call for an ambulance."

"No. I'll be all right."

"It's no use arguing. You're clearly injured. Your head

is bleeding and you're favoring your right shoulder. You need to get to the hospital."

Nicolas started to protest but then stopped himself. The truth was, his entire body hurt as badly as it had right after the car wreck. He knew a lot of it was tension but he needed to be checked out. So it was either take a ride in an ambulance tonight or a ride with Father Bernard the next morning. Either way, Nicolas had no doubt he'd be forced to seek medical attention.

Malcolm gave instructions for locating them, then slipped his cell phone back in the pocket of his sweatpants. "How did it happen?" he asked.

Nicolas hated lying but there was no way he could tell the truth. Instead, he settled for telling half of it. "I was tired and going too fast. I lost control of the chair and ran off the walkway."

"How are your legs? I can tell your shoulder is off— maybe dislocated—but can you feel any injuries to your legs?"

"They hurt. My whole body does."

Malcolm studied him for a moment, his uncertainty clear. "May I look?" he said finally.

Nicolas nodded, finally clueing into Malcolm's fear. Due to nerve damage, Nicolas had lost feeling in much of his legs. It was one factor that made his rehabilitation so tedious. He had to train his legs to do something whether he could feel them doing it or not. No one could know for certain the extent of the damage, but it was possible he could have a deep gash or even a compound fracture and might not be able to feel it.

Malcolm pulled out his cell phone and squatted down, using it as a flashlight to get a better look at Nicolas's legs. He held the phone with his left hand and ran his right hand up and down each leg, covering every inch from Nicolas's crotch to his ankles.

"I don't see any blood except for a bit on your sock," Malcolm said. "And I can't feel anything out of line. Doesn't mean there's not. I'm no doctor, but nothing is coming through the skin."

Relief swept through Nicolas. At least one hurdle was cleared.

"Father Malcolm? Father Nicolas?" Father Bernard's voice sounded behind them and Nicolas looked over to see the senior priest hurrying in their direction.

"It's all right," Malcolm tried to reassure the clearly concerned priest as he hurried up. "Nicolas took a spill off the walkway, but there doesn't appear to be any life-threatening damage. I've already called for an ambulance."

Father Bernard looked a bit relieved when he heard an ambulance was on the way. "What happened? Was there a problem with the chair?"

"No," Nicolas replied. "Only with the driver. I was pushing too hard and lost control. I should have taken more time but you know patience isn't my strong suit."

Bernard nodded. "Yes, well, I suppose we'll have to work on that some more."

The sound of the ambulance siren filled the night air and Nicolas glanced around at his scattered belongings. "Sounds like my ride is here. Can you help gather my things?"

"Of course." Malcolm reached for the backpack and picked up Nicolas's cell phone, which had fallen out. He started to rise, then frowned and took a couple steps forward. When he stood, he was holding the can of Mace. "Is this yours?"

"Yes," Nicolas said, seeing no point in lying when another half-truth would work as well. "It must have fallen out of my backpack. My mother...well, she worried, and I promised her..."

Malcolm's expression cleared in understanding. "Of course." He placed the Mace in the backpack and zipped it up.

"I'd like to take that with me if I could," Nicolas said. "In case they keep me. At least I'll have my phone and something to read."

Malcolm sat the pack on the walkway next to him. "Should you bring the chair as well?"

"That won't be necessary," Bernard said. "It will only be in the way in the ambulance and he won't need it in the hospital. When Father Nicolas is released, I'll take the chair when I pick him up."

Nicolas reached over with his left hand and clutched his right elbow, trying to prevent his arm from moving. Even a deep breath sent pain shooting through his shoulder and down his arm. He prayed it was only dislocated and could be put back in place. That would be painful and would definitely limit his mobility for some time, but it would be weeks and not months.

Paramedics entered the courtyard pushing a gurney and Malcolm waved them over. They helped Nicolas onto the stretcher and Malcolm put his backpack at his side. "Don't worry about anything," Malcolm said. "Father Bernard or I will be there shortly."

Nicolas nodded as the paramedics took him away. At first opportunity, he had to call Shaye and let her know what happened. And although it had crossed his mind before, Nicolas hadn't wanted to discuss with Shaye how to proceed if anything were to happen to him. First thing tomorrow, he intended to contact his attorney and make financial arrangements.

If the penitent made good on his threat, Nicolas would dedicate every dime in his trust fund to catching him before he could hurt anyone else.

IT WAS close to midnight when Shaye closed the door behind Jackson and drew the dead bolt. She felt sorry for him, knowing he had an early start again the next morning. Especially as his day hadn't yielded the results he and Grayson were hoping for. She understood their frustration and the way their desperation grew with every passing day. Abductions usually didn't allow much of a window of opportunity for recovery, if any. Past a certain point, detectives just hoped they could at least find a body and give the family some closure. Not the kind they were looking for, but Shaye was convinced it was better than not knowing.

She turned off the overhead light in her office but the lamp on her desk remained on. She left some illumination in all the rooms when she went to bed in case she needed to bolt up and open fire. Then she'd have a clear view of who she was shooting at. She'd gotten better over the years, moving from bright overhead lights that remained on 24-7 to lamps that gave a decent glow but didn't make the room look like the sun was shining directly in it. She had to admit that sleeping without bright lights in her eyes had improved the quality of her sleep, even if it hadn't lengthened the amount of it.

Beggars couldn't be choosers.

She'd take three to four hours of really solid sleep and another three of dozing in and out over the alternative. At least it had been months since she'd had a nightmare. When her memory had first returned, they'd been more frequent and more terrifying than before. Eleonore had said her mind was working overtime to process everything. But eventually, things calmed and the time between the nightmares grew longer until at least a month passed without a single night of interrupted sleep. Not interrupted by a nightmare anyway.

Shaye still slept so lightly that the slightest uncommon noise had her bolting upright. Two nights ago, it had been a slow drip in her bathroom sink, which was still awaiting repair. In the meantime, she had a washcloth in the bottom to stop the rhythmic noise. At least twice a week a car alarm went off and it took her the better part of an hour to get back to sleep every time. And the rain still bothered her. Nights when it was really coming down, she sometimes didn't sleep at all.

But the beauty of being self-employed was you could catch up in the daylight.

She grabbed a bottled water from the refrigerator and was headed for her bedroom when her cell phone went off. Assuming it had to be Jackson, she glanced at the display, and her pulse spiked when she saw it was Nicolas.

"Nicolas?" she answered. "Is something wrong?"

"Yes," he said, his voice wavering. "I'm in the hospital."

She gripped her phone. "Are you all right?"

"I'm stable or they wouldn't let me have my phone. I dislocated my shoulder, but they put it back in. No other damage but bumps and bruises, but they're keeping me overnight."

A bit of relief passed through her that he was stable and didn't appear to have any more serious injuries. "What happened?"

"He was there," Nicolas said, his voice cracking as he said the words.

Shaye stiffened. "Where?"

"At the church. I was running a committee meeting tonight in the administration building. The walkway connects that building to the one our living quarters is in, but the administration building is on the other side of the cathedral and our quarters are at the far end of the courtyard."

"Did he attack you?"

"No. But he was there. I heard him in the bushes and when I tried to go faster, I lost control of the chair and went off the walkway."

He was silent for a couple seconds and Shaye could hear him breathing heavily.

"I thought he had me," Nicolas said. "I managed to pull myself upright using the walkway, but my legs were spent, and my Mace came out of my pocket when I fell. He was moving closer. I knew when I turned around he was going to be right there...I thought I was dead."

Shaye's chest tightened as empathy for the young man swept through her. She'd thought that the end was near too many times, and the horror and dread you felt was indescribable.

"I am so sorry," she said. "I know how awful it is. How did you get away?"

"Father Malcolm heard me yell when I fell off the walkway and came outside to see if someone needed help. He was reading in our common living area and had the windows open to allow the breeze in. If he'd had them closed or been playing music..."

Shaye said a silent thanks to Father Malcolm and his desire for fresh air or to save money. Whichever one, it had probably saved Nicolas's life.

"Did you get a look at him?" she asked.

"Yes, but it won't do us any good. He was wearing dark pants, hoodie, and a mask, like the street kid said. His face was blanked out."

"What about size?"

"Maybe six feet or so, taking his height in comparison to the bushes. He seemed solid in build—not skinny or overweight." He sighed. "Which doesn't help much at all."

"What about movement? Could you gauge age at all?"

"No. I only saw him take two steps before I turned around to drag myself back to the sidewalk. I managed to pull myself up, but when I turned around again, he was gone. Then Father Malcolm showed up shortly after."

Shaye's heart clenched as the mental picture of Nicolas pulling himself up on the sidewalk flashed through her mind. "Can I get you anything? Do anything?" she asked.

"Catch this guy."

"I'm working on that, but it's clear that he's fixated on you for more reasons than wanting to unburden his soul or brag. He confessed to you to scare you."

"It worked. I'm terrified."

"And I'm sure that's exactly what he's enjoying. I promise I'm doing everything I can to figure out who he is, but I need your help. I need you to think hard about who might be targeting you. Regardless of reality, this guy believes you've done something wrong. If you have any idea what he fixated on, it might help."

"I swear I don't know. I thought about it a considerable amount this afternoon. I prayed for enlightenment, but I've come up empty."

"It's not going to be something obvious, or you'd already have the answer. So start thinking about your interaction with people over the last month or so. See if there's anything you can think of that someone could twist into something untoward."

"I'll try. I just don't see..."

"Don't worry about it tonight. You need to get some rest and make sure you didn't injure yourself further. And I'm afraid you're going to need to restrict your movement even more, at least for a while. I realize that makes things rather inconvenient."

"Actually, given how bad my shoulder hurts, I'm probably going to have to have some help for several days, at least."

"So no traversing walkways at night by yourself?"

"Not anytime soon. If you don't catch this guy, maybe not ever again. Maybe I should become a monk. I could move to Tibet."

If he hadn't been completely serious, it might have been amusing. But Shaye knew desperation when she heard it. And she understood it. Right now, Nicolas would do anything to feel safe again. Even if it meant cloistering himself in another country.

"I don't think you'll have to take it that far," she said. "But I have some ideas on the help end of things. Let me make some calls and I'll have some information for you in the morning."

"I appreciate all the help you can offer."

"I wish I could come see you, but I know that's not prudent. I would like to do some poking around at the church, though. Can you describe the location of the different buildings so that I can get a feel for the distance between them and the options for entrance and exit?"

"You're not going to go there, are you?" he asked, sounding a little panicked.

"No," she said. "But there's someone who helps me from time to time. He'll be able to give me the information I need."

"Photographer or something like that?"

She smiled. "Even better. An artist with photographic memory."

"That's cool," he said, his voice back to normal.

He gave Shaye a rundown of the various buildings and their location on the church grounds. His voice grew weaker as he talked, and she knew he needed to sleep.

"Thanks for this," she said as she finished up her notes. "I'm going to let you go so you can get some rest. If they offer you anything to sleep, please accept it. You're safe in the hospital. And you need your strength."

"I know. They gave me a sleeping pill. I didn't take it yet because I wanted to call you, but it took so long to get all the tests, then I had to convince Father Malcolm and Father Bernard to go back to the church. They have to cover my duties as well as their own. Nothing would be served by either of them staying here."

"You said Father Malcolm was reading, right? Where was Father Bernard?"

"In his bedroom. He heard Father Malcolm leave and when he came out of his room, found the front door standing open. So he dressed and went out after him."

"So neither of them would have seen anything."

"I don't see how. I didn't tell them about the man, of course. I just said I miscalculated because I was tired and fell. But if either of them had seen someone on the church grounds that late, they would have called out or at least commented on it because it would have been unusual."

"Is the cathedral open at night?"

"No. People sometimes go to the front entry to pray and leave flowers, but they aren't normally on the interior grounds that late. There's no reason for anyone to be in the courtyard at that time except me and Fathers Malcolm and Bernard. We're the only staff who live on-site and the rest had gone home hours before."

"Okay. I'll let you go now. Take that sleeping pill and get some rest. Call me tomorrow when you get a chance and let me know what the doctors say. If you want me to do more, just ask."

"Thank you. I want to maintain our secrecy for now, but I suppose there might come a time when my transgression will be exposed." He sighed. "I knew the risk I was taking when I spoke with you. If the church finds out and takes action against me, then I'll accept that. But I'll never regret my decision."

"Let's worry about that if the time comes. Right now, I need you alert and strong. Take care, Nicolas."

"You take care as well."

Shaye sat her cell phone on the kitchen counter and blew out a breath. Things had escalated from dangerous to dire in a single night. She put the bottled water back in the refrigerator and set a pot of coffee to brew. Sleep would have to wait. She needed to do some research on Nicolas. Something had prompted the penitent to target him.

She needed to know what it was.

———

HE STOOD across the street from the church, gazing up at the steeple on the cathedral. It was an impressive sight during the day, but with the moon big and bright behind it, it looked like something out of a movie or one of those award-winning photos you saw in magazines.

Don't worry, Father. Thy will be done.

There would be other nights. Other opportunities. He knew God would provide. And tonight wasn't the right time anyway. More of a test run, really. But it had yielded an interesting bit of information. Father Nicolas might have spoken to Shaye Archer, but he hadn't told anyone else about his fears. If he had, the police would have come along with the paramedics.

Maybe he'd been wrong. Maybe Nicolas had met with the PI for another reason altogether, but the timing had been highly suspicious. Still, it was possible, he supposed, that the young priest hadn't broken his vows. Hadn't committed another egregious sin.

Not that it mattered. The one sin was enough.

SHAYE GRABBED her cup of coffee and took another drink. It had cooled some, so she filled it up with what was left in her carafe, wondering if she needed to put another on to brew. She'd been at it for an hour so far, combing through every mention of Nicolas she could find on the internet. And there were many. The young priest was popular with his congregation. That meant tons of pics and mentions on social media—Nicolas christening babies and attending charity events.

She'd looked at every single mention going back a year and hadn't found anything that set off alarms. That might mean it was something deeper in Nicolas's past, something that very few people knew about, or it could mean that it was something the penitent had invented in his own damaged mind. With no way to determine which it was, she decided to keep pushing. She'd take it back another year and see if anything popped.

Some of the first hits were of Nicolas shortly after his car wreck. He was much thinner then and his eyes had that sunken look that came along with worry and a lack of sleep. She imagined the pain had made solid sleep difficult and worrying that he'd never walk again tipped it further in the wrong direction. It was a lot for a young man to process, especially when he was just starting his career.

She found a picture on social media of Nicolas and his mother. She was smiling down at him in his wheelchair and he was smiling back. The gaunt look was still in place but the smile was real. Shaye could tell Nicolas and his mother had been close. It was another huge blow, losing both of his parents so young, especially when he needed their help more than ever. Shaye gazed at the photo for a bit, then frowned. Reaching for her keyboard, she did a search for Nicolas's accident.

Pay dirt.

People had died.

Nicolas and another seminary student had been returning from a weekend event. The other student, Jason Roper, had been driving and the vehicle belonged to him. It was late at night and he'd fallen asleep at the wheel. Neither had been drinking. The Jeep Wrangler had crossed over into the oncoming lane and hit a sedan head-on. They'd both been thrown from the vehicle, so either the seat belts had broken or they hadn't been wearing them. Katrina Fontaine, the woman driving the other car, had died on impact. She'd been five months pregnant.

Nicolas survived but Jason died later at the hospital. Shaye did a quick check on Jason's family and found that his mother and father lived in Nebraska. He was an only child. She shook her head. That had to have been horrible for them, but she couldn't see any reason for them to blame Nicolas for the accident as it was Jason's vehicle and Jason had been driving. But the family of the other victim might not feel the same way. They were left with the ultimate loss and the person to blame wasn't available.

Shaye did a search on Katrina and located her Facebook account, which had basically been turned into a memorial. She saw a picture with Katrina and an older couple identified as her parents and clicked on her mother's account. They were local but they had obviously had her later on in life. Neither was young, and one of the posts referenced her father's Parkinson's. Not a good fit for the penitent.

Then she saw the father's full name. *Harvey Breaux.*

Her mother must have created her Facebook account under her maiden name because it wasn't Breaux. And granted, there were a lot of Breaux in Louisiana, so it might be a coincidence. But looking at Harvey's eyes and nose, she already knew what she was going to find. She scrolled down some more and found what she was looking for.

Jeff Breaux, the electrician, was Katrina Fontaine's brother.

Another picture sent her off to Katrina's husband's account, and her eyes widened when she scanned the posts. Jeff Breaux had been best friends with Katrina's husband, Damon. And Damon had committed suicide two weeks after Katrina's death.

She leaned back in her chair and blew out a breath. It was everything. Motive and opportunity. Granted, Nicolas hadn't been driving the car, but Jeff had lost his sister and his best friend because of the accident. If he was looking for someone to pay for it, Nicolas was the only target.

She closed her laptop and headed off down the hall for bed. Finally, she felt like she had a break in the case. Tomorrow—correction, later today—she'd ask Jackson if she could borrow his surveillance car. She wanted to find out how Jeff spent his free time. And even though Jeff was the best suspect, there was something else she wanted to know—if Father Malcolm could really hear a yell from the courtyard to the living quarters.

Malcolm had been outside the door to the cathedral when Nicolas pushed it open. It was Malcolm who'd given Nicolas the first letter from the penitent. And now, Malcolm had been on location when the penitent had stalked Nicolas on church grounds.

Be the first responder.

It was a classic fallback for the smarter criminal. Pretend you're assisting and people won't suspect that you were the perpetrator. Sometimes it was simply due to timing. They needed to explain why they were there, and playing the Good Samaritan was an easy out. Or sometimes they did it because they craved the attention and couldn't help pushing themselves into the limelight. Some forensic psychologists believed that they subconsciously wanted to be caught and that's why they inserted themselves into the investigation. Shaye figured that might be the case a handful of times, but mostly she believed some were so egotistical that they thought they could get away with the duplicity. That they enjoyed fooling law enforcement—proving how mentally and physically superior they were.

Yes, Jeff Breaux was the best fit, but Father Malcolm and Robert Croft weren't off the hook.

17

Hailey heard the sound of footsteps descending on stone stairs. She scrambled for the back corner of the room, panicked. If she pretended to be passed out, would he leave her alone? If he thought she was unconscious, would it give her an opportunity to bolt past him and run? She'd seen it work that way in the movies, but what if she ran past and then there was another locked door at the end of the stairs? Or what if she got out but had no idea where she was? She didn't even know how much time had passed. She could have traveled any distance away from New Orleans.

But if she didn't do something, then he might attack her. She knew that rape wasn't about sex. Some guys got off on the fear and the struggle. He hadn't assaulted her yet. She was a virgin and would have known. But maybe he was waiting for her to be conscious. Waiting so that she was awake and he could see her terror.

She heard a bolt slide back and dropped onto the ground, slumping against the wall, deciding that playing unconscious was her best bet. The door groaned as it opened and light flooded the room. She'd draped her arm over her face, but the light coming through the cracks between her body was enough to blind her.

She forced herself to remain still as he approached her. She could hear his footsteps on the stone. When she heard him breathing, she wanted to scream. She felt a finger poke her on the shoulder, and she struggled to remain limp as every muscle in her body wanted to tense.

"I know you're awake," he said. "God told me himself. It's his work I'm doing here."

What the fuck?

Hailey struggled to process the words. Even her father, with all his rigid beliefs, didn't say things that crazy.

The sound of an object being dragged across the stone echoed through the tiny chamber, and she cringed at the screeching. It stopped next to her and she felt the presence of the man right above her.

"Get up and sit in the chair," he said. "It's time for atonement."

She drew in a deep breath, trying to think. Maybe if she got on the chair, she'd have a better chance of making a run for it. Finally, she inched her head up to get a look at her captor.

Then wished she hadn't.

He was dressed in a long black robe with a hood. A

giant crucifix hung around his neck. But it was the face that bothered her the most. It wasn't there. He wore one of those solid material masks that eliminated features. It was black, like the robe, and utterly terrifying. All of the hard work she'd done to remain calm flew right out the window. She choked back a cry and every muscle in her body knotted. Her stomach roiled and the room began to spin.

He reached down with one gloved hand and pulled her up and into the chair. Any chance of running was dashed when he slipped the ropes around her hands, tying them together and then to the chair.

"There's a locked door at the top of the stairs," he said. "In case you thought about trying to get away."

"What do you want from me?" she cried out.

He stared at her silently and even though she couldn't see his eyes, she could feel them on her.

"I want to save you," he said.

She started to scream.

18

THURSDAY, MAY 19, 2016
St. Mary's, New Orleans

NICOLAS WAS in the courtyard again. It was night and a storm brewed overhead. The moon slipped in and out of the clouds, exposing parts of the lawn for seconds, then eclipsing them in darkness once more. He was in his wheelchair on the walkway to his living quarters but for some reason, the wheels wouldn't move. He leaned over, checking each side to see if something was jammed in them or if he'd run up against something on the sidewalk, but he couldn't find anything.

About twenty feet from him, the hedges rustled. He froze, staring at the foliage, trying to see what had caused the movement. It wasn't wind because the night air had suddenly gone still and silent. He couldn't even hear cars on the street. It was as if the entire world had been put on pause except for this little piece that he existed in. The moon slipped behind the clouds and he heard the rustling again.

He grabbed the wheels and tried to move the chair again, but to no avail. He even tried rocking them in reverse, but it was as if the chair were being held in place. As the clouds passed on, a dim glow of moonlight began to illuminate the courtyard. A figure stood next to the hedge from where the noise had come. He'd been trying to convince himself that the noise had been made by a feral cat, but he'd known a cat couldn't make that much noise. It was a man. It had always been a man.

He was nothing more than a shadow outlined on the lawn, and Nicolas knew that even if there were bright spotlights shining on him, Nicolas wouldn't be able to see his face. The man took a step closer and Nicolas shoved the wheels, twisting backward and forward, praying that whatever sorcery held them in place would let go of its hold on them. He kept his gaze locked on the man as he took another step closer. He never took two in a row. Just a single step, then stopped. Then another second later, he stepped again. Nicolas knew the action was intentional. It was just a way to scare him, and it was working.

He reached into his pocket and fumbled for the Mace, relieved that it was still in place. He slipped the cap off, making sure he kept his hands low and in his lap, not wanting to give away his advantage. When the man got close enough, he'd strike. The man's mask was made of cloth. The Mace should penetrate some of it. The man took another step closer and Nicolas prepared to fire. One more step and he'd be within feet of the chair. Two more steps and Nicolas would make his move.

One step.

Two steps.

Nicolas flung his hand up, but he wasn't quick enough. The man blocked his arm and shoved it to the side, causing him to lose his grip on the Mace, which went sailing across the courtyard. The man took one more step toward him and leaned forward, his hands reaching for Nicolas's neck. Nicolas opened his mouth to scream, but no sound came out. He tried again, this time forcing himself so hard that his lungs felt as if they were going to burst.

But he couldn't make even a strangled cry.

The man's hands closed around his neck. As he looked up into the blank face, fear coursed through him and a wave of dizziness passed over him. This was it. This was how it all ended. With the little strength he had remaining, he reached up with one hand and grabbed the mask, then ripped it from his attacker's face.

I know him.

THAT'S when he woke up.

He sprang upright and had to force himself not to cry out as pain shot through his shoulder and arm. His entire body was drenched in sweat and he could feel his heart pounding in his chest. He clutched his injured arm with his good one and leaned back against the elevated headrest of his hospital bed. He forced himself to take in a deep breath and slowly let it out. The steady beep of the heart monitor slowed and he felt his body relax.

What had happened?

His mind was all fuzzy. Probably because of the sleeping pill.

It was a nightmare. That much he remembered. He was back on the courtyard walkway and his wheelchair wouldn't move. The penitent appeared and attacked him. He frowned. There was something else. Something that flickered just at the edge of his memory.

The mask! He'd removed the mask from the penitent.

He squeezed his eyes shut, trying to force a face to appear, but all he saw was the black cloth stretched beneath the black hoodie. His breath came out in a whoosh and he realized he'd been holding it. Every muscle in his body was tense again.

He opened his eyes and reached for the glass of water on the tray next to the bed. As he dragged the glass over, something fell onto his lap. He looked down and his hands began to shake. No. It couldn't be. A single piece of folded paper lay on his blanket. The cup slipped from his hand and fell onto the floor, splashing water onto the wall. He reached down and picked it up. It contained one word.

Confess.

SHAYE PARKED in front of a café and looked over at Hustle. "You sure you don't mind doing this?"

He managed to hold in a sigh but just barely. It was only the third time she'd asked since they left the motel where he lived with his foster parent, an old friend of Shaye's.

"Mind doing what?" he asked. "Walking around in broad daylight at a church? Yeah, that's some serious risks—all those religious people."

"It's a potential crime scene, and for all I know, the perp could be one of those religious people."

He stared at her, not certain if she was serious or joking. "That's seriously screwed up. You know that, right?"

"Yeah, but I have to think that way. It's how I catch the bad guys."

He grinned. "You're not going to get any argument from me. I've seen crazy up close. I know it's out there. Any final instructions?"

"No. Just be careful. Try not to draw attention to yourself."

"Don't worry. I've got a cover story if anyone asks. I think you're forgetting which one of us has the street smarts."

She smiled. "Get out of here then, smarty-pants. I'll be in the café with a plate of beignets. If you're lucky, I'll save you one."

"Cruel," he said as he hopped out of the car.

Shaye had parked a block away from the church because she didn't want anyone who was employed there to see her nearby. Hustle hadn't asked her for details because he knew she couldn't tell him and in the big scheme of things, it really didn't matter. Shaye had a client, which meant someone needed her help and the police couldn't handle whatever it was. Hustle knew better than most how that felt. It was Shaye who had believed his story and helped him rescue his friend Jinx and ultimately get them both off the streets.

So when Shaye asked for his help with an investigation, his answer was always going to be a resounding yes. Because he knew exactly what kind of cases she took on and the difficulty involved in solving them. This one happened to be a really simple favor—walk the grounds and see how far it was from the courtyard walkway to the building with the living quarters. Take some pictures and give an assessment on the layout and how sound would carry. Living on the streets, he'd learned to make quick judgment about buildings and alleyways. Discerning all the potential pitfalls of a location was exactly what kept him safe.

What he did know was that her client was in a wheelchair and someone had scared him and caused him to fall off the sidewalk. The fact that someone was screwing around with a dude in a wheelchair made Hustle mad about the whole thing. He hoped whatever he saw helped Shaye find the asshole who'd done it.

He walked through the stone entry onto the church grounds, appreciating the structure in front of him. It was massive and old. And while he had no desire to work in any other art form than drawing and painting, he had a ton of respect for the craftsmen who had fit together all of that stone to create a work of art that would survive hundreds of years.

He pulled out his phone and took a picture of the

front, then started walking around, stopping occasionally to snap another shot. He was there to get information for Shaye, but already, his artist's mind was forming the subject of his next painting. He walked around the church and into the courtyard. It was a large area with elaborate and well-maintained landscaping. Winter had dragged on this year, so the azalea bushes were late to bloom and weren't quite done yet. He stopped to take a couple shots of the bursts of color with the stone building as a backdrop.

He located the walkway that Shaye had indicated and made his way toward it. It was easy to find the indentations where her client had rolled his wheelchair off the cement and into the grass. He backed up, pretending to study the massive wooden doors behind the walkway, and snapped several shots of the damaged area.

Once he'd documented the scene, he hopped up onto the walkway and headed for the living quarters. As he walked, he paced off his steps. When he reached the building at the end of the walkway he stopped and made a note of the distance. Then he began taking pictures of the building. He started with the front first, then walked around each side to get a picture of the windows. Then he returned to the front of the building and took a couple more shots of the walkway leading away from the building.

The photos didn't make any difference to Hustle. Once he'd seen something, it was imprinted on his mind forever. All he had to do was think about it and it was there as if he were looking right at it. But Shaye needed the pictures because for whatever reason, she couldn't go look herself, and he doubted her client had the luxury of waiting for Hustle to sketch it all.

"Can I help you?" A man's voice sounded behind him.

He turned around, forcing himself to remain relaxed and casual. The man behind him was probably in his middle thirties and was wearing a priest's collar. "No, thanks," he said. "I'm just taking some pictures for art class."

The man smiled. "I'm Father Malcolm. You're a student?"

Hustle nodded. "Southern Artists Academy. I'm first year."

"That's a difficult school to get into. And if you don't mind my saying so, you look very young. You must be extremely talented."

He shrugged. "I guess. Regular school wasn't really my thing, you know. So I did the GED and applied. I was lucky enough to get in so now I get to work on what I really care about."

"And you don't have to worry about algebra or grammar or boring history."

Hustle smiled because he knew the priest was joking with him and it was the expected response. "I guess so. Although there's still plenty of math that goes into painting. And I like history. Some of it anyway. That's why I want to paint this building. The architecture is incredible. And the grounds provide the contrast in color and texture. It's a great subject for my next assignment. We have to paint a local structure. I don't suppose you can tell me about the construction of the church, can you?"

"I'm afraid not. We don't have a shared love of history, and what I know about architecture wouldn't fill a thimble. But Father Bernard is quite studied on it and has regaled me with tales of the church construction many times. Let me get him for you."

Before Hustle could protest, the priest slipped back inside the living quarters. What the hell. Might as well talk to this Father Bernard and keep up the charade. Shaye might need him to come back for some reason and at least he had a good excuse for it. He took a couple more shots of the walkway leading to the courtyard and finally heard the door open behind him. He turned around and saw an older priest with silver-and-black hair step out, favoring his right knee.

"I'm Father Bernard," the priest said. "Father Malcolm tells me you're an art student with an interest in old architecture?"

"Yes. Can you tell me about the construction of the church?"

"Absolutely. New Orleans architecture is one of my favorite subjects and I've spent a lot of time studying this building in particular." Father Bernard launched into a detailed explanation of the construction process and materials and even the tools that would have been used.

Hustle nodded as he talked, impressed with the depth of the man's knowledge.

"What's unique about this church," Father Bernard continued, "is that all the additions and other structures were part of the original build. It showed either great forethought or great ego to assume this size would be necessary, but it worked out."

Hustle nodded. "One of the first things I noticed was that the stone is the same hue on all the buildings. And the mortar possesses the same amount of aging. When things were constructed at different times, it's impossible to match both. I mean, plenty of people won't notice but..."

"The artist, or builder, or historical architectural scholar would," Father Bernard finished. "But I agree. Most wouldn't. You have a good eye but then I assume that's why you were accepted to such a prestigious school. Have you determined what part of the church you'll use as the subject of your assignment?"

"Not yet. I'm walking around the grounds today and taking some pictures. Things look different in person than they do in photos, but the pictures help refresh my memory. Usually I get a feeling about something—like it calls to me to be painted. It's hard to explain."

Father Bernard smiled. "You're speaking to someone who understands a calling more than most."

Hustle laughed. "I guess you're right. I see very minor repairs on the outside surfaces, so I assume there has been minimal shifting. Do you know anything about the foundation?"

"Yes. A big part of the reason for the lack of shifting

is that a large portion of the church has catacombs beneath it."

Hustle perked up. Given flooding concerns, basements were rare in New Orleans. "Catacombs? Like a basement for dead people?"

"Exactly, although no one was ever interred here. I assume they decided flooding was too much of a concern."

"So what is the space used for?"

"Nothing now and not ever that I'm aware of. Given the lack of electricity and propensity for water seepage, they're not even good for storage. But the construction of the stone walls has served as piers for the structure, preventing a lot of movement that probably would have existed otherwise."

"That's really impressive," Hustle said. "That they created an underground structure so sound that it's held this kind of weight and only shifted a bit. They don't make buildings like that today, that's for sure. Heck, our doors stick every time it stops raining for more than a couple days."

Father Bernard nodded. "Modern buildings are necessary but not art. It's rare to see someone put in the time to conceive of this type of accomplishment, then carry it out with the building process. Everything today is about deadlines, which is about the bottom line, I'm afraid."

"People gotta eat, right?" Hustle looked over the building that housed their living quarters. "Is this where you live?"

"Yes. The building is designed with several bedrooms and a common kitchen and living area. Each bedroom has its own bath and a good-sized living area as well."

"And no problems with doors sticking?"

Father Bernard laughed. "Not so far."

"The windows look original. Do they still open?"

"Yes. We open them quite often when the breeze is nice."

Hustle glanced over at the street that was fifty feet away. "The noise from the street doesn't bother you? I try opening my window, but all the honking and tire squealing distracts me."

"We usually don't open them until late evening when we're retired for the night. The streets are a lot quieter by then given that there are no restaurants or bars directly across the street. But we do hear the occasional partygoer who imbibed a bit too much and is shouting at his friends rather than talking at a normal level."

"People here like their alcohol." Hustle stuck his hand out. "Thank you for your time. I'm looking forward to diving into this assignment."

"You're very welcome, and if you'd ever like to discuss the buildings further or decide to do something on the interior, please come speak to me again. I could talk for an hour on the woodwork alone."

Hustle nodded and made his way down the walkway. He officially knew more about the construction of the church than he ever wanted to, and no way was he ever asking about the inside. An hour's monologue on woodworking would put him to sleep. He didn't need to hear about every step of the process in excruciating detail in order to appreciate the artistry, but the priest was clearly passionate about the subject and probably couldn't contain himself when he found a willing listener.

He forced himself into a casual stroll as he left, pausing to take another couple shots for good measure. In the courtyard, he ran into Father Malcolm again and thanked him for his assistance. Once he was off the church grounds, he picked up his pace and hurried back to the café where Shaye was waiting.

As soon as she saw him come in, she waved at the server. "She's bringing you an order of beignets and a root beer float. Do you want any real food?"

"Please. I had real food for breakfast. You can only eat so much of that in one day."

Shaye shook her head. "One day, it will catch up with you and you'll be crying on a treadmill five times a week like the rest of us."

"All the more reason to get as much of the good stuff in as I can right now."

She laughed. "I can't argue with that. Okay, you were gone for a while. Did you run into any trouble?"

"If by trouble you mean being accosted by Father Malcolm who then fetched Father Bernard to educate me on the architectural history of the building, then yeah."

"Both priests saw you?" she asked, clearly dismayed.

"Don't worry." He told Shaye his cover story.

"Smart. And not exactly untrue. At least not all of it."

"Not any of it, thank you. I'll probably paint the front of the church for next week's assignment. It really is a spectacular structure."

"And what did you think about sound and distance?"

He pulled out his phone and accessed the pictures, starting in the courtyard. He described the layout and showed her the spot where the wheelchair had impacted with the lawn.

"I paced it off," he said. "I'd estimate it's thirty yards or so between the two."

"And the windows on the living quarters?"

"None on the side of the building facing the courtyard. All that's on that side is the door. There are windows on each side of the building. I asked Father Bernard about the noise level and he said they can sometimes hear people yelling on the street. That's maybe fifty feet away from the south windows, though. The courtyard is farther away and not direct."

"So what do you think?"

He shook his head. "I can't say for sure. Is it possible someone in that building heard a yell from the courtyard? Yeah. But I wouldn't swear to it. If the wind was blowing in that direction it would help. And that's assuming they didn't have the television on or radio or nothing else making noise."

"So no one's off the hook." She sighed.

"You really think one of those priests I met was spooking another one? I mean, I know you can't tell me what happened but given what you were asking for, I kinda made some assumptions."

"I hope they weren't up to anything," Shaye said. "Unfortunately, I can't be certain."

"If it helps, the older priest has a slight limp. Bad right knee, looks like."

"Interesting, and yeah, it helps. Thanks for doing this."

Hustle nodded. The thought of priests causing trouble for each other made him uncomfortable. The two men he'd met didn't seem like bad guys, and he usually had a feeling about that kind of thing. But he also knew that sometimes people fooled you.

"It was no problem," he said. "And besides, I really did get an idea for my next project. But I'm afraid I didn't help you much."

"You helped plenty. I needed something answered and you did what I couldn't risk."

"But I didn't get you an answer."

"In this business, sometimes 'I don't know' *is* an answer."

"Yeah, well, that answer sucks."

She nodded. "Massively."

19

Nicolas cringed as the nurse helped him into the wheelchair. His shoulder was in a sling and didn't hurt much when he wasn't moving it, but as soon as it was jostled around, pain shot up into his neck and down his arm to his wrist. He had attempted to use it to change positions in the bed and had almost yelled.

"Ready?" the nurse asked.

He nodded. That couldn't be a lie, right? Just nodding? Even though he wasn't ready at all. Wasn't ready for what might happen next. Wasn't ready to defend himself.

Wasn't ready to die.

He choked back a cry, covering it with a cough.

"Are you all right, Father?" the nurse asked. "I hope you're not catching a cold."

"I'm sure I'll be fine." If only a cold were the worst

thing he had on his plate. He'd take the most awful of colds over this. Anything over this.

The nurse pushed him out the emergency room doors to where Father Bernard was waiting with his sedan. The older priest opened the passenger door and helped the nurse get Nicolas into the car.

"Thank you," Nicolas said, and the nurse gave him a huge smile before going back inside. Nicolas reached over with his left hand to grab the seat belt and fumbled a bit trying to get it into the latch.

"Let me get that for you," Father Bernard said, and secured the seat belt. He gave Nicolas a hard look, then frowned. "You're in pain. Far more pain than you're letting on. You could have stayed in the hospital for a day or two. Maybe I should take you back in."

"Insurance says I'm good enough to go home."

Father Bernard snorted. "Insurance says whatever costs them the least amount of money. Your doctor would have been happy to argue with them. Given your other challenges, they would have eventually agreed. Besides, money isn't an issue for you. So what is it?"

"What do you mean?"

"Why do you want to go home when you're feeling so poorly?"

"I just don't like hospitals. I've spent enough time in them already. Please don't worry. I won't make any additional work for you or Father Malcolm. I plan on hiring someone to assist me during the day until bedtime. I have an interview this afternoon."

Father Bernard stared at him a second more, then nodded. "If home is what will make you feel better, then home it is. Did the hospital provide you with a list of possible care assistants?"

"They had several recommendations," Nicolas said. That wasn't a lie. He'd overheard a nurse talking to another patient about that option and knew they had a list. Nicolas just hadn't asked for it. He planned on hiring someone with a bigger range of skills than just health care. It was Shaye's idea and she'd given him a name when he called her earlier.

Not that he wasn't going to need some real help getting around. His shoulder had pretty much left him with no engine, so to speak. Since he was going to need help anyway, Shaye figured he might as well have someone who could pull double duty. It's not like anyone would have to insert needles or change IV bags. All he needed was help moving from one location to another. And Shaye preferred that the person doing that be armed. Nicolas preferred it as well.

So before Bernard had picked him up, Nicolas had made another phone call. This one to Colby Stringer, and Nicolas had arranged to meet him at the living quarters. Colby should arrive shortly after he and Father Bernard got home.

When they reached the church, Father Bernard parked in the lot just down from the living quarters and retrieved Nicolas's chair from the trunk of his car. Bernard then instructed Nicolas to lean out from the seat and the older priest grabbed him underneath his arms and helped him into the chair. Even though Bernard hadn't appeared to struggle with his weight, Nicolas knew it wasn't good for him to be lifting like that. Not just because of the weight, but because medical professionals were trained on how to do it correctly to minimize injury. After his accident, his mother had taken lessons from a nurse, in case an emergency occurred and she needed to help Nicolas when an aide wasn't available.

"I'm sorry you're having to do this," Nicolas said as he struggled to force his legs to cooperate, but he was afraid they weren't much help at all.

"Nonsense," Father Bernard said. "I'm not so old and creaky that I can't assist with minor things. And you're not exactly a heavyweight."

"Well, I appreciate all of your help, especially lately." He blew out a breath. "I know I've been even more trouble than you anticipated when you hired me."

Father Bernard gave him a serene smile. "We all have our challenges. Sometimes they are spread out over time —a little here and a little there. Those are the easiest to manage. But sometimes they seem to collect and hit us all at once. Those are the ones that test us. I have complete faith in your ability to come out of all of this an even better person, and priest, than you were before."

"I hope one day to have such a logical view of life."

"Oh well. That just takes years. Or maybe it's exhaustion. Speaking of which, let's get you inside so you can get on with your healing."

Nicolas clutched his right arm as Father Bernard pushed him down the walkway. He hated the feeling of overwhelming helplessness. Things had been difficult before but he hadn't felt so vulnerable. Now every short-coming was amplified.

"Here we are," Father Bernard said as he pushed Nicolas into the living room. "Would you like to shower or rest? Are you hungry?"

"I had breakfast at the hospital but I don't have much appetite. I don't think I have the energy for a shower right now and I have that interview shortly. You can just leave me here for now. I know you have a full schedule. I don't want to hold you up any more than I already have."

"Sometimes other things take priority. I'll get you one of those sodas you like so much and the television remote. That way you can watch something until your interview arrives. Will you be able to handle getting to the door?"

"Just leave it unlocked," Nicolas said, forcing his voice to remain steady as he said the words. He had his backpack with the Mace inside, but he wasn't about to pull it out until Father Bernard left.

"All right," Father Bernard said. "You have your cell phone. Father Malcolm and I are both on-site all day. If you need anything, call. And don't try to stand without help, or you'll injure that shoulder even more. Call."

"I will. And thanks again for everything. I'm really sorry to have caused all this trouble and additional work."

"Try to get some rest after your interview." Father Bernard exited the building, closing the door behind him.

Nicolas was seated toward the back of the living room. From his position, he could see down the hallway, out the living room window, and had a clear view of the front door. The window in the kitchen was at his back, but it was smaller than the others. Not exactly the first choice for someone breaking and entering.

Father Bernard had placed the remote on the table next to his chair, but Nicolas wasn't interested in background noise. That would just make it harder to hear someone coming. His backpack was on the floor beside him on his left side, so he pulled it up and located the can of Mace. It appeared to be in working condition despite its fall, so he stuck it in his lap and sat the book on Roman history on top of it.

He was just about to try to maneuver himself a bit back from the table when there was a knock at the door. He checked his phone for the time. It must be Colby Stringer. He took a deep breath and blew it out before calling for him to enter.

The door opened and a man about thirty-five years old with a shaved head stepped inside. Nicolas looked up at the guy who resembled the Hulk but not green and couldn't help smiling. Shaye really knew how to make a person feel safe.

"You must be Colby," he said, barely stopping himself from just throwing money at him and begging him to take the job.

Colby nodded and took a step forward, offering his left hand to shake. "And you're Nicolas, I take it."

"Did the wheelchair give it away?"

"Maybe a little." Colby scanned the room and leaned over. "Can we speak openly?" he whispered.

Nicolas nodded. "I'm the only one here. Would you like to sit down?"

"That would be more polite than towering over you." Colby angled a chair to face Nicolas and took a seat. "Shaye tells me someone is messing with you and it's escalating, but you don't want anyone to know so my role is undercover bodyguard."

"I know it seems foolish keeping such a thing a secret—"

Colby waved his hand. "People have all kinds of reasons for keeping things to themselves. Being that you're a priest, I figure you've got better reasons than most. And besides, Shaye wouldn't have called me if she didn't trust you. She may seem all casual and polite, but she doesn't miss a thing."

"Have you known her long?"

"Sort of. My mother and hers have done a lot of volunteer work together over the years. I remember the first time I ever heard Shaye really talk. She had been living with Corrine for maybe two years and she usually didn't come out of her room when Corrine had gatherings. On the rare occasions that she did, I don't think I'd heard her utter five words."

Colby smiled and shook his head. "So I'm back on

leave from the military and I'm at this gathering with my mom and my fiancée, and Shaye is sitting silently in the back corner of the kitchen. I'm standing next to the table where she's sitting and one of my mother's friends asks me about my fiancée's and my wedding plans. So I start talking about what we've decided on and I see Shaye frown. Then she snorts."

"Really?"

"Yeah. So I look over at her and ask if something's wrong. She looks me dead in the eyes and says she doesn't understand why I want to marry a woman who's in love with someone else. Then she looks at my fiancée and then my best friend. Both of them look at each other and I could see it in their expressions. She'd hit the nail on the head. I took off out of there and dumped my fiancée in the driveway."

"How did she know?"

Colby shrugged. "Women's intuition? Hell, I'd even believe it was magic. All I know is she saved me a lot of trouble even though Corrine was mortified."

"I guess when you've been through what she has, you get really good at reading people."

"It's survival. I learned quickly how to read expressions and body language when I was in the desert. The allies and enemies all look the same, you know. If you don't learn how to distinguish the small behaviors that signal which side someone is on, you can come back in a bag."

Nicolas shook his head. "I can't imagine...you probably lost people over there. Men you served with."

Colby nodded. "We all do."

"I'm very sorry. I know that has to be so difficult. But I appreciate your service and the lifestyle it affords me. My father was an army paratrooper for fifteen years. Knees finally caught up with him and he retired."

"Your father sounds like he was a good man. Fifteen years is a long time to jump from planes." He glanced around the room and Nicolas could see him assessing the door and windows. "Can you give me the rundown on these quarters? Then I'd like to take a look around. I won't tamper with the other priests' things, but I'd like to at least open the doors and check out all modes of ingress."

"Of course," Nicolas said, and gave him a description of the location of each apartment and the layout of the ones upstairs. Colby headed down the hall and Nicolas could hear the doors opening and closing, then footsteps on the back stairwell. A minute later, he heard footsteps above him.

It didn't take Colby long to do his assessment and he came back into the living room. "No one's been in the upstairs for some time," he said. "There's a decent layer of dust and none of it showed signs of disturbance. The windows are all locked from the inside and in good working order. I don't think someone would choose those as an entry point except a professional."

"And we'd hear them. I heard your footsteps above me. They almost echoed through the room."

"That's how the acoustics are sometimes with these old places."

"So what about the downstairs rooms?"

"The locking hardware is in good shape, but all the windows open easily. Shaye said you guys like to open everything up when there's a cool breeze. It's clear that the windows have been maintained and used for that purpose. I could slide them up with almost no noise."

"But there's no way to unlock them from the outside without breaking the glass."

"Or cutting it, but again, that leads us back to more of a professional job and Shaye doesn't think that's the case here. Do you lock the front door when you're all gone?"

"Yes. And the back door is never used, so the dead bolt remains drawn."

"Good. So how many people have keys to the building?"

Nicolas blew out a breath. "I don't know. I can't imagine that the locks are changed often, and Father Bernard hands out keys to visiting priests. I'm sure the cleaning crew has one, and probably some of the maintenance people. We don't...I guess we never considered that security would be an issue."

"And I'm sure things have been that way because it never has been."

"We don't really have much of value in here. I

suppose if it was left unlocked someone might lift a computer or iPad, but if someone is going to expend the energy to break into a residence, I assume they'd choose one with more content to take than what we have."

Colby smiled. "You're absolutely right. Priests wouldn't be the first on the list of any decent thief. A crime of opportunity would be the more likely thing to occur. But you have a stalker, so all bets are off."

Nicolas looked down at the ground, then back up at Colby, his gut clenching. "I did some reading on the internet last night...police stuff mostly. They say that if someone is stalking you, it's almost impossible to protect yourself."

"'Almost' being the operative word. I'm not going to lie to you—stalking is serious business. If someone is fixated on another person, then there's nothing in the realm of logic that's going to dissuade them from their task."

"So the only way this ends is with him dead or behind bars." Nicolas swallowed. "Or if he's successful and moves on to the next target."

"That last one isn't going to happen. I'm here to make sure that it doesn't."

Nicolas wasn't convinced. "I agree that attacking me with you standing there isn't likely, but that wouldn't stop him from shooting me from across the street. Or you too, for that matter."

"You're correct. If he wanted to, he could simplify things and end it all with one well-placed bullet. But I understand from Shaye that he's already had the opportunity to finish this and hasn't. That he's taunting you."

Nicolas nodded.

"Someone like that feeds off your fear. He won't settle for anything less than looking you straight in the eye when he makes his move. For stalkers, it's personal. He has an emotional investment in the outcome, and he wants more than your death. A bullet isn't good enough. He'll want to reveal himself before he finishes the job."

"That's a sobering and horrifying analysis."

"It is. And it's not mine. It's Shaye's. But I happen to agree with her."

"So what do we do?"

"You go about your normal routine—as much as possible, anyway. I go with you as your medical aide. I was a field medic, by the way, so I have the experience and lingo to maintain cover."

"That's helpful." Nicolas had to admit that he felt a little better about things knowing that Colby had actual medical experience. He didn't want things to go south, but if something went wrong, then Colby would know how to handle it.

"The best possible scenario," Colby said, "is that we go about the day as normal. Either I spot something unusual and it breaks the case, or Shaye tracks him down and it breaks the case."

"And what about the worst possible scenario?"

"He gets desperate because my presence prevents him

from moving forward with his original plans, and he makes a mistake."

"A mistake meaning he tries to kill me without all the pomp and circumstance."

Colby nodded. "And I'll be right there to nail him."

"Of course," Nicolas said.

Colby was an impressive figure with an equally impressive skill set. And Nicolas knew Shaye wouldn't have recommended him if she didn't have absolute confidence in his abilities. But Colby was still a man. The stalker might not be able to settle for an impersonalized death for Nicolas, but that wouldn't stop him from shooting Colby just to get him out of the way.

SHAYE PARKED in front of the weekly rental motel where Crystal Walker and her missing friend, Sunny Trahan, stayed. It was typical of this type of business in a rough area of town—in desperate need of repair and with a collection of people loitering around on sidewalks and corners. Shaye knew exactly what the loitering was for. It was mostly young men now, which meant drugs. Once night hit, the working girls would join them.

She checked her pistol and climbed out of the completely average and nondescript car that Jackson kept for surveillance. It was smart because the people she was trailing didn't notice it, and it wasn't high on the list for car thieves, either. She was dressed in street clothes—

jeans, T-shirt, and tennis shoes—but she wasn't fooling anyone. They knew she didn't belong here.

She hurried to the apartment and knocked on the door, hoping Crystal was home. She heard some movement inside and then the door opened a crack and a girl looked out at her. She held up her PI license.

"My name is Shaye Archer. I'm a private investigator. I hoped I could speak to you about Sunny."

The girl studied her a second, then unlatched the chain and motioned for her to come in. She closed the door, drew the dead bolt, and re-hooked the chain as soon as Shaye was inside. The inside of the room was as rundown as the outside of the motel, but it was neatly kept. Two full-size beds were on one wall and they were both made up with colorful comforters that looked more like college dorm linens than that of adults. A couch separated the living area from a kitchenette. There was no clutter on the counter. No dirty dishes or food wrappers in sight.

Shaye turned her attention to Crystal and the first thing she noticed was her age. The cop had been right. There was no way this girl was eighteen, regardless of what her ID said. Shaye put her at sixteen at the most, and she struggled with the difficulty this girl faced living the way she did at such a young age. It wasn't supposed to be this way, but it was for far too many young people.

"Are you with the police?" Crystal asked.

"No. I'm a private investigator."

"Doesn't someone have to pay you to investigate? Why are you asking about Sunny?"

Shaye had done nothing else on the drive over but consider how she was going to answer this exact question. She didn't want to scare the girl half to death but by the same token, she didn't want to gloss over the gravity of the situation.

"My client overheard someone saying he'd hurt a girl," Shaye said. "My client couldn't see the other man and didn't recognize his voice, but your friend fits the description of the girl who might have been hurt."

Crystal gave her a skeptical look. "So your client hears someone talking crazy and he hires you to find the guy? Is your client crazy too? Because in my experience, most people don't concern themselves with things that don't affect them, especially when it costs them."

"My client is not crazy, but he's got plenty of money and what he heard disturbed him greatly. He's a sensitive sort of person and gives all his time to helping others. That's really all I can say for confidentiality reasons. But rest assured, he's a normal person with a legitimate concern."

Crystal stared at her for a bit, then nodded. "I guess if I overheard something like that, it might freak me out too. I mean, not anymore but before. You hear a lot of crazy shit on the streets."

She flopped down on the couch and waved a hand at Shaye to join her. "What do you need to know?"

Shaye sat in a chair near Crystal. "I need to know

about Sunny—about her normal routine. The places she went, the people she interacted with."

"You think someone took her on purpose? It wasn't just random?"

"That's what I'm trying to determine. Anything you can tell me about her everyday life will help."

"That's easy enough. We don't have the money to do much. We work the south corner."

"Do you bring customers back here?"

"Customers...that's funny. Bunch of dirty old men, mostly. And usually married. But no, we don't ever bring anyone here. We agreed on that from the beginning. If they want the whole pretend thing, they can rent a room. But mostly, it's just cars."

Shaye had been afraid of that. It was common but so dangerous, as it was easier to attack or drug someone in an enclosed space without other people seeing or hearing. Then it was a simple matter of driving off. Depending on where and how they dumped the body, it might never be found.

"You were working the night she disappeared?"

Crystal nodded. "It was close to midnight. One of my regulars showed up. He's a room guy and usually springs for a whole hour, so I was gone for a bit. When I got back, Sunny wasn't there but that's not unusual. We were working, you know? When she didn't come back within an hour, I called her but her phone went straight to voice mail."

"Is that unusual?"

"Yeah. She usually just puts it on silent."

"Was anyone else around who might have seen her?"

"I asked and one of the guys who sells pot on the corner said he thought she got into a car, but he couldn't tell me what kind or what time, much less who was driving. Dude's always high, so I can't even be sure he saw Crystal at all."

"No one else saw anything?"

"If they did, they're not saying. People don't like to talk much, you know? If you get a reputation for talking about the business that comes to your area, those 'customers' tend to relocate. It's not the sort of thing they want other people to find out about."

"No. I guess it's not."

"But Sunny and I had that tracker thing set up on our phones. We thought it would be a good idea given what we were doing. But it showed her phone off-line and her last location was here. It's never showed since. I've called and checked day and night, usually every hour or so."

"I'm so sorry," Shaye said.

Crystal rubbed her nose with the back of her hand and sniffed. "It sucks. I know something bad happened because Sunny would have never taken off. Not without telling me. We made promises, you know? And I know that she's probably dead and that if I keep doing this, the same thing will happen to me. But at least here I'm getting paid for it. At home, my stepfather was taking it for free."

"What about your mother?"

Crystal sneered. "That worthless bitch? As long as it kept him from beating her, she didn't care what he did."

Shaye's stomach clenched and she pulled a card from her wallet, then passed it to Crystal. "This information is for my mother. She's building a huge facility to help house and protect minors who are living on the street. Everything is not yet in place, but it will be soon. In the meantime, I want you to contact her."

Crystal's eyes widened. "No. I can't tell anyone the truth. They'll send me back home. I'd rather die than be there."

"They won't send you home," Shaye assured her. "My mother has attorneys on staff who will file protective orders on your behalf. There will be an investigation, but you won't be forced to return to a home where you're being abused. Please contact her. She's helped out so many kids. She's dedicated her life to it, in fact."

"I'll think about it." She looked down at the floor, then back up at Shaye. "So do you think the guy your client overheard is the one who took Sunny?"

"I don't know. When you weren't working, did you frequent any restaurants or bars? Any place that someone might have zoned in on you and seen you more than once?"

"We buy groceries at the mini-mart two blocks down. We don't have the money for restaurants, and the bars hassle us. They don't like our kind in there taking business away from their own girls."

Shaye nodded. She already knew that some of the less

reputable establishments had their own girls on payroll, so to speak.

"Sometimes we'd get coffee and muffins at the corner bakery," Crystal said. "But maybe only once a week and not at the same time or same day. It was usually just when we'd had a really rough night and had a little extra."

"Is there anyone you noticed hanging around? Any customers that gave you a bad feeling—I mean, beyond the usual."

Crystal shrugged. "There's always people hanging around but we know them all. I don't think anybody around here is a stellar citizen or anything, but I can't see them hurting Sunny, either. There's been a couple customers that got too strange, but all the girls started turning them down and they moved on. I haven't seen any of the weird ones in months."

Shaye put her card on the coffee table. "This is my cell phone. If you think of anything or see anything that might help, call me. Day or night. It doesn't matter. And please think about calling my mother. She can help you."

The tiny flicker of hope in Crystal's expression broke Shaye's heart. It was so hard to trust when you'd been living in hell. So hard to believe that anyone else could have your best interests at heart. Shaye knew exactly how she felt. But Corrine had saved her life. She was going to save others.

20

Jackson lowered his binoculars and called Grayson on his cell phone. "I hope we're not wasting our time here. He hasn't shown any sign of leaving."

They'd been watching Michael Pitre since he left for work that morning. So far, it had been uneventful. He'd driven straight from home to the office and hadn't left the building. It must be a day for phone calls and paperwork and not direct customer interaction. Jackson was watching the front of the building and Grayson was watching the rear where Pitre's car was parked.

"It's almost one," Grayson said. "If he doesn't head out for lunch soon, we'll cut out and get a unit to cover him this evening."

Jackson put his cell phone down on the seat of his truck and blew out a breath. He was beyond frustrated. They were making no headway on this case and any thoughts of locating Hailey alive were fading. Hailey's father had all the makings of a great suspect but without evidence, they had nothing. Jackson didn't figure Pitre for much of a tough guy, but they needed something to break him with. If they could find something, anything, to pressure him with, Jackson thought he would fold. In Jackson's opinion, Pitre was a nut but not a sociopath.

His cell phone rang and he glanced down then grabbed the phone when he saw the call was coming from headquarters. Maybe one of the cops reviewing videotape had spotted something.

"Lamotte, this is Brewster," the detective said. "You were asking about missing girls the other day and I told you about the pro that the roommate reported."

"Yeah, you got anything else?"

"A body. Tourist found it in Metairie Cemetery. And get this, she was tied to a cross on a crypt by her hands and feet and had a crown of thorns on her head. I know crazy isn't limited to atheists, but when these religious fanatics lose it, they really go hard. That's some seriously sick shit."

Jackson winced. "Agreed. Do you have a cause of death?"

"Nothing official yet. You know the drill, but she was strangled. The bruises on her throat were consistent with handprints. Maybe that wasn't what ultimately did her in, but it was definitely the route he took. I didn't see any other wounds. No blood."

"Rape?"

"Can't say for sure until the autopsy, but her clothes

were intact and no bruising on her thighs. If I had to guess, I'd say no, but given her profession I doubt there will be any shortage of hair and fibers."

"Yeah. Thanks for letting me know."

"Do you think this has something to do with your missing girl?"

Jackson had gone looking for the information for Shaye, not himself, but he couldn't exactly say that. "I was leaning toward no when I asked, and now I'm definitely hoping it's no. But you have to cover all bases."

"Gotcha. Well, good luck. Let me know if you need more info. The autopsy is scheduled for this afternoon."

"That's quick given the backlog."

"Brass is in a snit over young girls going missing. It looks bad in the press. And it doesn't help if tourists find them strung up on crosses, so they're pushing it ahead of other cases. I think they're probably operating out of your camp, worried that these two cases are related. My guess is they're not about to be caught back-burnering a murder that might have led to finding a victim alive."

"I'm sure you're right. Thanks again. I owe you one."

"I'll take payment in beer the next time we both get off at a decent hour."

"You got it."

Jackson disconnected and blew out a breath. If Sunny Trahan wasn't Shaye's victim, then it was an enormous coincidence. The strangulation. Lack of sexual assault. Blatant religious signaling. It fit the profile she'd given him in its entirety. Which meant her priest's instincts had been correct. The confession had been legitimate. Jackson knew he didn't have to tell Shaye how dangerous someone was who stood behind religion for the awful things they did. She'd lived it firsthand. And if the man who'd strangled the life out of a girl and strung her up in a cemetery was messing with a priest, then that priest was in serious danger.

He lifted his phone and called Shaye. "I've got some news," he said when she answered. He filled her in on Sunny Trahan. He could tell by her response that she was saddened but not surprised.

"I talked to her roommate this morning," Shaye said. "Honestly, I wasn't holding out much hope, but this is way worse than I imagined. The dramatic placement, I mean."

"I know I don't have to tell you all the implications," he said.

"No," she said quietly. "I know what I'm up against, and I've been putting some measures in place. I'm on my way to see my client now. This is going to devastate him. Especially given the girl's age. If she was the same age as her roommate, no way that girl was an adult."

"The detective investigating doesn't think so, either. I'm really sorry about the girl and what it means for your client, but I'm even more worried for you. Promise me you'll get backup if you have to go anywhere questionable, especially after dark. If I'm not available, you've got people you can call."

"I know. And I will."

Jackson's cell signaled another call and he saw it was Grayson. "I have to go. Call me later and let me know if there's anything else I can do."

"Thanks."

He disconnected with Shaye and answered Grayson's call.

"Pitre is on the move," Grayson said.

"Driving?"

"No. He walked out the back entrance and is headed south. I'm about half a block behind."

"I'll be right there." Jackson jumped out of his truck and took off down the street at a decent run, dodging people as he went. He was probably a good two blocks behind Grayson but assuming Pitre was walking normally, it wouldn't take him long to catch up.

A couple minutes later, he spotted Grayson crossing the street half a block in front of him. He picked up the pace a bit and caught up with him right after he'd crossed the street.

Grayson looked over at him and grinned. "I'm impressed. I didn't figure you'd catch up for another block or so."

"Helps that we're in casual clothes today. Couldn't have done it in dress shoes."

"Or if you had you would regret it later." Grayson pointed to Pitre, who was about to cross the street a half block ahead of them. "There's our man."

"Probably going to lunch," Jackson said. "And I hurried for nothing."

"But you never know. Hey, he's going into the church grounds."

"Let's pick up pace. I don't want to lose him in the courtyard."

They increased to a slow jog, dodging pedestrians as they went, but stopped at the corner and waited for the crossing light. The last thing they needed was a bunch of cars honking at them. That drew attention. If Pitre turned around and saw them, there was no doubt he'd know what they were up to.

When the light changed, they hurried across and through the big entry into the church courtyard. Jackson pointed to the left where Pitre was on a walkway headed for the cathedral. They slipped down the bushes and saw him enter the cathedral through a door in the courtyard.

"Side entry," Grayson said. "What do you think?"

"If he spots us, it's over. And I don't know how the church is laid out, do you?"

Grayson nodded. "I've been here a few times. That door leads into a hallway that runs to the confessional to the left and another door straight ahead leads into the cathedral."

"You think he's going to confession?"

Grayson shook his head. "This is the exit side. I took my neighbor one day when he was on driving restriction because of a foot injury. I went inside in case he ran into trouble."

"Okay, so I'll go around front and enter the cathedral. It's a wider opening and gives me more chance to duck behind something if Pitre heads my way. You watch this door."

Grayson nodded. "Text me when you lay eyes on him."

Jackson avoided the walkway and set off across the courtyard instead, just in case Pitre exited. He slipped through a thick hedge and made his way to the massive front entry. He stopped behind a column and scanned the vestibule but it appeared empty. He pulled his hoodie up and hurried inside, leaving his sunglasses in place. It wasn't much of a disguise, but it went past most people.

Unless they were expecting to be followed. Then all bets were off.

He headed into the cathedral, scanning the rows as he went. Finally, he spotted Pitre kneeling in the second pew from the front. Jackson made a quick right and hurried down the back pew to the far end, then took a seat and pulled out his cell phone.

Pitre in cathedral praying.

He hit Send and a couple seconds later, Grayson's reply came through.

Let me know when he leaves.

Jackson watched Pitre's bowed head, waiting for any sign of movement. Several minutes later, he rose from the pew and made his way up front to the altar. He reached over and lit a candle, made the sign of the cross, then turned around and looked across the cathedral. Jackson dropped onto his knees and lowered his head, peering up through the small space between his hoodie and the pew.

Now Pitre was looking to his right and frowning, his expression one of indecision. He stood there for at least a full minute without moving. Finally, his expression shifted to anger and he whirled around and strode for the side exit.

Coming your way.

Jackson waited until the side door closed behind Pitre before heading to the main entrance, not willing to risk following him. Besides, Grayson had him covered. As he exited the cathedral, he spotted a familiar face coming toward him pushing a man in a wheelchair. Correction—a priest in a wheelchair. He hesitated for a moment, trying to place the face, then it clicked and he cursed silently. Colby Stringer was former military and current security detail for hire.

Shaye had introduced them at a restaurant one night.

The priest must be Shaye's client.

Damn it all to hell.

21

SHAYE WAVED AT COLBY AS HE PUSHED NICOLAS INTO the café. The priest looked exhausted and the way he winced as the chair bumped over the entry let her know he was in pain. She really hated what she was about to tell him. He was already on the ragged edge. She'd been there herself enough times to know what it looked like and where his mind was. He wasn't ready for this, but she didn't have a choice. He was her client and he was paying her to provide him with information, not withhold it.

She gave Colby a nod as he moved a chair and pushed Nicolas up to the table. "How are you doing?" she asked the young priest.

"I'm okay, I guess," Nicolas said. "As long as I have Colby to shuttle me around, that is. I'm afraid my shoulder is going to limit my mobility for a while."

"How bad is it?" she asked.

"It was dislocated. No other damage, so it's mostly bruising and general soreness. The doctor said it will be 80 percent better in a couple days as long as I limit its use to showering and such. But with Colby helping during the day and Father Malcolm and Father Bernard there to assist if I run into a problem at night, I figure I can keep from overusing it."

Shaye hoped that Nicolas's nights were as calm as he anticipated. "Well, I'm glad you weren't hurt any worse than you were," she said. "I can't imagine how frightening that must have been."

Nicolas gave her a small smile. "No. I'm sure you could, which is why you're such an empathetic person."

Nicolas glanced at Colby then back at her and Shaye could see his hesitation and understood where it came from. Nicolas needed to speak with her about things he didn't want to share with Colby.

"Colby, can you please give us a minute?" she asked.

Immediately understanding, he rose from the table. "I'll be right out front. Come get me when you're ready to leave." He headed out of the café.

"That man looks like the Hulk, except for the green thing," Nicolas said.

Shaye smiled. "He's got a better temper, but I'm guessing he's just as deadly."

"Well, I appreciate you recommending him. He's made me feel better already and this morning, I didn't think that was possible." He looked out the window, then back at Shaye. "I got another note."

Shaye straightened. "When? How?"

"It was on the tray next to my hospital bed when I woke up."

Shaye's stomach clenched. She'd thought Nicolas was safe in the hospital, but she'd been wrong. Granted, it would have been difficult for the penitent to strangle him, but there were plenty of other ways to kill a person, especially when they were immobilized.

"I don't know why I was so surprised," Nicolas continued. "He was probably still lurking around when the ambulance came. It wasn't difficult to guess where I would be."

Especially if you were the one who called the paramedics.

The thought ripped through Shaye's mind, and she struggled to keep it from showing on her face. The last thing she wanted to do was terrorize Nicolas even more when she didn't have proof.

"He would have known where to find you," Shaye agreed. "But he still had to get in past hospital staff. It's a big risk. Did you ask them if someone was in your room?"

Nicolas nodded. "They said the only people there after Father Bernard and Malcolm left were hospital staff. Which then caused me to panic thinking he might be on the staff. That's possible, right?"

"At this point, a lot of things are possible."

"Even if he was medical staff somewhere else, he could have just strolled in there in scrubs and people probably wouldn't have looked twice."

Shaye nodded. "Especially in the middle of the night when there are fewer people around to see anyone to begin with."

"I know the hospital has cameras. Do you think there's any way..."

She could tell by his tone that he already knew the answer, but he couldn't help asking anyway. "They'll only provide footage to the police."

"So my only option is to throw away my future to protect my present. I know some people would call me crazy, but I'm not willing to do that just yet." He sighed. "Maybe I am crazy."

Shaye felt her heart clench at the defeat in his voice. "I am so sorry," she said. "I should have come there to stay with you."

Nicolas shook his head. "We couldn't risk Father Malcolm or Bernard seeing you there. Besides, you couldn't have known this would happen...that he'd be so brazen. Neither could I."

"But we know now, and I feel a million times better knowing Colby is on the job. If anyone tries to hurt you, they'll have to go through him. I'm not saying it can't happen, but he'll defend you to the death."

"I'm really hoping it doesn't come to that."

Shaye reached across the table and put her hand on his good arm. "Me too. But I'm afraid I have some bad news for you."

Nicolas stared silently at her for several seconds, then looked down at the table. "They found her, didn't they?"

"There's no way to know for certain but I suspect she's the one he talked about."

"Strangled?"

She nodded.

"Who was she?"

"A girl, my guess is a teen. A runaway who was working as a prostitute."

Nicolas's eyes filled with tears. "A child?"

"Yes. Although she wasn't living as every child should be. I spoke with her roommate yesterday. Let's just say staying at home wasn't a better option for the roommate. I'm guessing it was the same for our victim."

Nicolas frowned. "But surely an untimely demise isn't uncommon in that line of work. Even strangulation seems more likely than something premeditated. Is there something else that makes you think she's the one?"

Shaye took in a breath and slowly blew it out. Then she described the staging of the body as Jackson had conveyed it to her. As she spoke, the color drained from Nicolas's face and she pushed his glass of water closer to him. He lifted it and his hands shook. He spilled some when he took a sip.

"I don't know what to say," he said finally. "That's beyond horrific."

She nodded. "But it definitely speaks to religious fanaticism."

"Yes. Although the word 'fanaticism' seems underwhelming in those circumstances."

"I know this is a lot to take in, and I wish I didn't

have to tell you all of this, but you have a right to know. And it's my job to keep you informed."

"I appreciate your concern. Greatly, in fact, because I know it's genuine. And I also appreciate your honesty. I suppose some would have withheld the facts in order to spare my feelings."

"I have spared feelings before, but never on the job."

A twinge of guilt passed through her because she wasn't telling Nicolas that she was going to take a closer look at Father Malcolm. But she didn't want to frighten him more than he already was and she had no reason to believe Father Malcolm would attempt anything in their living quarters. Not with Father Bernard right there. And Colby would remain with Nicolas until all three priests were in for the night. She'd make sure of that.

She also had something else in mind. Something she might as well pitch to him now. "I've been thinking," she said. "Given the situation with the courtyard and now the hospital, I think the penitent is enjoying getting close. How would you feel about putting a security camera in your bedroom?"

Nicolas's eyes widened. "You think he would enter our quarters?"

"If he wanted to send your fear into the stratosphere, there's no better way than violating the one place you feel safe. Colby said the building is well maintained but the lock on the front door is old and could easily be picked. You can't draw the dead bolt when you all leave so that leaves the quarters vulnerable to break-in during the day. I figure asking Father Bernard to upgrade the locks might look a little odd, and I don't want to violate the privacy of the others by putting a camera in the main living area, so this is the next best option."

Nicolas frowned. "I suppose if we did it and the penitent took things to that level, then we'd have him. It almost sounds too simple."

"Most criminals make a foolish decision at some point. Their ego won't allow them to believe they can get caught. And that's exactly how the police catch most of them."

"If it could mean an end to all of this, then I don't see a reason not to do it." He glanced at her, then looked back down at the table. "It records everything, right? You would see whatever goes on inside. I...it's difficult to dress in the bathroom because it's so small..."

"Don't worry. When I review the footage, I'll fast-forward past any time you're in residence. I won't review anything until you're out of the room."

Nicolas relaxed a bit. "How would you hide it?"

"Colby can cover installation, so don't worry about that part. No one will ever know it's there."

"Okay then. I guess I'll be on candid camera."

"I'm going to figure this out," Shaye reassured him. "He's going to slip up. He's already taking foolish chances. I just need you to keep it together for a bit longer. I think this will all be over soon."

"I was thinking, would it help if I left? I have money and I'm sure Father Bernard would give me time off given my medical condition."

"Honestly? I don't think it makes a difference in the long run. Once someone is fixated on you, it usually doesn't go away until they've accomplished what they wanted or they're caught. You would be safe in the short term but how long would it take for him to track you down? And if you don't plan on staying gone forever, he'll still be here waiting when you get back."

"Unless the police catch him before then."

"It's always possible but they have very little to go on. Even if they get DNA off the girl, my guess is the penitent isn't in the system."

Nicolas sighed. "I know you're right, but I feel so helpless. Quite literally sitting around, hoping he doesn't get to me."

Shaye nodded. She knew exactly how Nicolas felt.

She'd lived it the majority of her adult life.

"Nicolas, I think it's important that we figure out why the penitent is fixated on you," Shaye said.

"I agree. I've thought about nothing else, but I can't think of any reason, even tiny, that someone could have turned into this much hatred."

Shaye studied Nicolas for a minute, trying to figure out the best way to broach the conversation she needed to have. But ultimately, there wasn't a good way to say "I'm investigating you even though you're my client."

"I did some work online," she said finally. "Seeing if there was anything printed about you that might give me a clue."

"I can't imagine what would be on the internet besides fund-raisers and babies."

"That was mostly what I found. And stories about your accident."

Nicolas frowned. "I've intentionally avoided reading anything about it. I just wanted to put it behind me."

"I understand. But someone died."

"I know," Nicolas said, his expression pained. "But I wasn't driving. I wish I had been, then maybe it wouldn't have happened."

"Can you tell me what happened?"

"Not firsthand."

"What do you mean?"

"I have no memory of the accident. I don't even remember leaving the hotel. The last thing I remember is hanging out in the lobby with the other students the night before—or early in the morning, I guess. I know we were exhausted, but we had to be back in class the next day so we couldn't stay over." He shook his head. "I don't even remember packing. Everything between that night and when I woke up in the hospital is simply gone."

She was disappointed but not surprised. Given the severity of Nicolas's injuries, gaps in his memory were normal.

"So what *do* you know?" she asked.

"What people told me. That Jason and I left late that morning. It was an eight-hour drive back to seminary. The policeman who talked to me when I regained consciousness said that Jason fell asleep at the wheel and crossed into the oncoming lane. The woman driving the other car tried to avoid him but couldn't. The Jeep hit her car on the side. She was killed on impact."

His voice broke and he downed some water.

"I guess neither of us were wearing seat belts because we were both thrown from the Jeep," he continued. "Jason was conscious. They rushed us to the hospital but there was nothing they could do. He...he had them call a priest to give him last rites, then he died. His parents didn't even make it there in time."

Tears spilled out of Nicolas's eyes. "He was an only child. The lady in the other car was pregnant. So many lives ruined, and I slept through the whole thing."

Shaye's heart clenched and she put her hand on Nicolas's arm. "You weren't sleeping, but I understand what you're saying. And I know that the accident wasn't your fault. It was simply one of those horrible things that happen sometimes."

"I wish every day that we could go back and redo things. That one of us would insist on missing a day of seminary so that we were rested. But I can't change what happened. I've made my peace with it—as much as I ever will. But you think, perhaps, someone else hasn't?"

Shaye told Nicolas about the electrician's connection to the woman who'd died in the accident and his relationship with her husband and his subsequent suicide. The color drained from Nicolas's face as she gave him the details.

"That's horrible," he said when she finished. "I had no idea. I tried contacting the woman's husband and her parents but neither returned my calls. I only called twice and then let them be. I didn't want to cause more pain." He stared out the window for several seconds. "You think he blames me?"

"Maybe. I know it's not rational, but you're the only person left alive for him to blame."

Nicolas nodded. "It's rational if you're in his head, with his loss. But it doesn't explain the other murder. Why would he strangle that poor girl? She had nothing to do with the accident."

Shaye had thought extensively about that very question and every time she tried to figure it out, her thoughts went directly back to her conversation with Robert Croft. How his personality seemed to have done a 180 and how uncomfortable his religious fervor had made her.

"I don't have an answer for that," she said. "But it could be that he's been suffering since the accident and then something else happened to send him over the ledge that he'd been teetering on."

"A mental break?"

"It would have to be. Unless you are willing to believe that God is really calling people to commit murder."

"Then if I'm the source of his pain, why not kill me first?"

"Maybe he needed to practice first. Maybe he really is hearing voices and believes God called him to that victim first. Or maybe simply because when he kills you, it's over."

"You think by killing other people and taunting me with it, he can punish me for longer."

Shaye shrugged. "We have no way of knowing for sure, but yeah, that's one possibility."

"Well, if that was his plan, it's working. I don't suppose there's any way to get the police investigating the girl's death to look into the electrician."

"Not officially. That would require you filing a report. We have opportunity and a motive for harassing you, but we don't have proof that he killed the girl. Unless you told them about the confession, they would have no reason to assume the two things are connected."

"I'm not willing to put everything on the line without more. Perhaps he left evidence on the other victim, but then they'd have no way of matching it unless they focused on the electrician as a suspect."

He shook his head and Shaye could see what little hope he had slipping away.

"Don't worry about that. I might have a way to filter information to the detective on the case."

"That's something at least. Do you think you can get more evidence?"

"Yes. But we might have to wait until he makes another move."

Nicolas blew out a breath. "I guess that's why I have Colby, right?"

22

―――――――

JACKSON ENTERED SHAYE'S APARTMENT, HIS USUAL happy-to-see-her expression nonexistent and replaced with one of concern. Shaye knew his case wasn't going well and after seeing him, she was afraid things might have gone completely south. She'd been tailing Jeff Breaux for about an hour when Jackson had called, asking to meet with her immediately. Given that it was only three in the afternoon, she knew something was up.

"What's wrong?" she asked as she closed the door behind him.

"We have to talk about our cases," he said as he made his way into the living room and flopped on the couch. "Seriously talk about them."

"But neither of us is supposed to do that." Shaye couldn't even fathom what had happened that had Jackson ready to spill facts about an ongoing investigation.

"I'm afraid your case may overlap with my missing teen, Hailey Pitre."

She drew in a breath and sat next to him. "What makes you think that?"

"Grayson and I were tailing Hailey's father today."

Her stomach clenched. "You suspect him?"

"Let's just say his reaction to some things has been outside what we consider normal. And we have a fairly wide range. Based on some statements he made to us and to others who know him, he's very serious about his strict moral code. He also failed to inform us that Hailey's best friend from their old neighborhood disappeared before they moved. Pitre had a fight with the girl's father shortly before, claiming the girl was leading his daughter down the wrong path."

"Did they ever find the girl?"

Jackson shook his head. "It's still an open case, but it's been over a year."

"I assume you saw Pitre do something that set off more alarms?"

"Yeah, he spent his lunch hour at St. Mary's, praying and lighting a candle."

Shaye's eyes widened when Jackson said the name of the church. "Plenty of fathers are strict about their daughters, and lighting a candle is normal under the circumstances," she said, not wanting to go to that place in her mind where a man killed his own daughter because she was a sinner.

"That's true. But something is off. I have a bad feeling about Pitre."

Shaye felt her back tighten. If Jackson thought something was off, then it probably was. His instincts were excellent, which was exactly why Grayson had requested him as a partner. "You really think it's him?"

"He's my number one suspect at this point. I already had a bad taste in my mouth when I saw him go into the church. Then after lighting the candle, he stood at the front of the cathedral for a full minute, staring at the door that leads to the confessional. Then he got this pissed-off look and practically jogged off. On my way out, I caught sight of Colby Stringer pushing a priest in a wheelchair. He's your client, isn't he?"

Seeing no reason to lie at that point, she nodded. She'd introduced Jackson to Colby and he knew exactly what the former military officer did for a living. He also knew Shaye's case had something to do with a priest, so it wasn't exactly a huge leap to figure out that Nicolas was her client.

"We need to exchange information," he said. "I won't repeat anything about your client to anyone with the police department. But I need to know exactly what you're dealing with and you need to talk to your client and see if he knows Michael Pitre."

"Okay," she agreed. "Might as well start from the beginning."

She started with her initial meeting with Nicolas, relaying the confession and Nicolas's inability to identify the person. Then she went on to describe the notes the penitent was leaving for Nicolas and his run-in with the penitent in the courtyard the night before. She ended with the note he'd found on his hospital tray.

Jackson listened intently without speaking. When she was done, he ran one hand through his hair and leaned back. "Your client is in serious danger. This guy is certifiable. That body they found today...sneaking into the hospital to leave notes. He's risking a lot just to antagonize your client."

Shaye frowned. "Was Hailey harassed at all before she went missing?"

"Not that I'm aware of. Neither her best friend nor her boyfriend mentioned anything like that and I'm sure it would have come up."

"So why the change in MO?"

"You're right. That's not consistent. Damn it. Just when I think I'm going to catch a break in this case, things are all mixed up again."

"I'm not saying they're not related. Maybe they are. But if so, then there was some reason the penitent focused on Hailey. If we knew that reason, we might be able to break this open."

"Assuming it's the same person." He blew out a breath. "The longer I think about it, the less likely it seems. Hailey and Sunny were both teenage girls. What could a disabled adult priest possibly have in common with them?"

"They're sinners."

"We're all sinners. But why focus on those people?"

"Looking at it logically, the girls would have been easier targets than boys. And Nicolas's disability puts him at even more of a disadvantage than a healthy teen girl."

Jackson nodded. "So they're easier to overpower. That I could go along with, but he's picking his victims out somehow. There has to be some reason he chose those people. Again, assuming it's the same guy."

"Yeah, God told him, remember?"

"Right. Well, God had to point them out somehow."

"Sunny is easy enough to figure out. She worked a street corner. He could have driven by and seen her at any given time. Prostitutes aren't exactly an uncommon target."

"True. And maybe that's where he started. With someone who wouldn't necessarily be missed."

"And who he knew for certain was committing a sin. The thing that makes it difficult is that he didn't have to know her personally before picking her. He could have selected her without even speaking a single word."

"So in this case, the victim isn't personal. She might have simply been the one that was easiest to try his hand at."

"Why not? It's as good a reason as any other."

"Okay. So if we go with that, there's two huge unknowns—what was Hailey's sin and what was Nicolas's? Did you come up with anything on your background search?"

"Maybe." She told him about the car wreck and the woman who had died.

"But Nicolas wasn't driving?"

"No. The other priest was and he died in the hospital shortly after the accident."

"And that's how Nicolas wound up in a wheelchair?"

"Yes. But that's not all." She told Jackson about the electrician who was on-site at the church the day of the confession and his connection to the victim.

"That complicates things. I guess it's possible this guy is looking for someone to blame and the only person left is Nicolas."

Shaye nodded. "It's opportunity and a somewhat sketchy motive, but I can't make it logically fit with Sunny. If his problem is personal with Nicolas, why kill someone else?"

"To mess with him? Scare him into heart attack mode before he finishes him off? Practice?"

She nodded. "And I considered all of those. But he could have scared Nicolas without actually killing someone. The confession alone was enough to cause him to break his vows. And then there's the way the body was displayed. I can't believe that was done to scare my client when he wasn't even aware of who the victim was and might not have ever heard about the circumstances of how she was discovered if I wasn't involved."

"That's true. Damn it. I really hoped I was onto something."

"I'm not saying that you're not. If the person who

killed Sunny and kidnapped Hailey is also Nicolas's stalker, then he's picking his victims for individual reasons. But it's equally possible that Sunny is the victim that the penitent told Nicolas about and Hailey was abducted by someone else entirely."

"And God tells the penitent who to kill," Jackson said drily.

Shaye put her hands up in the air. "It wouldn't be the first time."

He shook his head. "I'm more confused now than when I walked in. I saw Colby and the priest at the church and I was convinced everything was related. Maybe I'm completely off. Maybe I'm so desperate to find Hailey that I'm seeing patterns that aren't there."

"That's possible. But it's more likely that you've gotten a bad feeling because our cases have something in common even if they're not related. Trust me, I'm struggling with this as well. I feel like I have so much information but nothing fits together properly."

He nodded. "I'm in the same boat. I'm going to press Hailey's best friend and the boyfriend harder—see if I can get anything out of them that might have triggered setting Hailey up as a victim for this penitent."

"If they get DNA off of Sunny, any chance you can run Pitre and my electrician by the lead detective?"

He frowned. "I could probably manage something, although to be honest, I don't have a good idea how to do it just yet. Are you looking at anyone else for this besides the electrician?"

"For the first time ever, I have too many suspects."

"Who else are you looking at?"

She told him about her visit with Robert Croft. "He totally creeped me out, and that's not an easy thing to do."

"He sounds like a good fit."

"I know, right? And I thought so too, until last night. Right before I left his office, Croft told his assistant to make sure his jet was ready. He said he was going to New York. So assuming he made that flight..."

"He wasn't in New Orleans to stalk Nicolas last night. Do you have any others?"

"One more, but it's an opportunity thing. I'm short on motive."

"Who?"

"Father Malcolm."

Jackson stared. "The priest who came to Nicolas's rescue in the courtyard."

"Did he?"

He rubbed his temples. "Jesus H. Christ. You're right, of course. In fact, there's no one else with that kind of opportunity that fits the bill, and he's got the religious end of things wrapped up as well. You run a background on him yet?"

"On my list for tonight."

"Do they both live at the church?"

"Yes. Along with the senior priest. They share living quarters. Common kitchen and living room, separate bedrooms."

"What about the other priest? You looking at him too?"

"No. Hustle said he has a knee injury and walks with a limp. That's something the street kid would have noticed. And even though he didn't see much, Nicolas would have recognized his walk in the courtyard last night. I'll probably run a background on him just because, but I doubt I'll come up with anything. He's been running St. Mary's for decades."

"At least there's three of them living there. Nicolas isn't alone."

"And I had Colby install a security camera in his room today. I don't anticipate anything happening to him there with three in residence, but I thought maybe the penitent would get bold and leave him a note in his room. And at this point, I'd rather play it safe."

"I'm beginning to think there's no safe way to play this."

Shaye nodded. She'd felt that way ever since Jackson had given her a description of the body placement of the first victim.

* * *

HUDSON SQUIRMED a bit and adjusted the collar of his T-shirt before pulling on his leather jacket. "You're sure she won't be able to see anything?"

"Do you plan on getting naked?" Grayson asked.

"No! No way," Hudson said.

"Then she won't see the wire," Grayson said. "Even if you take off the jacket. It's really small. Unless the fabric of a shirt is the clingy type, which yours isn't, it won't show."

"Okay. Are you sure I have to do this? I mean, every time I think about having to pretend I like that girl, I get so angry I want to punch a wall." Hudson looked down at the floor. "I know I shouldn't say things like that, but I don't like being blackmailed."

"I don't blame you," Jackson said. "But we need to know if Marcy had anything to do with Hailey's disappearance. If anyone can get that out of her, it's you."

"Yeah, I know," Hudson said. "And I want to help, I swear. I guess I'm just having trouble seeing Marcy as capable of something that big. This blackmail thing is totally her but making someone disappear...I don't know."

"And neither do we," Jackson said. "But the point of all of this is to find out. The less time we spend looking at Marcy the more time we have to investigate others."

Hudson swallowed. "You really don't know what happened to Hailey, do you?"

Jackson's heart clenched a little. "No. I'm sorry. I wish we did."

"Me too," Hudson said. He looked up at Jackson, his expression one of sadness and fear. "I was on the internet earlier, looking stuff up about this kind of thing. It's already too late, isn't it? I mean, there's practically no chance she's alive anymore."

"There's always a chance," Jackson said. "You have to maintain hope until we find out the truth."

Hudson nodded but Jackson didn't see even a shred of hope in his eyes. He couldn't really blame him. Jackson knew the facts about abductions as well as any professional, and God knew the internet never focused on the rare positive outcomes. If Hudson had spent time googling abduction cases, Jackson was surprised he wasn't halfway in a bottle.

Grayson looked up from the receiver he'd been adjusting. "We're all set. We'll be able to hear you from a good distance, but buildings interfere so we need to keep the airways as direct as possible. Take it easy when you drive. If we can maintain line of sight, then we should get everything."

"But you have backup in the car, right?" Hudson asked.

"Yes. There is another unit recording in the car," Grayson said. "Are you ready?"

Hudson shrugged. "As ready as I'm getting. Jesus, I'd rather do family dinner night and listen to my mother piss and moan about all my bad decisions than be locked up in a car with that bitch." His face flushed a little. "I better not find out she did anything to Hailey."

"Don't do anything stupid," Jackson said.

"Stupid's a matter of opinion," Hudson said. "Like most things."

Jackson struggled not to smile. He was starting to like Hudson.

The young man grabbed his car keys off the counter and set out for the back of the auto shop where his car was parked. Grayson and Jackson headed for Grayson's car and pulled out behind Hudson as he left. There was no reason to create distance until he picked up Marcy, so they followed closely until he turned on the block where the teen had told him to meet her. Jackson figured she didn't want Hudson showing up at her house. Despite her tough-girl demeanor, Marcy had rules to play by just like everyone else.

Grayson pulled to the curb at the beginning of the block and they watched as Hudson stopped halfway down the street. Marcy hurried out of a shop, beaming at Hudson.

"If my teenage daughter ever dressed like that, I'd ship her off to one of those nunneries," Grayson said.

"Do those still exist?"

"If not, then I'd build one."

Jackson didn't like to pass harsh judgment on young people, as he figured most of them were still finding their way. But in this case, he had to agree with his partner's sentiment. The glittery spandex pants, top that plunged to the bottom of her elevated cleavage, six-inch spike heels, and dark makeup were more commonly seen on working girls than the average citizen. Clearly, she was pulling out all the stops to attract Hudson, but given that Hailey had more of a geeky thing going, Jackson doubted the look would get her the compliments she was looking for.

Hudson didn't bother getting out to open the door for Marcy, even though she stood next to it with a pouty look for several seconds. She must have decided it was open her own door or stand on the street all night because she finally pulled it open and climbed inside.

"You look great," Marcy said. "I love the jacket."

Hudson grunted.

"Aren't you going to say anything about the way I look?" she asked.

"Don't know how you walk in those shoes," Hudson said. "Looks like you'd break an ankle."

Jackson smiled. It definitely wasn't the response Marcy was looking for. He only hoped Hudson didn't make her too mad before he got anything useful out of her.

"You're just not used to seeing the way a sophisticated woman dresses," Marcy said.

Hudson must have remembered that he had to play a role because he shifted into his "poor, pitiful me" routine.

"I'm sorry," he said. "I just can't stop thinking about Hailey. I'm afraid something bad happened to her, you know? But at the same time, I don't know why anyone would want to hurt her. She was so nice and so good."

"Not according to her father," Marcy said.

"What do you mean?"

"Hailey always complained about how he treated her. He locked her up like a criminal with her phone. 'Text me the instant you get home. Don't leave the house again.' He even had a tracker on it that read her texts."

"Seriously?"

"Yeah. I removed it for her. I don't know why adults think they know more about technology than we do. We were practically born with these things."

"Did her father ever hurt her?"

"You mean hit her or something?" Marcy asked. "I don't think so. But he was really strict. Made her read Bible verses after dinner every night, then explain to him what she'd read and how it applied to life today. He would have a stroke if he found out about you."

"I didn't realize it was that bad. Hey, you don't think *he* did anything to her, do you?"

"What? No!" The surprise in Marcy's voice was apparent. "He's an asshole. He's not some crazy psycho killer. Jesus, what kind of crap do you watch on TV?"

"Actually, that's the kind of crap that's on the news."

"That's why I don't watch it or read it on the internet," Marcy said, sounding more like a teen than the woman she was pretending to be. "That stuff freaks me out. It's one thing to see it in a horror movie, but I don't want to know about that stuff in real life."

"You probably need to know about it," Hudson said quietly. "You're a girl. Lots of things can happen to a pretty girl."

There was several seconds of silence.

"Maybe this isn't a good idea," Marcy said. "If my parents found out I was with someone as old as you, they'd freak. I don't want to be punished for months."

"What about the movie?" Hudson asked.

"I've changed my mind. You can drop me off at that café on the corner."

"Let me take you home, at least. You shouldn't be walking by yourself."

"I'll call an Uber."

Hudson pulled over at the curb in front of the café. Grayson parked half a block back, and they watched as Marcy jumped out of the car and bolted inside the café without so much as a backward glance.

Jackson looked over at Grayson. "Well, that was interesting."

Grayson nodded. "I think we can cross Marcy off our list of suspects. She's scared silly."

"Yeah, not exactly the makings of a killer."

"Twenty bucks says she thinks Hudson is the bad guy."

"Yep," Jackson agreed. "I think it finally dawned on her that she was in a car with a strange man whose girlfriend was missing, and that no one knew where she was. Not exactly a smart move."

"Nope. But the noose is tightening around Michael Pitre," Grayson said, his voice grim. "If he was as strict as Marcy claimed and somehow found out about Hudson..."

Jackson nodded. "I know we wanted more evidence, but I think it's time we press Pitre about Melissa Greer."

"Me too."

23

Nicolas looked up as the door to the living quarters opened and Father Malcolm and Father Bernard walked in. They both hesitated when they caught sight of Colby, and Nicolas hurried to introduce them.

"This is Colby," Nicolas said. "He was a battlefield medic and he's going to be assisting me until my shoulder is better. This is Father Malcolm and Father Bernard."

The two priests moved forward and extended their hands to Colby.

"I hope you'll find this assignment a bit less stressful than the battlefield," Father Bernard said.

Colby smiled. "I'm sure that will be the case. Little I experience here could compare to what I saw over there. I consider this type of work semiretirement."

Father Bernard gave him a curious look. "Pardon me for saying so, but you have the physique of someone who would have favored a more strenuous type of work."

"It's true I never miss a gym workout," Colby said. "And this work isn't always easy. Sometimes it takes a bit of strength to lift someone from a chair. Not everyone is as fit as Father Nicolas. Nurses know how to lift properly. But if you combine that with all the walking and pushing, it's a bit of a workout for the average person if they're doing it all day long. This kind of situation is tailor-made for me."

"Of course," Father Bernard said. "Well, we're very happy that Father Nicolas has such capable help. He values his independence so much. I know he was concerned about further limitations because of his shoulder."

"Colby has been a great help today and I am happy to have found him," Nicolas said. "His strength is definitely an advantage. Most home aides are women. I'm sure they're absolutely capable, but I don't think I would have felt comfortable with certain things..."

"Your propriety is above reproach," Father Bernard said. "And while I'm sure the church places no stipulations on gender when it comes to medical care, I understand and appreciate your comfort level. Will you be staying for dinner, Colby? Father Malcolm always makes more than enough."

Father Malcolm, who'd been standing back and studying Colby, started a bit. "Yes, yes, of course. There's plenty."

"No, thank you," Colby said. "My duties are fulfilled when Nicolas is in for the night. I was just staying until someone else arrived...just in case Nicolas needed further assistance."

"Thank you so much for your help today," Nicolas said. "I'm already changed into my nightclothes, so the only thing I'll require after this is a push to my bedroom, which I'm sure Father Malcolm won't mind assisting me with."

"Absolutely," Malcolm said.

"Then I'll say good night," Colby said. "I'll see you tomorrow morning, Nicolas. I'd prefer it if you'd wait on my assistance to shower. What time would you like me to arrive?"

"I'm an early riser, I'm afraid," Nicolas said. "I'm usually up by 6:00 a.m."

Colby grinned. "Slacker. I get up at four. I'll see you tomorrow morning." He headed out the door and Father Malcolm closed and locked it behind him.

"What an imposing man," Father Bernard said.

Nicolas nodded. That was exactly the point.

SHAYE WAS busy doing a background check on Father Malcolm when she heard a knock at her door. It wasn't Jackson. He and Grayson had a stakeout planned and depending on how it went, they were planning on watching Pitre for a bit afterward, just to see if anything was out of the ordinary. Shaye checked the security camera and saw Colby standing there, so she headed to the front door.

"You want anything to drink?" she asked as she waved him inside. "Beer? Water? Sweet tea?"

"Water would be great," he said and followed her into the kitchen. "Sorry for barging in like this but I wanted to give you a rundown of my observations, and I was close by so figured I'd do it in person."

She grabbed two bottled waters from the refrigerator and they sat at the counter. "And?" she asked.

Colby chugged back a quarter of the water, then sat it down. "First off, I like your client. He's got heart and most people don't these days."

She nodded. "It's becoming a lost art. How did your afternoon go?"

"He didn't have much to do in the way of priest work. That senior dude let him out of most things until he's sure he's equipped to handle them. He made a quick stop by his attorney's office after we met with you. Then he had a meeting with two horribly annoying women who spent an entire hour bitching about the wood oil being used in the church. Is that really part of a priest's job duties?"

"I guess so, but yuck. I hadn't thought about their job requiring the totally mundane."

"This went right past mundane into borderline emotional assault. After that hour of good times, he went to pray—also for an hour. I figure it took that long to rid himself of bad thoughts. Then we went to the church library and he spent the remainder of the afternoon studying."

"Any hair raises? Tickle on the back of your neck?"

Colby shook his head. "If anyone was following us, I didn't catch sight of them." He frowned.

"What? Did you think of something?"

"It's not really something, per se, but it felt a little off. You know that priest, Malcolm? I'm positive he saw us in the library but he never came over. He was dressed in street clothes so I didn't know he was a priest until I met him at the living quarters tonight. He pretended it was the first time he'd laid eyes on me, but I know that's not the case. And I got the impression that my presence made him uncomfortable."

Shaye smiled. "I think your presence makes a lot of people uncomfortable."

"People who are up to something, sure. But a priest? The senior guy invited me to dinner and even though Malcolm was looking right at me, he wasn't paying attention. I don't know what he was thinking about, but he looked nervous about my staying."

"Maybe you don't fit his idea of a caretaker."

"That's probably part of it. Nicolas gave them my credentials and I made the point about my strength being an advantage in cases like Nicolas's."

"Did they buy it?"

"Bernard agreed with his hiring a man for propriety. Malcolm didn't say anything."

"But?" Based on his tone, she figured there was a "but" in there somewhere.

Colby was silent for several seconds, then shook his head. "I don't know. There was an undercurrent, I guess is the best way to explain it. But I couldn't tell you why."

"Probably because it could stem from anything—Malcolm having to pick up more of Nicolas's slack, concern for Nicolas but an unwillingness to talk about his personal business in front of you."

"Because he has something to hide," Colby suggested.

She sighed. "People are always hiding something. I suppose priests are no exception. Figuring out whether it's relevant has always been the problem."

Colby nodded. "Did you check the camera feed?"

"Yep. Clear as a bell. If the stalker is brave enough to leave one of his nastygrams in Nicolas's room, we'll get him."

Colby chugged back the rest of the water, then rose from the stool. "I really hope I get to take him down. Someone harassing a priest is bad enough, but a disabled man to boot? I'd like two minutes alone with him."

"I'm thinking it would only take ten seconds."

"Maybe. Well, I'll be back there tomorrow at 6:00 a.m. If I see or hear anything, I'll let you know. Anything else you want me to look out for?"

"I'm going to send you images of a guy I'm checking into. He's an electrician who's been working at the church so he might be around. If you spot him, pay special attention to what he does."

"You got it. Have a good night."

"Good night to you. And thanks for taking this case."

"You know I'll always take work from you." He grinned. "You're the only client I have who pays net ten."

Shaye laughed and followed him to the front door. She locked it behind him and headed back to the kitchen, pulling up the security camera on her phone as she went. Nicolas wasn't in his bedroom yet, but the lamp was on and she had a clear view of the entire room and the entry into the bathroom. Maybe this one would be easy. Maybe he'd be egotistical enough to waltz into Nicolas's bedroom as he had his hospital room.

She hoped so. Because the only thing that mattered was catching him before he could hurt Nicolas. Whoever he was.

24

HAILEY BOLTED AWAKE AT THE SOUND OF FOOTSTEPS outside her stone prison. With no cell phone and not even a ray of sunlight visible, she had no idea how long she'd been a captive. Long enough to go through hunger pangs then have them subside, her stomach apparently realizing no food was slated for the near future. Her captor had left water, claiming it was the source of life and would sustain her long enough for him to save her.

She shuddered and tucked her knees up to her chest, wrapping her arms around them as her captor's last visit flashed through her mind. He'd tied her to the chair and then started reading from the Bible. Passages about repentance and forgiveness and salvation. She knew them because her father had read them many times after dinner. She'd always been uncomfortable with her father's strict religious adherence and the way he insisted that she interpret every verse exactly as he did. The intensity with which he spoke to her about her responsibilities to God and her soul sometimes frightened her.

But her captor terrified her.

He'd held her there for what seemed like hours, his fervor increasing with every spoken verse. He'd yelled at her to confess her sin, promising her absolution. But no matter what she confessed to, he shook his head and kept reading, kept praying. He'd thrown holy water on her and screamed for the demons refusing to allow her to speak the truth to leave her body. Frantic to make him stop, she'd told him about lying to her parents about her older boyfriend. About her secret phone. About sneaking off after school to see him. But every time she confessed something, he just shook his head, his faceless expression making everything more horrifying.

She'd even made stuff up—told him about horrible things that she hadn't done, but no matter how much worse the next item was than the one before, it didn't even make him pause. Finally, exhaustion had taken over and she'd slipped into unconsciousness. When she'd awakened, she was on the floor, alone, and the chair was gone. Now, as the footsteps grew closer, she started to hyperventilate and had to force herself to take longer breaths.

What did he want from her?

What had she done that he wanted her to confess to?

The door opened and light poured in, blinding her. She put her arm up in front of her face, but as she heard the familiar scrape of chair legs on the stone, she began to sob.

"Are you ready to confess?" he asked. "I've decided to help you this time. God spoke to me. He said that as hard as it is for me to understand, you don't know what I'm asking for. What he is asking for."

"Please," she begged. "Please, just let me go. I promise I won't sin again."

"You're right. You won't sin again. But you have to confess first."

He grabbed her arm and pulled her up from the floor, dropping her into the chair. She didn't even bother to fight as he tied her hands together behind her and then to the chair. What good would it do? He'd already told her that past this door was another locked door. There was no escape. No windows that she could see. Just a narrow hallway with a set of stone steps at the end that rose into darkness.

He moved around in front of her and even though she couldn't see his face, she knew he was staring at her. Studying her. Looking for something, but what? Contrition? Fear? If only she knew what he wanted, she'd give it to him. Then maybe he'd let her go.

"Tell me," he said.

"I don't know what you want me to say. I've told you everything."

"No. Think back to Monday. Where did you go after school?"

"I went home, like I always do."

"And after that?"

She sucked in a breath. Had he been following her? Was it possible that he'd been following her and she hadn't even known? She knew exactly where she'd gone Monday. It was the last thing she remembered before waking up in her stone prison. But she hadn't told anyone, not even Gina. Because Gina didn't know about Hudson, so Hailey couldn't tell her about Monday.

"I went to the clinic," she said. Was this it? Was this the horrible sin he wanted to hear?

"For what purpose?"

"I...I got birth control."

"Because you're fornicating before marriage."

"No! I haven't—I didn't—"

"Perhaps not yet. But that was your plan."

"But I haven't done anything," she wailed. "How can I repent for something I didn't do?"

"You've already done it in your mind. And you would have followed suit with your body. Do you know what happens to the children of teen parents? How hard their life is? Most live in poverty with little chance of escape. They're beaten by the parade of men that the mother allows through the house. They're sold to sexual perverts for drug money."

Hailey gasped. "I would never..."

"That's what they all think, but then their family and friends abandon them. The man who fathered the child disappears. She's alone, with no skills and no means of support. Desperation leads to horrible choices, and the child suffers the most."

"But the birth control is so I don't have a child," Hailey said, already aware that reasoning with him was impossible but unable to stop from trying.

"You can't be sure of that. You know the risks and you were willing to risk a child's future for your lust. Repent for your sin."

Hailey stared at him and for the first time since she had woken up in her stone dungeon, the attitude every sixteen-year-old was supposed to have coursed through her.

"No," she said.

Several seconds of absolute silence passed, then he took a step closer to her and slapped her across the cheek with his gloved hand, striking her so hard, the chair fell over. With her hands tied behind her and to the chair, she couldn't reach out and break her fall. Pain shot through her shoulder as it connected with the cold, hard stone, then her head hit a split second afterward and her vision blurred.

He towered above her, the blank face staring down at her. "You will repent. I don't understand why you refuse. Once you repent, you're free."

Hailey blinked. Had she heard him correctly? Was he really going to let her go if she said she was sorry for something she didn't even do? Surely it wasn't that simple. She rolled her tongue over her swollen bottom lip and tasted blood. It must have split when she fell. She tried to force her fuddled mind to think. She pretended to care about a lot of things with her father. It was the easiest way to get away from him, even though she didn't believe half of what she said. Maybe this guy was like her father. Maybe telling him what he wanted to hear would be enough.

"Okay," she said. "I'll repent."

"Excellent." He reached down and pulled her and the chair back upright.

"I'm sorry for getting birth control. I'm sorry for impure thoughts. I know I'm supposed to wait until marriage and I promise that is what I'll do. I'll flush the pills. I'll break up with my boyfriend. He's too old for me anyway. And I'll tell my parents about everything I did. All the lies."

She stopped and sucked in a breath. Surely that was everything.

He stared down at her and every silent second was torture. Finally, he nodded and relief coursed through her. It was almost over. And she hadn't lied about everything. She was going to tell her parents everything, but first she was going straight to the police station and telling them.

"Now I'll set you free," he said and took a step toward her, placing him so close to her that his leg was almost touching hers.

Then he stretched his arms out and his gloved hands grasped her neck.

The horror of what she'd done washed over her and

she screamed as his hands tightened. He meant to kill her. That was how he planned on setting her free. He'd never intended to let her go. Why had she been so stupid? All the secrets she'd kept, thinking she was saving herself from problems at home, and instead, she'd managed to draw the attention of a crazy person. She was going to die here and worst of all, her father would be justified in all the things he'd tried to force her into believing.

She didn't even bother to struggle. There was no point. Her hands were bound. And even if they weren't, she was too weak to fight off an adult twice her size. Instead, she said a quick prayer for forgiveness, a true repentance, and slipped into darkness.

25

COOL AIR BLEW ACROSS HAILEY'S FACE AND SHE FORCED herself to remain still. She was lying on dirt, not the cold stone of the room, and she could no longer feel the ropes cutting into her wrists and ankles. She felt the breeze on her bare feet. Her pulse ticked up and she struggled to remain still. If she was free of the dungeon, this might be her chance to escape. But she had to time it perfectly. She held her breath, listening for any sound that indicated he was nearby, and heard a noise off to her left. Her left arm was partially draped over her head, so it provided her a tiny bit of cover to barely open her eyes.

He was there, just five feet away, doing something with a rope over the cross on a crypt. Rows of crypts stretched in both directions. She was in one of the cemeteries! Her jaw stiffened until it ached, holding in the cry that wanted to burst out. He thought he'd killed her. That's why they were here.

At the moment, he was turned sideways so he could see her if she moved. But maybe if he faced the other direction, she could jump up and run. She had no idea where she would run to, but as long as she kept moving away from the monster, she should be able to find help. Every agonizing second ticked by as she watched him working with the rope. Then he reached to the side and pulled a small ladder over.

Her pulse quickened. That was her chance. When he was on the ladder, she'd make a run for it. She watched as he placed it in front of the crypt and gathered the rope in his left hand. He used his right hand to guide himself up the ladder. When he was poised on the second-to-last rung and reached up with both hands to stretch the rope over the cross, she drew in a deep breath and shoved herself up from the ground.

Then fell back down with a thud.

The monster spun around and looked down at her, and even though she couldn't see his eyes, she knew they were locked on her. The lack of food and being in the same position for so long had made her body weak, and something was wrong with her ankle. But no way was she going to let the monster hang her from that cross.

The monster took two steps down the ladder and then jumped off the remaining steps and took a running leap for her. Adrenaline coursed through her and she pushed as hard as she could with her arms, gathering her legs beneath her to force herself up from the ground. As she made it to her feet, he grabbed her arm, his gloved hand squeezing her bruised and cut wrist so hard she cried out in pain.

She yanked her arm, trying to break his grip, but he was too strong for her. Then she remembered the self-defense lessons they'd gotten during PE class at school. The students had joked about it, mostly because no one wanted to think that something bad could happen to them. But the teacher had persisted with lessons, forcing them through the moves.

So instead of trying to pull her right arm away from him, she did what he wasn't expecting. She spun around to face him and at the same time, struck his wrist with her left hand and yanked her right arm as hard as she could, twisting it to break his stranglehold. As soon as her wrist broke free, she swung her right leg out between the middle of his legs and connected as hard as she could with his crotch.

He yelled and stumbled backward. As he moved away from her, she spun around to run. But as she fled, she stepped on something sharp, like a track of needles, with her right foot. She screamed as pain shot through her foot and up her leg, but she forced herself forward and sprinted off between the crypts. She had no idea where the cemetery ended, but if she kept running in one direction, she should be able to find an exit. The sky was cloudy but the moon peeked out enough from the clouds to cast a dim glow. It was enough to allow her to run without slamming into one of the crypts or the trees that sprang up occasionally between them.

Trees!

It was Metairie Cemetery.

That was the only one she knew of with trees. That meant the interstate was somewhere nearby. She just had to find it. There would be cars there. People. Surely he wouldn't continue to pursue her with witnesses around.

She heard him running behind her and it sounded like he was gaining on her. But she couldn't take the chance of looking. The only way to do it safely would be to slow her pace and she wouldn't risk that. To turn while she was running through the uneven ground, dodging the stone and cement structures, might cause her to trip or slam into something. Then it would all be over. He wouldn't make the same mistake next time, and she had no doubt that he'd throttle her until every breath of air had left her body.

She sobbed as she ran, the ragged ground tearing at her tender feet, sometimes jabbing directly into the punctures made by whatever she'd stepped on while trying to get away. Her shoulder ached so much that she lowered her right arm as she ran, and every step she took it felt like someone was hammering nails into her ankle. The lack of form slowed her down a bit, making it harder to maintain stride, but she focused on her legs and tried to ignore her broken body.

She burst out of a row of crypts into wide-open space and slowed a tiny bit until she spotted a wrought iron fence just ahead, its brick columns stretching out in a line like tombstones. Without even pausing, she turned up her speed and ran straight at one of the columns. When she was a couple feet away, she leaped up and grabbed it, screaming in pain as she scrambled up the side and over the top.

Momentum carried her all the way over the structure, but she was going too fast to control her landing. She slammed into the ground and pain shot through her shoulder and head again, but she didn't care. As soon as she connected with the turf, she sprang up and kept running, weaving a bit as wave after wave of dizziness coursed through her. But it was there, right in front of her.

The street.

Headlights.

She ran into traffic, causing the cars to slam on their brakes and angle off to the side to avoid hitting her. A man jumped out and started yelling but then got a good look at her and rushed over.

"Call 911!" he yelled to the other motorists who'd stopped. "What happened?" he asked her, his hands outstretched but hesitant like he was unsure if touching her would hurt her more.

"Kidnapped," she said. "He's in the cemetery. Call the cops."

The stranger caught her as she collapsed.

26

FRIDAY, MAY 20, 2016
  French Quarter, New Orleans

AT 2:00 A.M., Jackson and Grayson practically ran down the hallway of the hospital, catching sight of the doctor as he exited Hailey's room. They put on the brakes and waited as he gave them a rundown of her condition.

"She's weak from lack of food," the doctor said. "Her shoulder is seriously bruised and she has a sprained ankle and a mild concussion. Her wrists and ankles are raw from being tied up, and the bottoms of her feet are pretty ragged from running through the cemetery. She also stepped on something with the right foot—looks like small nail holes."

"Is she going to be all right?" Jackson asked.

The doctor nodded. "Physically, yes. She'll make a full recovery, but the other..."

"Yeah, we're hoping we can help with that end," Grayson said. "Can we talk to her?"

"I know you have to," the doctor said, "and I won't bother asking you not to stress her because there's no way around it. Trust me, I want you to catch the guy who did this as much as you do. But if you see her getting overwrought, then please call the nurse. We haven't given her a sedative yet because we knew you were on the way."

"Thank you," Grayson said, and they entered the room.

Hailey was propped up in bed, her right arm in a sling, her wrists wrapped with bandages. A large bruise was forming on one side of her face, its purple hue almost glaring against her pale skin. She looked up at them as they entered and Jackson could tell she was uneasy.

Grayson pulled out his ID and showed her. "I'm Detective Grayson and this is Detective Lamotte. We were assigned to your missing persons case. I can't tell you how happy we are to see you here. Are you all right? Do you need the nurse to bring you anything?"

Hailey had relaxed when Grayson introduced them, and now she shook her head. "I'm okay," she said, her voice weak.

"I know this is hard," Grayson said, "but we want to catch the guy who did this to you. The sooner we hear your story, the better. Will you talk to us?"

"Yes," she said, her voice stronger. "I want him caught. I want him strung up on a cross like he was planning to do to me."

Jackson stiffened, then glanced at Grayson, who frowned. He'd heard about the other girl found in the cemetery and the circumstances of her placement, but he didn't know about the connection of that case with Shaye's case. Jackson could barely contain his frantic mind. He'd been right! The cases were related. He'd just been wrong about the perp because it wasn't Pitre. Hailey's parents had been in Covington visiting a sick relative and were now en route to the hospital, probably breaking every speeding law in the state.

"Where do I start?" she asked.

"Start when you were taken," Grayson said.

She shook her head. "I can't remember that part exactly. I remember putting the chicken out for my mom and then I got a phone call that my prescription was ready. I went out to get it—I know I'm not supposed to leave the house after I get home, but I did, okay. And after I left, I was going to see a, uh, friend."

"We know about Hudson," Jackson said.

Hailey's eyes widened. "Do my parents know?"

"We didn't tell them," Grayson said. "But you need to."

Hailey looked down at her bandaged wrists. "My dad is...he's not easy."

"It's okay," Jackson said. "We don't have to talk about that right now. It's more important to catch the man who did this to you. What do you remember after picking up the prescription?"

"That's where it all gets fuzzy. I know I took a shortcut across the park and I remember tripping. I think that's how I hurt my ankle. A man helped me up and gave me a bottle of water, and I kept going until I got to a bench. I remember sitting and taking off my shoe and sock to look at my ankle, and then everything goes blank until..."

She took a deep breath and slowly blew it out. "I woke up in a room," she continued. "It was small and made of stone with a thick wood door. It was locked from the outside. There was no electricity. The only light I had was when he came and that was from a flashlight."

"Can you describe him?" Grayson asked.

"He was fairly tall, maybe six feet, and solidly built. But I couldn't see his face. He had this blank mask. It made him look like he had no face at all."

Jackson felt his back tighten. He'd been pretty sure before that Hailey had been abducted by Nicolas's stalker, but now he was positive.

"Did you recognize his voice or was there anything that stood out about the way he walked or moved?" Grayson asked.

"No. I don't know anything that can help."

"That's okay," Grayson said, trying to keep Hailey from getting more upset. "Just start from when you regained consciousness and tell us everything from there."

She nodded and started talking, telling them everything that had happened. The inquisition and requirement to repent her sin. Her inability to give him the answer he was looking for. And then his final visit. When he coached her into confession. Into repentance.

And then when she realized how he intended to set her free.

It was all Jackson could do not to punch the wall. He was a cop. He was supposed to have better self-control. But listening to this girl recount the horror she'd been through made his blood run hot. That someone was so demented they could do such things to a child. And all of it made him remember what Shaye had gone through for years on end.

If it was the last thing he did, he was going to catch this guy.

"He thought I was dead," Hailey said as she described what happened in the cemetery. "I think he was going to hang me on that cross. Over birth control pills." She choked as she delivered that statement and Grayson poured her a glass of water.

She took a sip and wiped her nose with her bandaged hand. "How can someone do that?" she asked.

"I don't know," Grayson said. "How did you get away?"

Hailey told him about pretending to be dead and waiting for him to climb the ladder. About how when she tried to spring up, her body wouldn't comply, and she was almost caught again. Then she told them about remembering the self-defense move from PE class and kicking him. Then she ran and ran until she was safe.

"You are so smart and so brave," Jackson said. "Most adults wouldn't have been able to do what you did. You should be very proud of yourself, Hailey."

Hailey sniffed and the tears that had been lurking at the edge of her eyes finally spilled over. "All I could think of when I reached the road was how glad I was that I'd disobeyed my parents and done all that running. If I hadn't..."

Grayson nodded. "I have no doubt it saved your life. Your speed and endurance, despite being so weak, were too much for him to match."

"He was gone before the police got there, wasn't he?" she asked.

"Yes," Grayson said. "But I want to go back to something for a minute. The guy who helped you when you fell in the park—can you describe him?"

Hailey opened her mouth to respond, then frowned. "No. I can see him bending over, but I can't make out his face." Her eyes widened. "Was that him? Was there something in the water? I had a horrible headache when I woke up. Like I was hungover. Oh my God, why can't I remember? That was him. If I could just remember, you could catch him."

She started to sob, and Jackson placed one hand on her arm, his heart breaking. "We're going to catch him. And he'll never hurt anyone else again."

A choked cry sounded behind them and Hailey's

mother rushed into the room. Her father was right behind but stopped in the doorway, staring at Hailey, his expression a mixture of disbelief and horror.

"Oh my God, my baby!" Hailey's mother cried and hugged her daughter, causing her to grimace.

Mrs. Pitre realized what she was doing and released her. "I'm so sorry. Your shoulder, your hands. Oh, Hailey, I am so sorry that we weren't there to protect you." Then she burst into giant heaving sobs and Hailey began again as well.

Grayson pulled a chair over next to the bed and helped Mrs. Pitre into it. She draped her arms over the bed, holding Hailey's arms and continuing to cry. Pitre still stood in the doorway, not making a move to come near them.

"This is my fault," he mumbled and fled the room.

Jackson and Grayson stared at each other for a second, then Grayson asked Mrs. Pitre and Hailey to excuse them, and they set out after him. They caught up with him in the parking lot, laid across the hood of his car, weeping like a baby.

"Mr. Pitre?" Grayson said as they approached. "I know this is hard to deal with. I can't imagine seeing my daughter that way, but Hailey needs you to be strong for her. She's doing a fantastic job keeping it together given what she's endured. You need to pull yourself together and be there for her."

"I can't," Pitre said. "We heard everything she said. The doctor stopped us outside the door so that she could finish telling you what happened. I heard..." He began to choke.

"I heard everything he did," Pitre continued. "I heard why. It's all my fault."

Suddenly, Jackson got a feeling that something else was going on. Something more than what had happened to Hailey. He could tell Grayson was getting frustrated with the man and put his hand on Grayson's arm before he could speak.

"How is it your fault?" Jackson asked.

Pitre stood up and looked directly at them. "This is retribution. God sent his emissary to settle the score."

"What score is that?" Jackson asked.

"The score with Nathan Greer," Pitre said. "My daughter for his."

Grayson's eyes widened and he glanced at Jackson.

"What are you saying, sir?" Grayson asked.

"That I killed Melissa Greer," Pitre said. "It was an accident, but that doesn't matter. She's still dead and I hid it from everyone...allowed her mother and father to go on without knowing what happened. I can't risk something happening to Hailey again. I have to tell the truth about what happened, no matter the consequences."

Pitre thrust his arms out toward Grayson. "Arrest me. I'll confess to everything. It will keep Hailey safe. It's my fault this happened to her. My fault."

Grayson looked over at Jackson, his expression one of complete disbelief, then he pulled out his handcuffs and secured Pitre's wrists.

AT 4:00 A.M. Shaye opened her front door and rushed Jackson inside. She'd just fallen asleep two hours before when he'd called and told her that Hailey had been brought to the hospital and he and Grayson were on their way. That had sent her straight out of bed and to the kitchen to brew some coffee. No way would she be able to sleep until she knew Hailey was all right.

About an hour later, she'd gotten two texts.

Hailey escaped. In stable condition. Our perp is the same.

Pitre confessed to murdering Melissa Greer.

After that, she'd been unable to think of anything else. She'd turned on the television, played music, tried sitting, standing, eating, and finally settled on pacing. Even a hot shower hadn't stopped her mind from racing with all the questions she had. Her emotions were all over the place from elated that Hailey was alive to frustrated because there were so many unanswered questions. How had Hailey escaped? How did Jackson know the perp was the same? She was certain they hadn't caught him because Jackson would have said so. Did Hailey even see him or was he simply unknown to her? And why did Pitre confess?

Jackson trudged into the living room and slumped down on her couch, and she hovered over him.

"Can I get you something to drink—beer, water?"

He looked up at her and she could see how exhausted

he was. "Can you brew a pot of coffee? I don't even want to try sleeping. Not yet."

"I'm on my third pot." She hurried to the kitchen to pour him a cup, then returned to the living room to sit beside him. "Tell me," she said.

And he did.

He only paused occasionally to sip the coffee as he recounted Hailey's story and Pitre's confession right up to the point where Grayson arrested him. She managed to keep from interrupting, letting the story flow as he remembered it. Several times, she was unable to control a gasp and she didn't even bother to try to contain the horror she felt as he told her what Hailey had endured. When he recounted her escape, she hadn't realized she'd been holding her breath until Hailey got to the road.

When he finally stopped, she filled his mug again to heat up the coffee that had gone cold in the bottom, and he took a big sip. Shaye shook her head, still marveling over everything that had transpired in such a short amount of time.

"I can't believe it," she said. "It's all so unreal."

"I know. I'm still trying to wrap my head around it and I was there."

"I have so many questions, I don't even know where to start. But the first is how is Hailey?"

"She's banged up a bit but nothing that some time won't fix. Emotionally, she's been pushed to the edge and I'm afraid once she finds out about her father, it might tip the scales in the wrong direction."

Shaye nodded. She had firsthand experience in finding out the people you loved weren't exactly who you thought they were. "She's going to ask why he isn't there to see her. Why he left the hospital without even saying a word."

"Yeah. It was hard enough telling his wife. All the joy she had because Hailey was alive just drained out of her. She told Hailey that her father went to the police station to help us with the investigation, but that will only hold for so long."

"Their lives are changed forever. Did Pitre give a full confession at the police station?"

Jackson nodded. "The long and short of it is he came home from work early one day and Melissa came into the house through the back door to see Hailey. Her mother had taken her to a doctor's appointment after school, so Pitre was the only one home. He got into it with Melissa and she taunted him, refusing to leave the house. He pushed her toward the back door and she fell down the steps, breaking her neck on the way down."

"And I suppose it never occurred to him to call the police."

"He said she was dead on impact and he figured there was no use for two families to be ruined over a stupid accident. He hid her body in his shed until after everyone was asleep, then took it to the bayou and dumped it. He told us the location, but you know how those things go."

Shaye felt her stomach roll. The likelihood of the police recovering any part of Melissa was so remote it wasn't even worth hoping for. The Greers would have answers and Michael Pitre would pay for what he did. But they wouldn't have their daughter to bury.

Still, her immediate concern was Nicolas, who was still at risk.

"So you were right about the cases being connected," she said. "The ritual posing of the bodies of the first victim and Hailey. The blank face mask. It's the same guy." She frowned. "Even the punctures on Hailey's feet..."

"Yeah. I'm guessing she stepped on the crown of thorns when she was running away. I didn't clue in on it at first but when it hit me, I had a whole other round of wanting to punch a wall."

"So can I assume you'll be finishing this coffee, hitting the shower, and heading back out to find the penitent?"

Jackson's expression flashed with anger. "No. Grayson and I were pulled."

"What? Why?"

"Because detectives are already working on Sunny Trahan, and since every indication is that Hailey's abductor is the same guy, the chief sees no point in having four detectives on the case, especially when there's no shortage of work to go around."

Shaye didn't even bother to hide her disappointment. Jackson had information about the penitent that the other detectives didn't have and couldn't obtain. If he and Grayson had remained on the case, he could have worked her suspects in somehow. But with other detectives in charge and Nicolas unwilling to make an official statement, getting information to them would be far more difficult. Maybe even impossible.

"I'm pissed off about it," Jackson said, "and Grayson is mad as hell. But there's nothing we can do. Grayson pleaded to let us work it for just another day, but the chief wouldn't have it. But that doesn't mean I'm going to stop."

Shaye stared. "You can't risk your job. You've invested too much. If the chief catches you..."

She didn't finish her statement. She didn't have to. Jackson knew he was on tenuous ground with the department, mostly because of his relationship with Shaye. Even though she'd been the victim, uncovering her past had brought a lot of damage and heartache to the department, and there were still hard feelings, especially from those who had been there for decades. As far as some of the old guard were concerned, Jackson was part of the problem because he was dating Shaye. There were a lot of people watching him, just waiting for him to screw up.

"Then I'll just have to be sure he doesn't catch me," Jackson said. "I'll still work as hard as I always do on whatever case we're assigned, but there's always some downtime during an investigation, and I'll put in evenings and nights when I've got them to spare. I'm not telling Grayson. He'd insist on helping and he's already stuck his neck out enough for me."

Shaye's hopes ticked up a notch. Even if Jackson

couldn't be officially involved, the information he had access to could definitely make things easier. They'd just have to be careful. Make sure no one could come back on Jackson. But she already knew that when they caught the guy, and linked him back to Hailey and Sunny, shit would hit the fan at the police department. Jackson knew it too, but there was nothing he or Shaye could do about it unless she was willing to drop the case, and neither one of them wanted her to do that.

27

FRIDAY, MAY 20, 2016
  St. Mary's, New Orleans

COLBY PUSHED Nicolas away from the breakfast table and into the living room where Malcolm and Bernard were sitting to watch the morning news. It had become a ritual, of sorts, for the three men, watching the local news before they headed out to take care of their respective duties. Often, the reports led to additional items on their prayer lists and a good bit of sorrow, but Father Bernard felt it was important for them to be aware of what was happening in their city because their congregation was affected by it as well.

After positioning Nicolas next to the recliner he usually sat in, Colby took a seat at the kitchen table. It was interesting, Nicolas thought, to see how the other priests reacted to Colby's presence. Father Bernard had invited him to breakfast, of course, which Colby had declined, stating he'd already eaten. But he'd taken coffee while the priests ate French toast that Malcolm had made and had answered all of Bernard's questions about his military service. Malcolm had been unusually quiet and Nicolas could tell something was bothering him. But despite being a very outgoing person, Malcolm was also a private one. Nicolas figured that whenever he was ready to talk about what was occupying his mind, he'd seek out Father Bernard for a talk.

In the meantime, Nicolas felt secure, knowing the bodyguard was only feet away and literally watching his back. The news began with the usual traffic report, letting commuters know which streets to avoid during their morning drive, then a report on a meeting at city hall over budget cuts.

Nicolas half listened to the reporter drone on about the infighting among the local politicians, but his mind was in other places. Would the penitent try to contact him again? Would Colby be enough to protect him? Would Shaye figure out who he was before he struck again?

And despite the fact that he'd managed to fall asleep fairly easily and had slept for a good amount of time before waking, Nicolas still felt sluggish and tired. He knew he'd dreamed because he'd awakened with a sheen of sweat covering his body and his heart racing, but he couldn't recall any of the jumbled images that seemed to vanish from his memory as soon as he awakened.

"And now for a special report," a lady reporter said. "We received a call yesterday from a tourist with a harrowing tale about her visit to Metairie Cemetery."

The reporter shifted the mic to a stressed woman. "I was researching my family tree and looking for a crypt, and that's when I saw her—tied up on a cross just like Jesus. She even had a crown that looked like it was made of sticks. It's the most horrible thing I've ever seen."

The reporter moved the mic back. "Police will only say that the woman was strangled, and they are withholding her identity until her family can be notified. They had no comment on the investigation or the horrific placement of her body."

Nicolas gasped. Shaye had told him the police were keeping everything quiet until they had a better grip on things. He'd never expected to see a story about that poor girl on the news, but apparently the tourist who had found the body had decided people needed to know.

"Are you all right?" Father Malcolm asked him.

"Yes," Nicolas said. "I mean, no, not really. That story..."

Malcolm frowned. "It is troubling. We should add that young woman and her family to our prayer list."

"And the woman who found her as well," Father Bernard said. "I can't imagine it was a pleasant experience."

Nicolas gave Father Bernard a hard look and he

barely shook his head. Malcolm rose and grabbed his wallet from the kitchen counter.

"I need to get to the business office," Malcolm said. "It's payroll day and the new system is giving us a bit of trouble."

He said his goodbyes and left the apartment. Father Bernard looked over at Colby.

"I wonder if you could give us a minute in private?" Bernard asked.

"Of course," Colby said. "I'll just step outside for some air. Let me know when Nicolas is ready to leave."

Colby left the apartment, closing the door behind him, and Nicolas looked at Bernard, struggling to maintain a semblance of composure. "What if that was her?" Nicolas asked.

"You don't know that," Bernard said.

"She was strangled and arranged on a cross with a crown—"

Nicolas began to choke and reached for his bottled water.

"I agree that the circumstances fit what you heard. But even if you made the decision to break your vows and speak to the police—which is not something I support—what could you possibly offer that would help?"

"Time of day, maybe? They could eliminate people if they were somewhere else when I took the confession."

"But you don't know that they have a pool of people to eliminate from. You can hardly suggest they alibi all of New Orleans."

Nicolas sighed. "I know you're right. But it feels wrong to sit here and do nothing."

"There is someone far more powerful than you who can provide help. How about we have a special candle-lighting service for the police on Sunday?"

"That would be nice," Nicolas said, trying to force an ounce of enthusiasm into his voice. He knew Father Bernard was trying to make him feel better and a candle service was a nice gesture. But it didn't help identify the penitent. And it didn't put him behind bars before he could hurt someone else.

Like Nicolas.

Father Bernard rose and placed his hand on Nicolas's shoulder. "I have a budget meeting to prepare for. Please be kind to yourself today, Father Nicolas. You are doing everything you can."

Nicolas nodded because he knew that's what Bernard wanted him to do. "Thank you for your counsel. You always put things into perspective."

Even when it wasn't what Nicolas wanted to hear.

Bernard exited the apartments and a couple seconds later, Colby stepped inside.

"I got a text from Shaye," Colby said. "She needs to see us as soon as possible."

Nicolas felt his back tighten. "Did she find him?"

"I don't know. She said we needed to meet in person. I wasn't sure what your work schedule was so I said I'd check."

"Actually, I'm duty-free until later this afternoon. Where does she want to meet?"

"She gave me an address. It's to the facility her mother is building. She can provide you with documents that will make it appear as if you had a business meeting about St. Mary's contributing to the facility. In case anyone asks."

"Not perfect, but better than meeting in a public place. Let's get going then." Nicolas was anxious to hear what Shaye had discovered. At this point, she wouldn't have risked a meeting unless it was necessary.

Hopefully, she was closing in on the penitent.

SHAYE GREETED them at the front door and directed them down the hallway to a small meeting room. A table was already in place with a gap for Colby to place Nicolas's chair. Once Nicolas was situated, Colby excused himself and closed the door behind him.

"Do you know who he is?" Nicolas asked, barely waiting for the door to click closed.

"Not yet," she said. "But a lot of things happened last night. Too much to tell over the phone and I wanted to ask you questions and show you some pictures as well."

"What happened?"

She told him about Hailey Pitre's kidnapping and her escape. Nicolas listened as Shaye described every detail of what Hailey had endured, and she could tell he was struggling to keep his emotions in check as he processed the horror the young girl had experienced. When she finished, he took in a deep breath and blew it out.

"I heard about Hailey's disappearance on the news, but I never once thought...it's unbelievable. It was him."

Shaye nodded.

"But who is he? Do the police have any idea?"

"Not that I'm aware of. Prior to Hailey's escape, the police were watching her father."

Nicolas stared. "Her father? Surely not."

"It wasn't him. He has a solid alibi for when Hailey escaped from the cemetery. But he wasn't exactly an innocent party." She told Nicolas about Pitre's confession.

"That's horrible! That poor girl. So much to handle already and now her father... What will happen to him?"

"I don't know. It's his word that it was accidental, and the fact that he hid the body doesn't bode well for him with the DA. I'm afraid Mr. Pitre will probably go to prison for a while."

She pulled out her cell phone and showed him some pictures. "I wanted to see if you recognized Hailey or her father."

Nicolas studied the images but ultimately shook his head. "I don't think so. If they attend St. Mary's, they're not regulars. At least, they're not part of the volunteering or complaining crowd. That's usually the ones I get to know."

"St. Mary's wasn't their regular church, but it is close

to Pitre's office. He came here yesterday to light a candle."

Nicolas looked up at her in obvious surprise. "You saw him?"

"No. The police did. The man I date was assigned to Hailey's case."

Nicolas felt his hope surge. "So the police are looking for the penitent. You can give your man information without disclosing my name, right? Because he'll trust you and take your word."

"Yes, I can and have already given him information. Unfortunately, he's been pulled from the investigation. The perpetrator is the same man who killed Sunny Trahan, and there was already a detective assigned to the case. Since Sunny's death was first, the original detective gets both cases."

Nicolas struggled to contain his disappointment, but she could see it written all over his face.

"Your friend can hardly pass along suspects without a reason," he said.

"No. But he's not letting this go. He's going to help me, but he has to be very careful about it because it could cost him his job. Still, he has access to information I don't, like details from Sunny's and Hailey's cases and all the watercooler gossip surrounding them."

"I suppose it doesn't matter much as our suspect doesn't look so good anymore. The electrician might have a motive to hate me, but he had no reason to target those two other girls."

"No reason that we're aware of. But from the beginning, we've known the person we're looking for has a different thought process than the norm. I've seen first-hand what a misguided interpretation of religion can do. And I know how much a single event can affect a person to the point that it changes them completely. Look at Michael Pitre. After killing that girl, he moved his family away and became a fanatic, attempting to control his daughter's every action and thought."

"So what happened to the electrician's sister and his best friend could have sent him over the edge."

"It's possible, and at that point, regular logic doesn't apply. The penitent took Hailey for acquiring birth control pills. Maybe the electrician thought this teen didn't deserve to have a child when his sister and her child were gone. Maybe he felt Sunny Trahan didn't deserve to live because she was destroying her life while his sister was living correctly but didn't have a choice."

"I understand what you're saying, but to kill them?"

"He killed them after they confessed. In his mind, he's saving them. If they die right after he absolves them of their sin, then they go to heaven. His sister didn't have that luxury. She died on impact."

"You really think it's him?"

"I think he's a possibility. But it could be someone else." She hesitated a moment, trying to figure out the best way to frame the discussion she needed to have. "More importantly, I need to talk to you about how we proceed," she said finally.

"What do you mean?"

"Hailey's escape was a huge blow for the penitent. He's failed and I doubt he's going to take that lightly. And there's also the fear that the police will focus on her interaction with the man from the park and she's able to identify him. He doesn't know that she can't remember."

"Surely he won't try to take her again."

"No. I don't think he'll risk that. But he might be more desperate to please, and in a hurry to finish his business here."

Nicolas gasped, the full force of Shaye's words finally hitting him. "You think he's going to come after me now because he's afraid he's about to be caught."

"Yes. So you have a decision to make. Your first option is to leave town. He can't hurt you if he can't find you. There's a lot of pressure on the police right now and they'll throw resources at this case. They'll pull available camera footage from everywhere that Hailey went that day, and they'll have her looking at photos as soon as her memory returns. There's always the possibility of DNA."

"But that won't help identify him unless he's already in the database. What are the odds of that? The truth?"

"Honestly, I don't think they're very high. I think the penitent was a normal person with a normal life until the day he wasn't. And while the DNA probably won't help identify him, it will definitely help convict him."

"But you have to catch him first," he said slowly. "And reality is, you have no way of knowing how long that will take. Or how long Hailey's memory will take to return. If it ever does. He could walk around this city for years without being discovered."

"He would be taking a huge risk to do so."

"Then he could simply disappear. And then what? When would it be safe for me to return? A week? A month?" He shook his head. "How do we know he won't come back or go looking for me somewhere else? If he's not caught now, I could spend every moment of the rest of my life waiting for him to appear. You know what that's like."

"I do."

Nicolas leaned forward and looked her straight in the eye. "Then let me ask you, if you'd had the opportunity back then to end it all, to keep him from ever hurting another person, to not have to constantly look over your shoulder, would you have done it? Even if it meant putting yourself at risk?"

"Yes," she said, without hesitation.

He nodded. "Then that's what I intend to do. I can't live with this hanging over me. And because of my health, I'm at a huge disadvantage and will be for some time. Maybe forever."

"You realize what you'll be doing?"

"Stringing myself on a fishing hook? It's still better than the alternatives. Even if it costs me my life, it's still worth it."

She nodded, immense respect for Nicolas's bravery flooding through her. Most people wouldn't make the decision he had. Especially people with the means to easily flee.

"If this is the course you want to take, then we have to be smart," she said. "You have to be extra diligent about what you do and who you see. The more you can limit your movement to the church and avoid open areas, the better. I'm going to inform Colby that the threat is elevated and to be on alert for a strike. He already has photos of the electrician and is on watch for anyone who is paying attention to you."

"What about at night? Is there anything more I can do?"

"No. I think the building is as secure as it can be without involving Bernard to change things. The camera is working fine, so if anyone were to enter your apartment, I'd see it. And I'm going to figure out the best way to watch on location as well, even if it means walking the block all night long. I'll also devise a schedule to have you check in before you go to bed."

He gave her a small smile. "Watching over me while I sleep?"

"Whatever it takes."

"What about Father Malcolm and Father Bernard? Am I placing them in danger by remaining?"

She hesitated before answering. "There's no way to know for sure, of course, but my inclination is no. The penitent is obsessed with ritual. I don't think he'd kill two people, especially priests, just to get to you. It is more likely he'd take a shot at Colby during the day and attempt to take you then."

"I've been afraid of that since the beginning and even mentioned it to Colby when we first met."

"And how did that go?"

"I think he was more amused than concerned."

Shaye smiled. "That sounds right. Don't worry about Colby. He's been in situations far worse than this and he's always come out on top. He's very good at what he does."

Nicolas nodded but Shaye could see the doubt.

She didn't think Nicolas questioned Colby's qualifications, and neither did she. But in war, Colby had known who the enemy was. With this, he could be blindsided. And if he were, she knew Nicolas would blame himself. Shaye could tell that hearing what had happened to Hailey had both distressed and frightened Nicolas.

If the penitent got Nicolas on that chair, would he have the answer the penitent was looking for? He had claimed all along that he didn't, and Shaye believed he was telling the truth. Not that knowing the answer mattered, she supposed. Ultimately, all roads led to the same endgame.

But unlike Hailey Pitre, Nicolas had no hope of fleeing.

28

Jackson entered Shaye's apartment, frowning. After the big reveal the night before, he'd gone to his apartment for a shower and to grab a couple hours' sleep. He and Grayson had already been given the day off since they'd worked back-to-back shifts the day before and hadn't yet been assigned to a new case. That meant he had time to work with Shaye to identify the penitent. But since he wasn't at the police station, he lacked access to the gossip on how Hailey and Sunny's investigation was progressing. Catch-22.

"What's wrong?" Shaye asked as soon as he stepped inside. He'd been fuming the night before at being removed from the case, and she couldn't blame him. Jackson cared about his work. He cared about the victims. And when something this horrific happened, you wanted to see it through to the end, not pass it off to someone else and hope they made the right calls. It wasn't that Jackson didn't trust the detective in charge of the case. He'd already told Shaye that he was highly experienced and excellent at his job.

But he didn't have inside information like Jackson did. And as of last night, they hadn't figured out a way to filter it back to him. Not just yet.

Jackson pulled his laptop out from under his arm and put it on the kitchen island, motioning for her to sit next to him. He pulled up a document and pointed. "Your instincts were right. There's a problem with Father Malcolm."

Shaye's pulse quickened. "What kind of problem?"

"He appeared out of thin air fifteen years ago in San Antonio. Prior to that, there is no record of Malcolm Warner. No address, no work records, not even a Social Security number."

"What the hell?" Of all the things Shaye had imagined, this one hadn't even been on the list.

"I know. Normally when I see this, it's someone with a nefarious past having a do-over to escape, either through witness protection or by their own means. But Malcolm is thirty-three years old. He would have been eighteen when this happened."

"Assuming he's really thirty-three now."

"That's true enough but if he's not, he can't be far off."

Shaye nodded. Father Malcolm looked to be midthirties max. "But for the past fifteen years, he's trackable, right?"

"Yes, and it's definitely him. I've matched photos from his driver's license to pictures on the St. Mary's website as well as the church he worked at prior and the seminary school in San Antonio. It's the same guy."

"So not an elaborate identity theft where the bad guy offs a priest and turns up at a new church to stalk a new set of victims."

"Not unless he offed a high school student about to attend seminary. That's some serious advance planning. And a whole lot of schooling just to set up a cover."

"I agree, but no way someone disappears off the planet to reappear as someone else without something to hide."

"Nope."

Shaye frowned. "I wonder if something happened to him when he was a teen. Something that allowed him to legally change everything."

"You mean like being a witness to a crime?"

"Or a victim of one. Plenty of victims would start over in a new place as a new person if they had the option. It's not easy to have a normal life when everyone knows all the horrible things that happened to you."

"You'd know that better than anyone. But if that's the case, then it only lends more weight to Malcolm potentially being our guy. If he went through something horrible as a child, then something could have triggered a break now. Even becoming a priest could have been part of trying to get a grip on his emotional health."

Shaye nodded. She didn't like to dwell on how many victims became perps, but she was well aware of the statistics. If it weren't for the tireless work of her mother and Eleonore, she could have been one of them.

"Is there any way to find out more?" she asked.

"No. If I were legitimately on the case, I'd try putting out feelers to the lawyers in the area where he made the switch. Sometimes you can convince one to give up some gossip, as long as it's not about their client. Or if I have any idea where the person might have originated from, I send photos to the local PD and ask if anyone recognizes them. But in this case, I'd guarantee you Malcolm didn't grow up in San Antonio and we have no earthly idea where to start looking."

"Hustle said his accent is Southern, and Nicolas said he's always playing country music, but I suppose that still leaves a large part of the country as an option. And then there's the part where you're not assigned to the case and have to be careful about what can be tracked back to you." Her back tightened. "How did you pull the background? They're watching everything you do. Won't you have to explain?"

"That's why I grabbed my laptop and did it at a café. I masked my IP address and used another officer's log-in to access the system."

She blinked. "Whose log-in did you use?"

"Vincent's."

"Oh wow." Detective Vincent had been Jackson's senior partner when she'd first met him. He was a sexist, lazy, useless lump, occupying a desk until he could ride into retirement. He'd gone out of his way to make things difficult for Jackson and had insulted Shaye more times than she could count.

"How did you know his password?" she asked.

"It's 123456."

"You've got to be kidding me."

"The department's computer security requirements are lousy, and with budgets constantly being cut, there's not much chance of improvement anytime soon."

"But what if Vincent notices?" Of all people, Vincent wanted Jackson off the force more than anyone.

"He'd have to give a shit before he noticed anything. You know how lazy he is. And since he's still working the Clancy records, he pulls a ton of background checks every day. Even if he sees it, he'll just assume he input some information wrong or that it was a system error."

"And if Malcolm turns out to be our guy? Then someone will notice a background has already been pulled."

"Yeah, there's that. But they still have no proof it was me."

"That doesn't mean they won't know. And that's all brass needs to cause you problems."

"If they do, then I'll deal with it. This isn't the only law enforcement agency in the state. I have options."

Shaye knew he was saying it to make her feel better.

She also knew that if Jackson were dismissed from the PD for any reason to do with impropriety, he'd have a tough time securing a good position in a large agency. And she doubted he wanted a future that included arresting cow-tippers and drunk-and-disorderlies or writing speeding tickets. But the damage was already done. He couldn't take back the background check and if Malcolm turned out to be their guy, then someone at the department finding the check was only a matter of time. Whether or not they could pin it on Jackson wasn't the issue. They'd know even if they had no proof, especially if the whole thing exploded and everyone learned that Shaye was involved.

"In other news," Shaye said, changing the subject, "I've verified that Croft *did* fly out to New York. In fact, according to social media posts, he's still there."

"So he's off the list. That's good. What about the electrician?"

"I watched him several hours yesterday evening and didn't see anything out of the ordinary. He went straight home after the job. He lives in Metairie, so not exactly a convenient base for things here."

"No. But it's convenient to Metairie Cemetery."

"Yeah, I thought that as well."

"Does he live with anyone?"

"A young woman opened the door for him and greeted him with a kiss, so I'm assuming girlfriend. But I don't know whether or not she lives there. I got as far as finding out that he doesn't own the house and I ran down the rental company last night. I was planning on calling today to see if I could get any information."

"Let me do it. They'll answer quicker to a badge and I don't have to give them much of a reason for the questions. Not like you."

She nodded. "I feel like I should be doing more, but I can't think of what."

"You're worried he's going to make a move on Nicolas."

"Yes. He knows Hailey escaped and even though she never saw his face while she was held captive, he doesn't know she can't identify him from the park."

"But assuming she'd never seen him before then—and I believe that's the case—she won't be able to point directly to someone, even when she remembers."

"The penitent knows Nicolas hired me, remember?"

Jackson swore. "That's right. And if he doesn't already know, it wouldn't take much to find out about our connection. But he doesn't know I was working Hailey's case."

"Are we sure of that? If the penitent is Malcolm, he could have seen you the day Pitre was at St. Mary's. It wouldn't have taken much to figure out why."

Jackson blew out a breath. "So the penitent has every reason to believe that the noose is tightening. You're right. If he's still determined to follow through with Nicolas, he's going to move quickly. Have you told Nicolas your concerns?"

She nodded. "He understands all the implications, but he wants to stay put and draw the penitent out."

"I have to give him credit. Most people wouldn't stick around for that, much less volunteer. Colby's with Nicolas all day, right?"

"Yes, and I've already told him the situation has escalated. That the person harassing Nicolas is suspected in one strangulation murder and another attempted one. But he's still unidentified and for now, we have to keep it quiet as Nicolas doesn't want the cops to know about his situation."

"How did Colby take that somewhat thin explanation?"

"In stride. I think he probably filled in the gaps enough to know the score."

"Probably."

"So I was thinking maybe we spend our day *and* night playing backup to Colby's backup."

"I think that's an excellent idea." He reached over and squeezed her hand. "We're going to get this guy."

"Yes. We are."

COLBY WALKED up to Jackson's surveillance car and hopped in the back seat. They were a block away from St. Mary's, and not visible from the church grounds. He'd just delivered Nicolas home for the night and was meeting with Shaye and Jackson to give them his impressions from the day.

He extended his hand over the seat to Jackson. "Good to see you again. I'm glad we have some help on board."

"Not in an official capacity, I'm afraid," Jackson said as he shook Colby's hand.

"I didn't figure," Colby said.

"How were things today?" Shaye asked.

"Quiet but weird," Colby said.

"Weird how?" Shaye asked.

"Nicolas took your advice about sticking inside. Aside from traversing the sidewalks between buildings, he hasn't had a breath of fresh air today. And we steered clear of the cathedral as well and mostly hid out in the priests' private library except for one meeting he had about some fund-raiser. I know you don't think it's likely this guy would enter a room with other people and open fire, but it's not an impossibility, either."

"Anything is possible," Shaye agreed.

"Anyway, Nicolas hasn't said much, but he's seriously spooked. Father Malcolm came into the library while we were there. I was walking the perimeter and he ran into me when he rounded one of the rows. Dropped the books he was carrying. Nicolas jumped like he'd been shot. Malcolm was practically tripping over himself to pick up the books. He muttered an apology over his shoulder and bolted out of there like he was on fire."

Colby shook his head. "I don't like it. I get a funny

feeling from that guy. He's not one of your suspects, is he?"

"I'm afraid he is," Shaye said.

"Jesus," Colby said. "Don't you think you should have told me that?"

"My not telling you was deliberate," she said. "I wanted to get your impression of Malcolm without any bias. I wanted to see what your instincts would tell you and not just your observations."

"Yeah, that makes sense," Colby said. "Well, my instincts tell me there's something off about him. My observations tell me he doesn't like me being around. If he's the one, I guess that's why."

"We don't know for certain that he's the guy," Jackson said. "There's still the electrician to watch for. He was on the church grounds working today as well. Did you see him?"

Colby nodded. "He was in the hallway when we entered the library. He nodded at Father Nicolas and gave me the side-eye." Colby frowned. "I could have sworn I heard the door to the library open about ten minutes later, but when I checked, there wasn't anyone inside or in the hallway. But he was the only person I had seen in that area of the building prior to that."

"Was he supposed to be working there?" Jackson asked.

"Nicolas didn't think so," Colby said. "But Malcolm is overseeing their work and sometimes wiring is run oddly in those old structures, so it's possible his being there was legit. You followed him yesterday, right?"

Shaye nodded. "Nothing much to see. He did his job then went home. Girlfriend let him inside. Jackson did some legwork today and found out he lives alone. The girlfriend has an apartment in the French Quarter and is a flight attendant."

"So no one to see his comings and goings for days on end," Colby said.

"Exactly," Shaye said. "And as Jackson followed her to the airport earlier, and she was suited up and had her travel bag, we're assuming tonight is clear."

"Nicolas stiffened when he saw him in the hallway," Colby said. "I couldn't see his face, but I could tell the guy made Nicolas nervous. He's not very good at acting normal, I'm afraid. I'm guessing you haven't told him that Malcolm is on your suspect list?"

"No. I don't want to freak him out," Shaye said. "What we have right now on Malcolm is completely circumstantial, although Jackson found out a bit more for us."

She gave him a rundown on Malcolm's appearance out of thin air fifteen years prior.

"Interesting," Colby said. "But like you said. Circumstantial. He could have been a victim or a witness or just hated his given name. I went to school with a guy whose parents were stoners. They named him Donald. Last name was Duck."

Jackson grimaced. "That's awful."

Colby nodded. "So how do you want to handle tonight? I've got to tell you, I'm feeling a little itchy about it now that I know Malcolm is as sketchy as he acted."

"Jackson and I will move the car closer when it gets dark. From the west, we can find a spot with a good view of the windows and the ones opposite the street side. You can park across the street from the courtyard and that should give you a view of the front door and the street-side windows. Nicolas will check in with me every hour or so by text until he goes to bed. At that point, we'll both have him on camera."

"So we sit and wait and hope Malcolm doesn't strangle him in his sleep before we get there."

"If anyone enters Nicolas's room, we move then," Jackson said. "Nicolas has been instructed to sleep with his Mace, so he's got a way to give us time to gain access."

"And there's also Father Bernard," Shaye said. "I don't think he could take Malcolm in a fight, but I think two of them could hold him off long enough for us to get there."

Colby blew out a breath. "Man, I hope it's the electrician guy. I really don't want to shoot a priest."

"Me either," Shaye said.

But she also knew none of them would hesitate if Malcolm was the penitent.

NICOLAS TOOK one last bite of lasagna before setting his fork on his plate. "No more," he said. "It's going to take me ten years to work off what I just ate."

Father Malcolm nodded. "And the thought of the treadmill right now makes me a little queasy."

"Today is one of those times I'm glad I'm on official treadmill hiatus," Bernard said. "So I take it you two enjoyed dinner?"

"I think we enjoyed it far too much," Nicolas said. "And we appreciate you making it. I know it's a long process, but the result is fantastic."

Bernard smiled at the compliment. "It's one of the best memories I have with my mother. Of course, she insisted we make the pasta from scratch, something I don't do, or we'd be eating at 3:00 a.m. rather than 8:00. But don't say that too loudly. She might hear and come back to haunt me."

Nicolas and Malcolm both laughed. Considering everything Nicolas had on his mind, the evening had managed to be quite pleasant. Nicolas and Colby had arrived at the apartments before the other priests and Colby had done a quick scan to check windows and doors to ensure everything was secure. Colby had left when Bernard and Malcolm arrived, and Bernard had set out on dinner while Nicolas had assisted Malcolm, who was combing through several years of photos to pick the best ones to add to the website.

When dinner was ready, they'd all gathered at the table and proceeded to eat themselves into a stupor. But

Nicolas had enjoyed the big, heavy meal. It had felt homey and nostalgic, and he imagined that was the primary reason Bernard insisted on cooking an Italian dish periodically, even though none of them needed the calories that came with it. Nicolas had managed—just for a few seconds—to forget everything that was going on.

But unfortunately, as quickly as the horrible things he had dwelling in his mind faded, they returned. He worried about tonight, even though he shouldn't. He was safe in the apartment with both Malcolm and Bernard in residence. And Shaye had a camera in his room, watching everything. And somewhere outside, she and Colby were watching the building. Even if the penitent risked trying to break in, Colby and Shaye would be there to stop him.

Nicolas couldn't help but wonder if he'd take that risk.

Yesterday, he would have said no. But now that one of his victims had gotten away, what was he feeling? Was he in a panic to meet some quota he thought he was being called for? Was he afraid that any minute the police would knock on his door? The whole thing was so far outside the scope of normal thinking that Nicolas didn't know what to believe. What to expect. What he was certain of was that he wouldn't be sleeping all that well until it was over.

Malcolm was recounting a humorous story about two children playing hide-and-seek in the cathedral that afternoon and Nicolas forced a smile. Bernard was softly chuckling and then he looked over at Nicolas and frowned.

"Are you all right?" Bernard asked. "You've lost color in your face."

Nicolas didn't even remember answering before he dropped into darkness.

29

NICOLAS AWAKENED WITH HIS HEAD POUNDING. Involuntarily, he tried to lift his arm to touch it, but his wrists were tied to a wheelchair and an IV was inserted into his right arm. Instantly, he panicked. It wasn't his wheelchair and this definitely wasn't his apartment. This was it. The penitent had him. But how?

He struggled to remember, but all that came to mind was dinner with Bernard and Malcolm and then nothing. He must have been drugged. But how had the penitent taken him? How had he gotten Nicolas out of the apartment with Malcolm and Bernard right there?

He sucked in a breath. What if the penitent had killed them? Just to get to Nicolas. It was the one horrible thought that had lurked at the back of his mind the whole time, and now that could be exactly what happened. But how had he gotten past Shaye and Colby? Had he killed them as well? Was all this blood on Nicolas's hands? He squinted into the darkness, trying to make out his surroundings, but all he saw was stone.

Exactly what Hailey Pitre had described.

In the far corner of the room, he saw something move. He narrowed his eyes even more, trying to make out the shape, and finally decided it was someone in a chair. But he had only moved once and hadn't again. Were Malcolm and Bernard being held captive as well? Or had the penitent taken someone else entirely?

He heard footsteps behind him and twisted around, trying to see who was approaching, but he could barely make out the figure in the dark hallway. As it drew closer, he saw the hooded figure emerge from the shadows, his blank face looking down at Nicolas.

A wave of dizziness washed over Nicolas, and he struggled to remain conscious while at the same time, his mind argued that slipping into an unconscious state might be a better way to go. But he knew the penitent would never allow him to leave this world that easily. He wanted repentance, then he wanted death. Unconscious men couldn't confess.

As Nicolas stared up at the blank face, his heart beat harder and faster until he thought his chest would explode. Every second of silence that ticked by was more miserable than the one before. This was it. After everything he'd overcome, he was going to die between these damp, musty walls at the hands of a madman who thought he was following orders from God. If he wasn't actually living it, he would have laughed at the absurdity.

Finally, the penitent reached up and pulled his hood back. Then he grabbed the edges of the mask and lifted it from his face. Nicolas gasped.

"No! It can't be."

The smiling face of Father Bernard looked down at him.

Nicolas stared at the senior priest in horror. "I don't understand. You, of all people, know what you're doing is wrong. Please tell me this is some sort of horrible joke."

Nicolas couldn't believe what he was seeing. It was surreal. He felt that at any moment, he'd wake up in his bed, covered with sweat from another nightmare. Only this time, the nightmare was real.

"You drugged me at dinner," Nicolas said.

Bernard nodded. "It was necessary to conduct my business. It's not the first time, either. I've ensured my secrecy several times by dosing your and Malcolm's drinks. It was the first time I've gone that strong on your dosage. But the flumazenil reversed the effect of the sleeping pills quite nicely, and quickly, I might add."

Nicolas's mind whirled. "Why do you know this stuff? And where would you get such a medication?"

"My mother is a nurse, remember? After my brother died, I found the bottles in her bathroom. She admitted to lifting them from the hospital where she worked. She used it on my brother when she was afraid he'd overdosed. With my brother dead, she no longer needed them and shouldn't have had them to begin with. So I took the medication intending to destroy them, but then that night, God came to me. Told me about my life's true purpose."

"You're crazy," Nicolas said.

"God told me you'd say that. You and others. Now that you know my truth, are you willing to share your truth with me? Are you ready to confess your sins before the Father?"

"I don't know what you want from me."

"Sure you do. It's in there. You just have to find it."

"Like you wanted Hailey Pitre to do? She was a child. So was that other girl you killed."

Bernard shook his head. "They were both sinners. Each likely to have children out of wedlock. Neither in a position to be a good mother. This town is already burdened with kids living on the street. Do you think God created rules for us out of folly?"

"Of course not, but he also didn't call us to kill people who broke them."

"I'm not killing them. I'm saving them."

A chill rushed through Nicolas at the sound of Bernard's voice. He was so calm, so matter-of-fact. As if he were telling Nicolas it was going to rain or the mail was running late. And that's when Nicolas realized, with complete certainty, that he was going to die. There would be no rationalizing with Bernard. He was so far gone that nothing Nicolas could say would negate the calling Bernard thought he had.

"And Father Malcolm?" Nicolas asked. "Is that him in the corner? Does he also have sins to confess?"

"We all have sins to confess, but I'm afraid Father Malcolm's biggest shortcoming was being in the wrong place at the wrong time. I never intended to make Father Malcolm part of this, but you gave me no choice when you hired Shaye Archer to investigate and that bodyguard to protect you. I prayed over it many hours and then God sent me the answer. So simple."

"What answer?"

"To take Malcolm as well. He's my salvation, you see. This time there will be no strangulation or placement on the cross. Poor Father Malcolm will simply go off the deep end and shoot you and then himself. I'll slip upstairs and take a good dosage of the sleeping medication that I gave you and wake up to all of this. Then the police and Shaye Archer can close their files, and I can let God direct me to a new place to continue his work."

Nicolas shook his head, his mind swimming with Bernard's thoughts. "What happened to you? You are not the man who hired me at seminary and welcomed me into his church."

"God's voice happened. The first time was two months ago. I was attending to my daily prayers for the congregation and I heard him as if he'd picked up a microphone and started speaking to me."

"And you think God is calling you to kill me and frame Father Malcolm for it? To let Malcolm's family suffer under the false belief that their son was a serial killer?"

Bernard's face flashed red with anger. "I am not a killer!"

Nicolas stared at him, incredulous. He actually believed that he wasn't a monster. Despair flooded through Nicolas and he felt the last ounce of energy drain from his body. Even if his legs were sound, escape was impossible. He was tied to the chair, he had no idea where he was, and Bernard had a gun. He closed his eyes and said a silent prayer, then opened them again and looked up at Bernard.

"What do you want me to confess?" Nicolas asked.

Bernard shook his head. "You already know."

"I don't know. I sin every day, but I can't imagine that any of those things is worth dying for."

"You killed her."

Nicolas stared. "The wreck? That wasn't my fault. I wasn't driving. I was knocked unconscious. There was nothing I could have done to render aid afterward."

Bernard studied his face, then frowned. "You really don't know. This whole time, I thought... It doesn't matter. A woman and an unborn child died because of the poor choices you made."

"I'll take responsibility for not insisting we wait until the next day to drive home. Is that what you want?"

Bernard gave Nicolas a sad look and shook his head. "You were driving. You just don't remember."

"No. Jason was driving. He told the police what happened."

"Jason told the police that he was driving to protect

you. He knew he was dying. He saw no reason for three people's lives to be over so he lied."

Nicolas shook his head, trying to fight the nausea that threatened to overtake him. "That can't be. I would have known. If I'd been driving, I would have remembered."

But would he? The accident had almost killed him. Could he be certain that it happened the way the police told him it did? Could Jason have lied for him? No. He refused to believe that. Besides, even if Jason had lied, there was no way Bernard could have known.

A thought flashed through his mind. One that cut like steel and made everything crystal clear. He looked up at Bernard.

"You performed last rites on Jason," Nicolas said.

Bernard nodded. "And took his final confession."

Nicolas lowered his head and began to sob as overwhelming guilt washed over him. So many lives ruined. He deserved to die. But God forgive him, he didn't want to.

"I'm so sorry," Nicolas said as he cried. "Please forgive me."

"Do it correctly, Father Nicolas."

Nicolas started to choke and then finally began to recite the Act of Contrition.

When he was done, Bernard nodded and extended his right hand over Nicolas's head and began the absolution. "God, the father of mercies, through the death and resurrection of his son, has reconciled the world to himself and sent the Holy Spirit among us for the forgiveness of sins. Through the ministry of the church may God give you pardon and peace. I absolve you from your sins in the name of the Father, and of the Son, and of the Holy Spirit. Amen."

Nicolas didn't even try to utter the "Amen." What was the point? He was forgiven.

Now he would die.

30

SHAYE SLIPPED INTO THE PASSENGER SEAT OF JACKSON'S surveillance car and passed him a large cup of coffee. "Anything?" she asked.

He shook his head. "Nothing on the camera in Nicolas's room, either, but it's only nine o'clock. They probably just finished eating. Or they're doing cleanup."

They were parked on a side street on the back side of the priests' living quarters. From that angle, they could see the windows on the side of the building that exited to the interior of the church grounds. Colby had wanted to be closer than the street allowed and had chosen to position himself in the church courtyard. He was concealed in the shrubbery, but with a clear view of the front door and the windows on the opposite side of the building. He could also make a sprint to the front door in a matter of seconds.

Nicolas had been instructed to text Shaye at the top

of every hour, or as close as he could come without drawing unnecessary attention to himself. At seven ten, she'd received a text saying they'd be sitting down to dinner in fifteen minutes or so and it would probably take a while. So when eight came and went, she didn't worry. But now that nine o'clock was upon them, she was starting to get antsy and found herself constantly looking at her cell phone display, as if silently willing the text to come.

As the minutes ticked by, her anxiety grew. Nine ten, then nine fifteen, then nine twenty.

"I don't like this," she said. "Something doesn't feel right."

"I agree," Jackson said.

She called Colby. "Do you see anything?"

"The lights are on in the front room, but the blinds are drawn, so I can't see any movement inside."

"What about Malcolm's bedroom?"

"Nothing. What about Bernard's room?"

"No light. And nothing on the camera."

"Then they're still in the living room."

Shaye blew out a breath. "Yeah, I guess so. But why hasn't Nicolas made contact?"

"He might not be in a position to. Do you want me to knock?" he asked, picking up on her anxiety. "I could always say I can't find my wallet and want to see if I left it there."

Shaye looked over at Jackson, who nodded. "Do it."

"Okay. Keep quiet. I'll stay connected and put my phone in my pocket."

Shaye heard muffled shuffling as Colby secured the phone, then shortly after, the faint sound of him knocking on the door.

"Father Nicolas? It's Colby. I think I might have left my wallet there."

Shaye clutched her phone, waiting for any indication that the three priests were alive and well on the other side of the door, but as the seconds ticked by, her worry increased. Finally, Colby spoke.

"I can hear the television, but there's no answer," he said. "And the blinds are so tightly fitted that I can't see inside."

"Call him," Shaye instructed Jackson. "Colby, can you hear a cell phone ringing?"

"Yeah. That's Nicolas's ringtone. But no one is moving in there. There's not a breath of noise except for the television and the phone."

"Break down the door," Shaye said. "We're on our way."

She and Jackson checked their weapons and jumped out of the car. It was several seconds before the street cleared enough to cross, then they jogged over, Shaye still clutching the phone to her ear. She'd heard the sound of wood splintering as they were waiting to cross, so she knew Colby had gained entry.

"Shaye?" Colby said. "This place is empty."

"That's impossible."

"Wait a minute. I found something in Father Malcolm's room. It looks like blueprints of tunnels."

"There are tunnels under the church!" Shaye said, remembering Hustle's conversation with the senior priest. "One of them must run under the living quarters. There has to be an entrance somewhere in that building."

"On it," Colby said.

Shaye sped up to a run, Jackson right beside her, scanning the area surrounding the building as they approached. When they got around to the entrance, the door was hanging off the hinges at the top. They ran inside, Shaye calling for Colby, but the building was quiet. She checked her phone.

"The call dropped," she said. "He must have found the tunnel. Check the bedrooms."

She ran into Malcolm's room and Jackson ran into Bernard's, but they were both clear. No secret doors in the closet, no trapdoors under the rugs. They already knew Nicolas's room was clear because they'd been watching it on the cameras, so they both ran into the room with the exercise equipment and spotted the closet door open at the back wall. A panel on the back wall had been shifted aside and a narrow set of stone steps led down into darkness.

A second later, a shot rang out and they both involuntarily ducked.

Jackson motioned for Shaye to get behind him and he slipped through the opening and started inching down the steps. Shaye stayed close, both arms clutching her firearm near her shoulder, ready to fire if Jackson went down. Going down the steps, they were open targets.

When they finally cleared the ceiling, they could see the end of the steps but not much beyond as there was no light except what was coming down the stairs from the closet. Jackson paused at the end of the steps and they listened, but it was as silent as a tomb. Shaye peered into the darkness, the stone walls closing in around her, and she struggled to keep her breathing steady.

She'd spent almost a third of her life in a place that looked a lot like this and it was all she could do to maintain focus. Jackson pulled out his flashlight and turned on the wide beam. They were in a hallway that was about five feet wide and stretched so far in front of them that they couldn't see the end. About thirty feet in front of them was a large lump of something on the ground.

"Colby," Shaye said, and they rushed forward.

Colby was slumped on the ground, facedown. Jackson grabbed his shoulders and rolled him over and they immediately spotted the entry wound on his stomach.

"He's losing blood fast," Jackson said. "He needs a medic now."

"There's no signal here," Shaye said. "Go back up and call for help. I've got to get to Nicolas and Bernard before Malcolm kills them."

"No way! You make the call and I'll go after the priests."

"You're a cop. You'll get a faster response than I will,

and we need backup. This has gone far beyond what we planned for."

Before he could say anything, she grabbed his flashlight and ran down the tunnel. She'd deal with Jackson's anger later. Ultimately, he knew she was right. One call from Jackson would send paramedics and cops to the church in a flash. She wouldn't get the same response and Colby's life depended on how quickly he got medical attention.

At the end of the tunnel was a sharp right turn. She stopped before the end and listened at the edge to see if she could hear anyone moving nearby. If someone was standing on the other side, waiting for her, she'd be an easy target. The tunnel was silent, and she was just about to spin around the corner when she heard voices echoing ahead of her. She couldn't make out what they were saying but one of the voices sounded like Nicolas.

Relief coursed through her. Nicolas might still be alive! But with Colby lying on the ground bleeding out behind her, she was sure that wouldn't be the case for long. Malcolm would kill Nicolas soon. Then he'd use one of these tunnels to escape and he'd disappear just like he did fifteen years ago. Become someone new. A new face for the same old serial killer.

She slipped around the corner and hurried down the tunnel as fast as she could without making noise. She kept the light small and directed on the ground in front of her so it wouldn't alert Malcolm that she was coming. The voices got a bit louder as she went, but not any clearer, with the sound echoing off the stone. Eventually, the tunnel turned to the left and she clicked the flashlight off as she approached the corner and stopped at the edge of the stone wall.

Nicolas's voice was clearer now and when Shaye realized what he was saying, chills ran through her. The Act of Contrition. Malcolm had gotten his confession and as soon as the ceremony was complete, he would kill Nicolas.

Her time had run out. The voices were closer but not close enough.

31

NICOLAS HAD INTENDED TO KEEP HIS HEAD DOWN AND his eyes closed while Bernard sent him to the hereafter. There was no dignity in death but he'd be damned if he gave Bernard the satisfaction of hearing him beg. But he couldn't keep his head down like a guilty dog. No. Bernard was going to have to look him right in the eye when he pulled the trigger. Nicolas could only hope that look haunted him the rest of his miserable and, God willing, short life. He lifted his head and looked directly at Bernard, who had pulled a gun from his hoodie pocket and was now leveling it at Nicolas's head.

And instead of the stark fear he expected to feel, anger coursed through him.

"I hope you burn in hell," Nicolas said.

Bernard blinked, then he started to flush, and Nicolas realized what he'd done. He'd sinned again before Bernard could kill him.

A noise to the right caused both of them to turn their heads and Nicolas saw Shaye round the corner, her gun lifted at Bernard. But when Bernard turned and she caught sight of his face, she froze. Nicolas could see the confusion and disbelief in her expression.

"It's him!" Nicolas shouted.

Bernard whipped his head around to face Nicolas again and squeezed the trigger. Pain exploded in Nicolas's head and his vision blurred so much he couldn't see at all. A second shot rang out almost immediately after the first, and then another. But he felt nothing more. Just life slipping away.

And then it was all there—playing like a video on fast-forward. Planting roses in the backyard with his mother. Fishing with his father. His acceptance into seminary. And the wreck. He *was* behind the wheel. Then it all started to fade into gray and he felt his body slump as the gray turned darker and darker and finally into black.

"Nicolas!" Shaye's voice sounded in front of him and he felt her hand press the side of his head. "Can you hear me? Open your eyes."

Confusion swept through him. Was this it? Had Bernard shot Shaye as well and they'd crossed together?

Then her words registered, and he realized that darkness had come because he'd closed his eyes, not because he had died. Slowly, he opened them and stared up at Shaye's concerned face.

"Try not to move," she said. "The bullet just nicked the side of your head, but it's bleeding. One second."

She moved around him and he felt his arms being jostled. Seconds later, the binding that held his wrists came loose and pain shot through his right shoulder as his hand automatically lifted to the side of his head.

"Keep your hand there if you can," she said as she moved around to cut his feet loose. "It will help stop the bleeding."

He pressed the side of his head, wincing from the pain. Then he heard the sound of footsteps running down the hallway and looked over to see a man burst into the room, gun in the ready position. A bit of panic ran through him before he realized he recognized the man from the news. He was a cop.

The cop scanned the room, his eyes widening at the sight of Bernard's body. Then he hurried over to Shaye.

"Are you all right?" he asked. "Are you hit?"

Despite his entire body being a mass of pain, Nicolas felt a trickle of warmth run through him. The cop's feelings for Shaye were so apparent and as she looked at him, he could see she felt the same way.

"I'm good. Nicolas got nicked in the head, but it's a surface wound."

"Where are we?" Nicolas asked.

"Tunnels, beneath the church," Shaye said.

"I didn't even know there was such a thing," Nicolas said.

"I don't think a lot of people did," Shaye answered.

"But I'm sure this is how Bernard moved about without being seen."

Nicolas bit his lower lip. "And Bernard?"

"Will never terrorize anyone else," Shaye said.

Nicolas had intentionally kept his gaze down or on Shaye, only catching a glimpse of the figure on the floor out of the corner of his eye. But now, he looked past her and saw Bernard's body splayed out on the stone, blood pooling around his head.

"Probably best you don't look too much," the cop said. "I'm Jackson Lamotte."

"Detective Lamotte," Shaye said.

Suddenly, Nicolas remembered the figure in the corner. "Father Malcolm! I think he's here. Over toward the back of the room. Bernard was going to frame him."

Shaye's eyes widened and she spun around, shining a flashlight into the corner. Malcolm was sitting in a wheelchair, just like Nicolas, his hands and feet bound and tape over his mouth. He was struggling to move but couldn't manage more than a twitch with all the binding. His eyes were wide with fright and Nicolas could see his chest heaving with panic.

Shaye and Jackson rushed over and Jackson eased the tape from his mouth while Shaye cut him loose. He dragged in a huge breath and then started to cry. "Thank you! Thank you so much," he said. "I thought we were both going to die. Father Bernard..."

His voice trailed off, full of confusion.

"Are you hurt?" Shaye asked as she scanned the back of his head. "You've got a good bump back here."

"He hit me," Malcolm said, his tone one of complete disbelief. "We had just finished eating and Nicolas looked odd. A second later, he passed out right there at the table. I jumped up to attend to him and something struck me in the back of the head. I don't remember anything until I woke up here. Father Bernard was forcing a confession out of Father Nicolas and I didn't understand. When I realized—"

Father Malcolm's voice broke and he started crying again. Nicolas felt his chest clench. Neither of them would ever be the same.

"Why would he do this?" Malcolm asked. "I don't understand."

Shaye put her hand on his shoulder and squeezed. "And there are things we might never understand. But we can explain some of what happened to you. Just as soon as we're certain you and Nicolas are all right."

"The paramedics are on the way," Jackson said. "Backup is already here. They're with Colby."

"What's wrong with Colby?" Nicolas asked.

"Bernard shot him," Shaye said. "But don't worry. Colby is tough. He's handled worse before."

Nicolas felt the last bit of energy drain from his body. So much pain and heartache.

And he still had no idea why.

MONDAY, MAY 23, 2016
French Quarter, New Orleans

SHAYE TAPPED LIGHTLY on the hospital room door and Nicolas looked over and smiled. It had been three days since she'd prevented Bernard from killing him. The color had returned to his face, but he still looked exhausted. She was all too familiar with that look. He wasn't sleeping well and he needed sleep to heal. But when you were in emotional turmoil, it was hard to still your mind long enough to be restful.

She pulled a chair next to his bed and sat. "How are you doing? And I don't want the standard answer you give everyone. I want the truth."

He nodded. "My head stopped pounding, so that's a

blessing. My legs still have random episodes of nerve pain, but the doctors said that's good. That all of this didn't cause more damage. My shoulder is still sore and will be for some time."

"That's your body. What about the rest?"

He looked down. "Days are all right. I've had a lot of visitors—all instructed not to talk about anything that happened lest they upset me, of course. And nurses pop in all day long. They're all so pleasant and kind. The police have spent quite a bit of time going over every detail with me. Malcolm isn't allowed out of bed yet and neither am I, so I haven't seen him, but he calls me every day to check on me."

Shaye nodded but didn't say anything.

Nicolas sighed. "But nights...nights are bad. Every time I close my eyes, I see his face and I feel that terror all over again."

"Have they given you anything to help you sleep?"

"They've tried, but I won't take it. I can't do it...I'm afraid."

Shaye nodded. "I understand."

Nicolas had been drugged and attacked. His fear of being unconscious far outweighed his desire for sleep. She knew that feeling all too well. And she'd made the same choice Nicolas had.

"I think it would be better if I understood," he said. "But then I know we probably never will."

"Actually, that's what I'm here for."

Nicolas straightened. "You've learned something?"

"Yes. And I think when I put it together with stuff you told me, it explains most of it. As well as they're going to be explained, anyway. I've just talked to the coroner. Bernard had a frontal lobe injury. Do you know what that means?"

"I think so. That part of the brain controls impulse, right?"

"It controls a lot of things. Judgment, behavior, emotion. Some people consider it our conscience, of sorts. It can also cause auditory hallucinations."

Nicolas nodded, then his eyes widened. "Bernard fell a couple months ago. He hit his head and injured his knee. That's why he limped. Although..."

He frowned.

"Bernard wasn't limping when you saw him in the tunnel," Shaye finished.

"No. I don't understand."

"I think, from watching you, Bernard figured out that a disability was a big advantage in making people comfortable around you. The limp combined with the priest collar and the silver hair made it easy for him to get close to victims."

He grimaced. "They trusted him. That's so insidious. So calculated. How could he be so clever with such an injury to his brain?"

"The injury didn't affect his intelligence."

"It still doesn't make sense to me. How does such a

thing change a person's morality so completely? And why that focus? Why sinners? Was it simply because he was a priest?"

"I think it goes deeper than that. I'm only surmising here, but based off the research Jackson and I have done in the last couple days, I believe that the death of Bernard's brother might have been the catalyst that sent him spiraling."

"His brother died shortly after Bernard's fall, but how would that matter?"

"His brother was a drug addict. Their mother enabled him and he used her. When he died, I think it might have set something off in Bernard. The way his brother had wasted his life. The way your mother covered for him, becoming part of the problem. His father went to prison for vehicular manslaughter when both boys were young. He was drunk when the accident occurred. He died in a prison fight."

"So the potential for the girls to become single parents, and the accident..."

Shaye nodded. "I think his mind created the voice of God so that he could deal with the things now that he couldn't deal with then."

"Do you know how he found the two girls?"

"We can only guess. A review of the clinic records showed that Bernard picked up a prescription for sleeping pills around the same time that Hailey Pitre got her birth control."

"So he could have overheard them talking. And she would have given her birth date to pick up the prescription, so he knew she was underage."

Shaye nodded. "Sunny Trahan worked a corner near a homeless shelter that St. Mary's donates to. Bernard dropped off a donation to the shelter the night before Sunny disappeared."

"Did he hold both of them in the tunnels?"

"Yes. The forensics team has found DNA there for both girls."

"And no one ever heard them or saw Father Bernard go in and out."

"He was very smart about things, and the tunnel system is vast. Bernard left those layouts in Malcolm's room to help with his frame-up, but they were very revealing. The place where Bernard held the girls and brought you and Malcolm is under an old delivery dock. He could drive his car between stone walls, and no one would be able to see him lift a body in or out of his trunk."

Nicolas recalled how easily Bernard had lifted him from his chair. "He was strong. The girls were light, but still, to carry Father Malcolm and me down the stairs, then all the way down the hall."

"He didn't. I'm pretty sure he dragged both of you down the stairs. Bruising on your body would indicate as much. And since he knew how easy it was to get someone around in a wheelchair, he had the chairs ready to push you from the living quarters to the area of the tunnel near the delivery dock."

"He thought of everything." Nicolas frowned. "But I still don't know how he made the confession and left without anyone seeing him."

"Because one of the tunnels is right below the confessional. He simply opened the door to the confessional to make you think he was leaving and while you were scrambling to rise, he slid back the panel on the side wall and left. The footsteps you heard were him descending the stone steps. Not footsteps in the hallway."

He stared at her, shaking his head. "It's still so hard to believe. It seems so impossible, and yet..."

"And yet."

"I saw Colby earlier. The nurse said he insisted on being wheeled in here. He apologized for letting me be kidnapped. Can you beat that? Like any of this was his fault. If I couldn't see what Bernard was how in the world could Colby have done so?"

"He couldn't, but he's an honorable and somewhat stubborn man. He doesn't like for people to get injured on his watch."

"I saw the look on your face when you saw Bernard holding the gun," Nicolas said quietly. "You were expecting someone else. Who?"

"Malcolm."

Nicolas stared. "Malcolm? Why?"

Shaye explained to him all the reasons she'd zeroed in

on the other priest. His ties to religion, his proximity to all the things that had happened to Nicolas, his discomfort with Colby, and his mysterious, disappearing background.

"How can you make your background disappear?"

"By legally changing your name and the judge agreeing to seal the records. It's like witness protection. You essentially become someone else."

"Malcolm was in witness protection?"

Shaye smiled, recalling how she'd felt when Malcolm had explained his secrecy. "Nothing like that. His father is quite famous. Country and western singer Chance Malcolm."

"That explains his taste in music. He often played songs by his father. He also has an excellent singing voice."

Shaye nodded. "Malcolm had a tough time in high school with people trying to get close to him to get at his father. So when he decided he wanted to become a priest, he knew he had to become another person in more ways than one. It was the only way he felt he could devote his life to his beliefs without worrying about being hounded by the press or fans. So Chance Malcolm Jr. became Malcolm Warner. Warner is his mother's maiden name. He said he made his last name his first because he knew everyone would call him Father Malcolm, and it would be easier to respond to."

"And that way, not everything was different."

"I'm sure that's part of it too."

"What about Colby? You said Colby felt he made Malcolm nervous. Was there any truth to that?"

"Yes. Colby had done a bodyguard stint for Malcolm's father when he was in town for a concert. Malcolm was backstage and was afraid Colby would recognize him."

"What are the odds of my hiring the one person who might give away his secret?"

"I have a favor to ask you. Malcolm gave me permission to tell you the truth, but he asks that you keep it private. He would like to continue his work as a priest without issue. Well, as soon as all the furor from this has died down, anyway."

"Of course I will keep his secret. It's the good kind." He sighed. "I suppose Malcolm will leave as soon as he is able. Not that I blame him. I can hear the distance in his voice when we talk."

"And you? Is your job in jeopardy?"

Nicolas shook his head. "I was surprised, really. I told the elders everything, including betraying the confessional. But I think in the end, they're more concerned about the reputation of the Church than one lowly priest."

"I suppose so," Shaye said, but the cynical part of her figured they were more concerned that without his collar, Nicolas would tell the entire world the whole truth.

"I think, though, that I am going to leave on my own accord."

Shaye stared at him, more than a little surprised.

After everything Nicolas had gone through, she'd figured his profession was the last stable thing he had and that he'd want to hold on to it.

"It surprised me too," he said. "But sitting here has given me time to think about things. A lot of things. For so many years, I did what I was told. I learned and I followed ritual, and I was okay with that. Until something challenged that belief system."

"The confession."

He nodded. "Don't get me wrong. I don't disagree with the requirements of the vows. I simply don't think I'm capable of keeping them. I've learned that justice on this earth is more important to me. I'm not patient enough to wait for the hereafter. Justice and a clear conscience. And I couldn't reconcile my silence with what I knew was right. Others can and they are the ones best left to the job."

"So what will you do?"

"The luxury of a trust fund is not having to do anything, I suppose. But like you, I don't think I'd find that life rewarding. Your mother came to visit me yesterday. Did she tell you?"

"No. We haven't had a chance to sit down and talk yet."

"She's a remarkable woman. There's an energy and kindness surrounding her that can almost be seen. She has a calling."

"She thinks so, and I would agree. She certainly saved my life."

"And you're not the first or the last. I asked her about her project and she said something that interested me. She told me they'd need adults to live in the building designed to house the children. Some of the children would be there temporarily. Others would be there longer. All will need a solid adult influence."

Shaye smiled, unable to imagine a better role for Nicolas. "And you'd like to be that influence. I think that would be wonderful."

Nicolas leaned over and placed his hand on hers. "I don't think I ever thanked you properly so I'm doing it now. Thank you, Shaye. For saving my life. You have a calling as well."

SHAYE KNOCKED on the door of Jackson's apartment, clutching a bottle of champagne. He opened it and gave her a wide smile, then pulled her inside for a kiss. After running off from him in the tunnel, Shaye had expected him to be angry with her. But his relief had been so great with how everything had turned out that he'd finally admitted she'd made the right call. She knew how much it had cost him to let her run after a madman and not follow. The amount of faith he had in her and his respect for her abilities made her love him even more. It was one thing to give lip service to those words. It was completely another to prove that you meant it, especially when the situation was life-and-death.

"Are we celebrating?" he asked when he caught sight of the champagne.

"I think we should. The list of things to be thankful for is getting pretty long. I'm not even sure one bottle is going to cover it."

"We'll just have to toast in compound sentences."

She laughed as she followed him into the kitchen and waited while he poured them each a glass of the sparkling bubbly.

"What do we toast first?" he asked.

"Success. Nicolas is safe. Bernard will never hurt anyone else. Colby is recovering nicely. And you pulling a background check for me will remain a secret since Malcolm wasn't our bad guy."

"I can definitely drink to all of that."

They lifted their glasses and clinked them together, then took a sip. Shaye looked at him and couldn't help smiling. She felt that way a lot around Jackson, even when things were tough. There was something about his presence. She didn't need protecting, but she knew he'd do it anyway, and that gave her a warm, cozy feeling. He challenged her without disrespect and made her a better investigator and person.

For weeks now, her mind had returned to a single thought that she'd been dwelling on. Something that once caused her great fear and panic but had turned into something different. Something slightly scary but also exhilarating. Finally, she'd made up her mind. The time was right.

"What shall we toast next?" he asked.

"Us," she said before she could lose her nerve. "And I'd like to stay the night. With you."

FOR NOTICE ON UPCOMING RELEASES, sign up for Jana's newsletter.

Printed in Great Britain
by Amazon